A MAN OF PARTS

Sir Westcott read from a folder in a flat, toneless voice. It was my list of injuries. If I had been feeling sick when the surgeon began his catalog, I grew sicker as he went on with it.

Then he coughed and read, "*Prognosis: terminal.*"

I remembered the punch line of an old tall story: *"So what happened to you then, Bill?" "What happened to me? Why, I died, of course."*

I gave a sort of hysterical titter. "What are you telling me? That I died and now I'm in Hell?"

"Nothing so sensational. Let me finish." Westcott pulled another sheet of paper from his folder. "Your brother. It tells the same story. *Prognosis: terminal.* For ten different reasons."

"It's been a month since the accident, and I'm still alive."

"Alive, and doing very well. But your brother Leo was in worse shape even than you were. He was sinking before we could even get him into the theater. I had to make a decision."

"*You killed Leo!*"

"No." He glowered down at me. "Your brother was a hopeless case, absolutely hopeless. And you were terribly injured. I had to make a decision. Save one, or save none. You died as much as Leo did."

"I'm here, and he isn't."

"Don't be too sure of that. You lost partial segments from three main brain lobes, but you had the brain stem and the midbrain completely intact. I took parts of Leo's brain, and used them to replace the lobe segments you lost."

"But Leo's dead. I don't feel half like Leo, and half like myself. I'm Lionel Salkind."

"All that proves is that you have the verbal part of the brain under control. That's all in your left hemisphere. If you want my honest opinion, yes, I think that Leo is still alive, in some sense, and he's inhabiting part of your skull."

He closed the folder. "And at some time—don't ask me when and where, or even how—I expect the two halves of the brain to integrate again. You'll become a single individual. And beyond that, I can't go."

BAEN BOOKS by CHARLES SHEFFIELD

MY BROTHER'S KEEPER

CHARLES SHEFFIELD

MY BROTHER'S KEEPER

A Baen Book

Baen Publishing Enterprises
P.O. Box 1403
Riverdale, NY 10471
www.baen.com

ISBN: 0-671-57873-1

Cover art by Gary Ruddell

First Baen printing, June 2000

Distributed by Simon & Schuster
1230 Avenue of the Americas
New York, NY 10020

Produced by Windhaven Press, Auburn, NH
Printed in the United States of America

MY BROTHER'S
KEEPER

Windhaven Press, Auburn, NH

Printed in the United States of America

PROLOGUE

I was sitting on a bench in St. James Park when Leo started work on me again. This time he was a lot more insistent.

He began with my left hand. My arm was stretched out loosely along the bench top. As I watched the fingers lifted and started to tap out a regular rhythm against the wood. I had been quite relaxed, enjoying the sunshine and watching ducks in the lake and young couples on the bank as they went through their elaborate courting rituals. So it took me a few seconds to realize that the finger-tapping was not my idea. Leo. It had to be Leo.

Da-da-DA-da-da-da-DA-da-DA-DA-DA.

Da-da-DA-da-da-da-DA-da-DI-DI-DI.

Over and over. My head was aching again, like a resonance to the tapped signal. The rhythm was inside me, and a harmony built to go with it.

Tom, Tom, the piper's son.

Da-da-DA-da-da-da-DA-da-DA-DA-DA.

Why in God's name would Leo be hitting me with that, an old children's song? He wouldn't. I had to be imagining it, mistaking a random thought of my own for Leo.

I sat quite still for another two or three minutes, trying to push the rhythm out of my mind. When it wouldn't go away I stood up and began to limp slowly west along Birdcage Walk and on past the palace. The stiffness in my right leg was less and less, but I didn't hurry. I had been told not to overdo things, even though the bone graft looked perfect on the X-rays. If only I were doing as well mentally as I was physically . . .

Leo was becoming more persistent every day. Last week there had been uncontrolled movements in my hand, and a couple of days ago it was double vision. If I could find out what was disturbing him, maybe we could get back to normal. No one at the hospital could offer any sort of explanation— relax, wait and see, was all they would say.

By the time I reached Brill's my fingers were under control. Even so, the sales assistant in the store looked at me oddly when I went in. No doubt the limp and the facial scars didn't help—that, and the fact that I suspected my left eye was roaming independently of my right one. I braced myself against the counter and did my best to look relaxed and casual.

"I'd like a book of nursery rhymes."

"Yes, sir." He looked surprised. "Er, what age group is this for?"

What age group indeed, sir? Only Leo could answer that one.

"Do you have a complete collection? I'd like a book that gives the alternative versions, if there is such a thing."

"I'll see what I can find."

When he brought it over and I had paid for it, I ignored the inquisitive look and leafed through on the spot to the right place. *Tom, Tom, the piper's son, Stole a pig and away he run. The pig was eat and Tom was beat, And Tom went howling down the street.*

I muttered the words aloud. Nothing. No surge of emotion, no sign that Leo was tuned in and getting the message. Second verse: *Tom, Tom, the piper's son, Learned to play when he was young, But the only tune that he could play, Was "Over the hills and far away."*

Now there was something. Something faint and vague, a prickling in the nape of my neck, as though a hairy-legged insect was crawling there. And that was all.

So what now?

I went back outside the shop and leaned on the wall. Even though I hadn't been able to pick up anything definite, the long scar across the back of my skull was still tingling with feeling, as though the stubbly regrowing hair there was trying to stand on end. I tilted my head back and looked up at the clouds, drifting along at the lazy pace of early autumn. The tune was right, I had no doubt about that—but could it be that I was tying in to the wrong set of words? Who else had taken that tune and used it?

Inside the shop again to where the assistant looked at me reproachfully.

"I wondered when you'd be back. You forgot to take your book."

"Never mind that. I don't really want that one. Do you happen to know where I could find a copy of the libretto to *The Beggar's Opera*? If you have the collected works of John Gay, it would be in that."

He was looking at me as though his worst fears were confirmed. He picked up the book of nursery rhymes.

"I'll take this back and give you credit for it. If you'll wait here for a moment I'll check in the other room and see if we have the other book."

He left—to look for my book, or maybe to summon reinforcements. I'm over six-two, and the accident has left signs of considerable wear and tear on my face. While he was gone I hobbled up and down in the store, trying again to control my arms and legs. Not so successful this time. Leo was excited, no doubt about it. But if I'd known where the events of the next five minutes would be taking me I'd have been excited too (and run out of the shop, assuming Leo would have permitted it).

Here he came again.

"This should do it, sir. Allowing for the credit on the other book, you owe us seventy pence." The man hesitated a little before he handed over the volume of John Gay. "We'll be closing in just a minute or two. If you would be kind enough to examine this outside, rather than in here . . ."

He didn't lie well, but I didn't mind. If this led nowhere, I'd shot my bolt anyway. Now, at what point in *The Beggar's Opera* had he used that tune? Some scene between Polly and Macheath, if I remembered it right. Here we are. I leaned against the wall again, feeling that strong itching in my scalp.

Were I laid on Greenland's coast, And in my arms embraced my lass, Warm amid eternal frost, Too soon the half-year's night would pass.

Da-da-DA-da-da-da-DA-da-DA-DA-DA.

And I would love you all the day, Every night would kiss and play. If with me you'd fondly stray, Over the hills and far away.

The prickling was stronger, and I was panting to myself as I read the words.

Something was coming, coming closer.

Second verse.

Were I sold on Indian soil, Soon as the burning day was closed, I could mock the sultry toil, When on my charmer's breast reposed.

Contact. As I read the words, a torrent of sensory inputs hit me and left me shuddering. The London street was gone. I was bathed in a bright, dusty sunlight, surrounded by a babble of familiar/unfamiliar language. There were strong, tantalizing odors, of spices, burning charcoal, flowers and musky oils. I felt a stab of lust, surprising and mindless, and my fingertips tingled as they moved over soft, cool skin. *On Indian soil, soon as the burning day was closed* . . .

I swayed against the wall of the shop, struggling to catch a breath. Leo had found a new way to get through to me. He was sure as hell making the most of it.

- 1 -

My reunion with Leo, like many incidents of my life connected with airports, had begun badly. I was held up in rush-hour traffic in central London, arrived late at Heathrow, and by the time I reached the right part of the terminal the passengers from his flight had all cleared Customs and left. It took me a few minutes to find that out, then I headed over to El Al to look for messages and have Leo paged.

"What's 'is name?" asked the young girl behind the desk. No Israeli she, but a genuine English rose, blue-eyed and pink-cheeked.

"Leo Foss. He was supposed to be coming in on Flight 221."

"That's in already. I'll page 'im, though. And what's your name?"

"Lionel Salkind."

"Righto. An' I'll keep an eye open for 'im, as well." She smiled at me—dimples, too. "Can you tell me a bit about what 'e looks like, so I'll know what to be watching for?"

"No problem there. He looks—"

"Lionel!" The familiar voice came from behind me.

"—just like me," I finished, as I turned.

I knew what the girl's expression behind me must be. I'd seen it often enough. The fact that Leo and I had different last names only made it more confusing. I looked back at the girl and shrugged apologetically as Leo and I approached to within a foot of each other to perform our usual reunion inspection and survey.

Most people would say we are identical, but of course we're not. We both are very aware that Leo is half an inch taller and usually five pounds heavier (Not this time, though. He was either a little thinner, or tired and worried). He was wearing his hair an inch shorter than the last time we had met, ten months earlier, but that was no surprise. So was I. We had become used to the built-in tendencies to favor the same actions at the same time. Now behavioral differences impressed us more than similarities. Today, for instance, we both wore dark sports jackets and red ties; but Leo was sporting a strange tie clip, rather like a little golden beetle. That was new, and rather surprising— neither of us liked to see men wearing jewelry, and we both shunned rings.

"Now then, about dinner plans," I said, after we had sized each other up and were walking side by side through the terminal to the usual accompaniment of turning heads. "Are you ready for a Chinese meal experiment?"

"Sorry, I can't do it this trip." Leo shook his head, and I noticed what looked like a love bite on his neck, low down near the collar. "I tried to call you from Zurich, but I couldn't reach you. There's been a change of plans, and now I'll have to fly on to Washington tomorrow morning."

"But that still leaves tonight. I'm not playing."

"I know—I found that much out from your manager. I'm relying on that. I have to talk to you, privately."

There was an odd expression in his voice. It confirmed my first impression. He was tired, and under some unusual kind of strain. Others might not have noticed it, but I could feel it under my skin.

"Do you still keep the apartment up north?" he went on. "The one you don't need."

"Of course."

It was a luxury, but when you travel as much as I do you really crave for a place where you can practice quietly and add to your repertoire. I've never been one of the Rubinstein types, who seem to be able to stay on top form without much daily practice. Maybe that's one reason I'll never be the world's number one. But if you want to get into even the top hundred concert pianists, you have to work at it—and don't believe anyone who tells you otherwise. It's hard work, too.

"I haven't been up there for a couple of months," I said. "But it's well looked after."

"Good. I want to go there so we can talk in peace for an hour or two." Leo was looking all around him as he spoke, very edgy. I was picking up his nervousness, and I didn't like it at all.

"We don't have time for a trip north if you have to leave tomorrow." I accepted his need for a place to talk privately without even thinking about it.

"Yes, we do." Leo managed a grin. "I called in here from Zurich and booked a helicopter. By the time we get over there the flight plan should all be cleared."

"Up to Middlesbrough?"

"Right. No Chinese meal tonight. You'll have to feed me on black pudding and tripe."

He faked a shudder. I'd been raised on them, but Leo's American palate had trouble with some of the delicacies from the north of England.

It was clear that he didn't want to talk any more serious matters until we were out of the airport, so I didn't push it. We chatted about trivia on the shuttle bus to the pad, about two miles away, and when we got there found a little BMR-33 four-seater waiting for us. She was a lovely trim job, blue and red painted, with the engines all warmed up for us and ready to go when we walked up to her.

"Want me to fly her?" I asked. Leo and I both fell in love with flying and with helicopters fifteen years ago, when we were still in our teens, and we both held current licenses.

He shook his head. "No way. That's my privilege as Big Brother."

Leo was forty-three minutes older than me, and we never forgot it. Other people suffered some confusion when he referred to me as his "younger brother," or I talked about his great age.

"All right, old man," I said, and went to stow his bag in the rear. While Leo signed off for the 'copter, I climbed into the passenger seat and checked the weather report. It was nearly six-thirty, just getting dark, and there was cloud cover at three thousand feet. Not the most perfect conditions. Leo was shaking his head in annoyance when he finished with the paperwork and climbed aboard.

"Lots of traffic, I guess. Look at this lousy flight plan. We have to head way off to the west before they'll let me swing up north."

"What do you have as the Middlesbrough ETA?"

"Eight twenty-eight."

"That's not bad at all. I've done this before. You'll find that everything clears up once we're past Cambridge—it's just this mess round London that's a pain."

He grunted, and settled in at the controls. Visibility was good in spite of the cloud overhead. I could see the dark flats of the Water Board reservoirs off to the southwest as we lifted, and away behind us the haze of London itself was a blue-grey ball over the city. We rose to two thousand feet and slid away to the west.

I hate to say it, but Leo was a better pilot than I was. That was a surprise to me, since on all the standard tests that we had been taking together since we were in our early teens, I scored higher on manual dexterity than he did. Leo had his own explanation for that. He said it was training, not talent, that gave me more nimble fingers. "What do you expect?" he would say. "You wouldn't expect a pianist to act as though he was all thumbs. It's mechanical aptitude that counts in being a good pilot." And of course, on mechanical aptitude he

usually scored a tiny fraction higher than I did—
but not enough higher, in my opinion, to explain
his easy skill as a helicopter pilot. I suspected that
was training, too, rather than talent. Leo simply got
in more flying hours, though it was hard for me to
see how his job offered the opportunity for it.

He had relaxed a good deal as soon as we lifted
off, and now that we were moving west towards
Reading he began to whistle softly, just loud
enough for me to hear him. It was the first movement of the *Unfinished*, taken a little slowly.

"You realize that you're a semitone flat?" I said.
"It's in B, not B-flat."

He turned his head and grinned at me. "Sorry,
Little Brother. I just wanted to see if you were
awake still."

He had the ear, all right, but he had simply
never got around to learning to play a musical
instrument. When I thought of the huge chunks
of my life that had been swallowed up on practice, I sometimes wondered if Leo had the right
idea and I was off my head. But it was too late
for that sort of thinking. I leaned back in my seat.

"All right, accept that I'm awake enough. How
about a little light on the big mystery, and the rush
to the north? It's not like you to miss the chance
at a good Chinese meal."

He nodded, looking straight ahead, and sighed,
"Too true. But this is really a tough business,
Lionel."

It was, too. I knew it as soon as he spoke. We
never called each other "Leo" and "Lionel" in private unless some really serious matter was involved.
I didn't speak, but just sat and waited.

"You know," he said after a few moments. "I've kidded you a lot about your job over the years, and told you you have to work your fingers off just to stay in the same place—you have the real Red Queen's Race. But sometimes I envy you. It'll pass in a few minutes, but I'm envying you right now."

"That's a first. You mean you're disenchanted with your job? I thought you loved those AID jaunts, hopping all over the globe and dishing out the dollars. What's up, have they stopped treating you like royalty all of a sudden?"

"Not quite." His tone had changed. I realized that he had not listened to me, and was only able to reply from an instinct as to what I must have said to him.

"What's wrong?" I looked at the instrument panel.

"She's not handling right." He was frowning at the gauges also. "Everything shows as though it's fine, but it's not. She's yawing, and I can't trim her to correct it. The hell with this, I'm going to take her back to Heathrow. Call in and request an emergency landing for us."

I reached for the radio, but before I could make connection it became irrelevant. The helicopter lurched sickeningly to the right, levelled for a moment as Leo struggled with the controls, then swooped sideways again, vibrating madly.

"I can't hold her at all," Leo grunted. His face was tense and flushed with exertion. "We'll never make it to Heathrow. What's down there on your side? I'll have to try and slip her that way and straighten us when we're really low."

Off to my right I could see a dizzying pattern

of fields and roads, leading a mile or two ahead to the more heavily built-up area of East Reading.

"As soon as you can," I shouted, still concentrating on the ground. "It gets worse the further we go. We're better off here than nearer the town."

Leo did not speak, but I heard his grunt of effort. The air was rushing past us and the helicopter was rolling and yawing crazily as we lost altitude. At three hundred feet we straightened for a moment. I could see a hedge, a muddy pool, and a plowed field, and beyond that the line of a major road with houses on the other side of it.

"Right here, Leo. Turn her *now*." My voice was high-pitched and panicky. "Watch out, you'll have us on the road."

He did his best, pulling us close to level at the last moment. It just wasn't good enough. I saw the ground coming towards me—much too fast—and in the moment before impact I could see so clearly that I could have counted the individual weeds that grew in the plowed furrows. When we hit there was a noise like the end of the world.

In a way, that's exactly what it was.

Nobody would believe me when I told them that I had not—repeat *not*—lost consciousness when we hit. They pointed to my injuries as proof that I must have been knocked out. I couldn't offer my proof for many months. But I was right. The idea that I had hallucinated in post-accident trauma was plausible nonsense.

To make this strictly and absolutely accurate, I actually did black out for maybe a second or two at the moment of impact, but I feel sure it was brief. I came to when the noise of settling metal and bending struts was still going on around me. Although I was in no pain, I couldn't move a finger—or a toe either. The helicopter had struck almost flat, thanks to Leo's last-ditch efforts, but fast. I had been thrown forward and to the right, to smash against the side panel and window as the machine jerked to a violent halt on the uneven ground.

It's hard to say how long I lay there, listening to the creak of twisted metal and wondering what I would do if the wreck caught fire. (Answer: nothing, which was all I could do.) The right side of my head was flat on the metal, and I was looking out of the window at the dark brown earth. From where I lay the perspective was distorted. It seemed that my nose was flat against the steel surface, just as though my head had been sheared in two to the right of my nose, and the left half laid on the cold metal panel.

All the fear and emotion that I felt before the crash had gone. I remember thinking, *About time, too,* when I finally heard footsteps moving on the broken frame of the helicopter. Surely it couldn't be Leo? He would have dragged me clear of possible fire before going to look for help. As the footsteps came closer I realized there were at least two people, stepping cautiously over the angled floor. There was a sound of labored breathing, and a grunt as some heavy object behind me was lifted and moved to one side.

"It's not on him, Scouse," said a voice a few feet from my head, "There's no sign of it."

"Bloody hell, it's got to be," said a second voice,

this one with a strong Liverpool accent. " 'Ere, you let me have a look at him, an' you try the other one. Mebbe he already gave it to 'im. Are yer quite sure yer got the right one 'ere?"

"Of course I'm bleedin' sure. He's unconscious, but that's Foss all right. See that tie pin, same as 'e 'ad on 'im last time? I'll take a look-see at this one, but that's Leo Foss."

A pair of black shoes, leather-soled and black-buckled, appeared a few inches in front of my face. Hands were moving lightly over my body, patting and probing.

"It's not on 'im, either," said the first voice. " 'Less it's underneath 'im. I'd 'ave to lift 'im up to see that."

"Well, get on an' do it, yer great git." Scouse sounded uneasy. "Lift him an' do it sharpish. We don't have all bleedin' night 'ere."

Up to that point there had been no pain for me, not even a twinge. But now hands began to raise and turn me, and that was murder. My long-suffering body began to protest, all the way from my toes to my neck. Streaks of agony were like darts shooting into my spine and my right side. It was too much. When I slid dizzily into unconsciousness I was very glad to go. My final thought was of Leo. I hadn't seen him since the crash, but the words of the two men told me that he was at least still alive. That was some comfort during my descent into darkness.

– 2 –

The first waking didn't count for much. It was a blurry, mush-minded few minutes of staring at an unfocused white ceiling, wondering who I was, where I was, and why I was aching all over. I didn't even try to move, which I later found out was just as well.

The second time up from the pit was better and worse. I found myself in a firm bed that was raised at the head end ten or fifteen degrees. I was in no danger of falling out, though—not with the tubes and wires that hung all over me like spaghetti. I was the central meatball. And I hurt even more than the first time.

I lay there, blinking. My right eye was providing me with a set of strange and uncoordinated images, and I spent the first few minutes trying to get things into focus. It was hard work until I learned the trick, which was to concentrate only on the object and not on the way my eye did the focusing. When the image in front of me finally became sharp it was debatable if the result was worth the effort. I was looking at a fat, bald-headed man with bulging eyes. He was sitting on a chair at the end of the bed, holding an apple in one thick-fingered paw and stolidly munching on it.

He nodded at me cheerfully when he saw that I was awake and finally focusing on him.

"With us for a while, eh? Good. I can stop guarding you for a little bit. D'ye know who you are?"

I made a miserable croaking noise, and he looked sympathetic.

"Try again."

"Ah—ah—Li'el Sa'ki'."

"Terrific." He threw the apple core somewhere out of sight, wiped his hands on the pants of his crumpled blue suit, and stood up. "That's the first question answered. I think you'd do well now to have another little nap. Don't go away now, and I'll bring the nurse."

His voice was deep and self-confident, with a West Yorkshire cut to the vowels. He moved out of my line of vision—I was getting nothing from my left eye—and I heard the squeak of heavy leather boots as he went out of the room. A minute later a nurse in a blue uniform slipped a needle into my right arm, and I went under again. As I did so I wondered why I needed the services of a policeman to guard me. My name is well-known enough, but I'm certainly no celebrity.

As I became unconscious I wanted to ask about Leo, but I had left it too late.

Third time lucky. I was improving a little

when I woke, and I knew it. My overall ache had progressed to sharp points of individual agony, but the feeling of being disembodied and unfocused was much less. My head still buzzed and reeled, but it felt like my head and not some anonymous cauliflower. I came out of a strange dream of my childhood, back before Leo and I were reunited. The familiar views of Middlesbrough and Stockton where I had grown up were overlaid with alien images of surf, flat palm trees, and fast-moving freeways. The harder I tried to concentrate, the more the images mixed and moved.

I finally worked my eyes open, to see the same fat man sitting there staring at me. He had taken a big clasp knife out of his pocket and was opening it when he saw my eyes blinking at him. He put the knife away again and moved quietly out of the room, still betrayed in his movements by the squeaking boots. When the nurse came in to crank my bed to a higher position for my head I turned to look at her.

"What's happening?" My voice was still rusty, but in better control. "Why do they need a policeman here to watch me?"

She looked worried, shook her head, and slipped out of the room again without answering me. I heard her voice nearby.

"I'm afraid we have a problem—a new one. He's awake, but he's rambling, something about being watched by a policeman."

"I'll be in in a moment," said a deep voice. "I don't like the sound of it, but all his other signs look good."

It was my fat friend again. There was another mumble from the nurse that this time I could not catch, then he appeared, grinning at me as he entered my limited field of vision. The nurse was behind him, a dark-haired woman with a great figure and with worry lines in her forehead. She was frowning at me accusingly.

"He did say it," she said. "I'm sure he did." Then, to me, "What was it you were telling me about a policeman?"

My left arm seemed unwilling to move when I tried to lift it. So even though my right forearm was a mass of IV tubes and monitor contacts, I managed to raise it far enough to point.

"Him," I said. "The policeman. Why is he here guarding me?"

She put one hand up to her mouth and her eyes widened. The worry lines vanished. "Ooh," she said. "Sir Westcott." And without another word to either of us she hurried out of the room.

The fat man pulled a chair towards the bedside and sat down on it with a grunt.

"She'll be back." He was scowling. "Gone to have a good laugh, if I know her. I think mebbe it's time I introduced meself. I'm Westcott Shaw. I'm the one who operated on you when you were brought in."

I looked at the hand resting on the back of the chair—the fingers were like a fat bunch of sausages—and shuddered at the thought. If he'd been pawing around in my delicate insides . . .

"Where am I? Is my brother Leo all right? And how long have I been lying here?"

"One thing at a time, and let's not rush it. You're

in the Queen's Hospital Annex, just outside Reading. Tomorrow it'll be four weeks since you were admitted."

That was a bad shock. Four weeks, and in that whole time I must have been conscious for a total of five confused minutes.

"What about Leo? Is he here too? Is he all right?" The questions came buzzing up without any conscious control.

"No, he's not all right." He saw my expression. "But it's a lot more complicated than you think. I don't want to start on that now, but I promise you I'll tell you all about it next time." He looked down at the catheters, intravenous feed tubes, monitors, and sensors that ran from my body to a variety of drip-feeds, waste bags, and electronic recorders. "I even think we can start to get rid of some of this plumbing, You're coming on faster than I hoped. We'll get Tess to take care of some of that this afternoon. How much do you hurt?"

"A lot."

"I'll believe it. You've had a fair hack about. I'll put you under again if you want me to, but if you can stand to stay awake for another half hour I'd like you to do something for me."

"I'll try. But it will have to be something easy. My brain's like cottonwool."

"It should be easy. I want you to think about your childhood, and about your life before you came in here. Just let your thoughts run where they want to, but do it in as much detail as you can. Don't worry about forgetting, or making any sort of note. Just let yourself go." He stood up.

"I know it sounds daft, but it's important for your treatment and recovery."

He came closer to me and peered into my face. "You're coming along fine. Anything coming in yet from that left eye? Blink each one, and try and look at my finger here."

Sausage—no sausage—sausage—no sausage.

"No. My right eye seems fine, but what's wrong with my left one?"

"Nothing. You'll see all right in a while. Give it time." He was off around the end of the bed before I could ask more, and I heard again that familiar squeak of boots—somebody should tell him he needed oiling. I closed both my eyes and felt dizzy again. Why couldn't I see out of my left eye? That hadn't been injured, I was sure of it—I had seen things with it right after the accident. What had happened when they brought me in here? And what had happened to Leo? It was difficult to see why the surgeon didn't want to talk to me about him.

In a minute or two I heard the nurse beside me, muttering and grumbling to herself. "I knew it, I knew he'd get you all excited. Your pulse is up again and so's your blood pressure. I *told* him to wait a couple of days more."

She saw that I had opened my eyes and was staring up at her miserably. She shook her head.

"Honestly, a *policeman*." She smiled, the worry lines disappeared, and she was suddenly very attractive. "I had to leave when you said that."

"Are you Tess?"

"Nurse Thomson to you." (But her smile took the edge off it.) "I know how you felt, when I first saw Sir Westcott I thought he must have stopped in at the hospital to deliver meat to the kitchen. A policeman's a new one, though—what made you think that?"

"It was his fault. He said he was guarding me."

"He meant he was keeping his eye on you—you're his prize patient." She had finished checking the monitors, and seemed happy with the result.

"Tess, what's happened to me?"

"Nurse Thomson." She bit her lip. "I shouldn't talk about it, really I shouldn't. But you're going to be all right—you've got the best doctor you could ever get. You were in a very bad accident." She moved to look into my face, studying it. "I'll be taking the catheters out later, and I don't think you want to be awake for that. I can tell you're hurting, but Sir Westcott told me to leave you as you are if you can stand it. Will you be all right to stay awake for a few minutes more?"

"If you'll stay to hold my hand." As I said it, I wondered what was happening. I would *never* try a line like that—particularly when I was quite incapable of following up on it. My concussion must be worse than I knew.

She just smiled. "I'll be back in twenty minutes. It's always a good sign when a patient gets fresh. Shout if you need me sooner."

I lay back and closed my eyes again, to assess my pains jointly and severally. Right leg, ribs, and head were the worst, with stomach and neck a close second. They competed for attention. It was a poor time to try for boyhood reminiscence, or for thinking of any kind, but if it would speed my recovery, I ought to at least give it a try.

✧   ✧   ✧

Being drugged is certainly no obstacle to recalling your childhood; I would say that it even helps. In the next twenty-four hours, drifting in and out of sedated sleep, I tried to obey Sir Westcott Shaw's request and worked my way forward from my earliest memories. I took his word for it that the exercise would have some value, and the order of recollection didn't matter.

I suppose that by my third birthday I already knew that I was a "twin," and that being a twin somehow made me special. It was unfair. I didn't know my twin, and Uncle Fred and Aunt Dora did. They would talk about him and about me when I was presumed to be asleep or watching the television.

"It's not fair to bring them up apart like this," Uncle Fred would say. "They have to get to know each other. We should send him out there for a visit with Leo."

"Don't be daft, Fred. We don't have the money for anything like that, and you know it."

"Well, mebbe Tom could find some way to send Leo over here for a holiday to see Lionel."

"It's a long trip from out there. It would cost a lot."

At the age of six I knew that "out there" was Los Angeles, a location as far away to me as the Moon. It seemed farther away. After all, I could see the Moon. In a way, Leo and I were true Moon-children. We were born on July 20, 1969, the day that humans first landed on the Moon and so far as we were concerned the Space Age began.

When we were one year old, Mum and Dad had been killed. They had gone down to Leeds for a day out, a casual shopping expedition, and they had stayed there for dinner. At seven o'clock in the evening, a big truck had gone out of control in the middle of the town and smashed in through the front of a restaurant. Fourteen people were killed. That was a statistic. Mum and Dad were at a window table and died instantly. If that was also a statistic, it was one that changed our lives forever.

Big Brother Leo went to live with Mum's brother and his wife, Tom and Ellen Foss. In 1972 Tom lost his job with Marconi and was offered a good one with Standard Oil of California in La Habra. Leo and I, two years old, had a final meeting in December, 1972. Later we both claimed to remember it, but I think we were recreating it from other people's descriptions.

I stayed on in Middlesbrough, living with Dad's brother, Fred, and Aunt Dora.

They could have no children of their own. It took me many years to learn that the two deaths they would have given anything to prevent had enriched their life together and given it a new meaning.

The earliest memory I can positively identify came at Christmas, when I was four years old. We had a telephone call from America and I talked to Leo. I was enormously excited when I was told that my "twin" was on the phone, and enormously disappointed when he said nothing more than the sort of things I might have said myself.

Memories came thicker after that. As I lay

there in the Reading Hospital I did my best to work my way steadily forward in time, but it was hopeless. Either I was too sick, or I was too full of drugs and mental confusion. Instead of the quiet years at Middlesbrough, through elementary school and then on through grammar school, I conjured up a distorted, surrealistic collage of events. The cold front room where I had practiced on the black upright piano was there, but the used-only-at-Christmas furniture with its shiny covers had vanished in favor of casual, low-slung chairs and couches with bright patterned upholstery, lit by a fiercer sun than the north of England ever knew. My solo performances on the piano, at school and later in the Town Hall, were clearly remembered; but they had acquired a different audience, full of tall, tanned girls with long hair and perfect teeth. They were noisy and cheerful, crowding in toward the stage while I struggled with a Mozart sonata.

I sweated in the hospital bed, tossing and turning, peering into the past until the night nurse, looking in, gave me an injection to bring the relief of a deeper sleep.

The next morning I couldn't avoid trying again, the way we tend to pick at a half-healed scab once we realize that it's there. Memories came easier after Leo and I had our first *real* meeting—which is to say, the first meeting where we were able to understand our relationship to each other.

It happened when we were nearly twelve. A big medical conference took place in Edinburgh, and one of its key sessions had as a theme the psychology and physiology of identical twins who had been reared apart. Uncle Fred had the brain-wave of his life. At his suggestion, the conference committee arranged for Leo and me to attend together and to submit to a couple of days of tests and questions. All our expenses were covered.

My inferiority complex probably began with that meeting. Raised in a house with no other children, I had become used to spending time alone and I was shy with strangers. My public recitals somehow didn't count; they were encounters with an anonymous and faceless audience. Leo had the advantage of me. Tom and Ellen Foss already had one child, a girl, before they took Leo, and a year later they had another daughter. Leo grew up in what sounded to me like a rowdy, active household, full of visiting California nymphets who came to see his sisters. At the conference in Edinburgh I met a relaxed, tanned version of myself, already a bit taller and heavier (blame those American meals and vitamins), far more self-confident, and with a developed line of small talk that allowed him to meet and impress any girl he happened to fancy. I watched and imitated, but there was no doubt who was the expert.

We had a great time in Edinburgh in spite of all that. Even the tests were fun. We came out with the same IQ's, rather differently distributed as to skills.

Our memories were about equally good, but I knew more English words. Thank crossword puzzles for that—the only Sunday newspaper that Uncle Fred would allow in the house was the *Observer*, and I cut my teeth on the "Everyman" crossword puzzles.

In spite of that evidence of wordpower, it was

Leo who showed more aptitude for and interest in languages. Concert travels eventually have brought me to the point where I can ask my way to the airport in half a dozen foreign tongues (and sometimes even understand the answers). But Leo was really interested, and by the time he was twenty-five he was fluent in five languages, and had a passing acquaintance with three or four more.

When the Edinburgh conference was over we had a few hours to ourselves before we had to take the train back to Middlesbrough. There was no need to sit and talk any more—we already knew that we got on better together than anyone else in the world. So we hit the fleshpots. I introduced Leo to skate and chips with salt and vinegar, and then to knickerbockerglories, with five flavors of ice cream, pineapple crush, whipped cream, strawberry sauce, chocolate flakes and grated nuts. He insisted he could eat another one. So did I.

On the train back to Middlesbrough I was sick out of the window on one side and Leo was sick out of one on the other. Two days later we watched a shuttle lift-off together on the television in Aunt Dora's bedroom. That same afternoon we had our first fight.

I was trying to bring back some details of that when I fell asleep again, and woke to find Sir Westcott Shaw sitting in his favorite place at the end of the bed.

He was holding two apples in one paw (did the man live on them?) and nodded amiably to me when he saw my eyes were open.

"How are you feeling?"

"Terrible." My ribs were killing me, and so was my right leg.

"Right. I thought you might be. I dropped your dose of painkillers in half."

"You're very kind."

"I thought you ought to be as alert as possible for this session."

"How's Leo?"

"If you'll give me a minute, I'll tell you. But first off I want to ask you just a few questions. All right?"

"Whatever you like." I didn't try and hide my impatience.

He reached down and picked up a pad from the floor next to his feet, then fished out a stub of pencil from his inside jacket pocket. I looked again at the heavy boots, and the fat, banana-bunch fingers.

"Are you sure you're a doctor and not a policeman?"

He looked at me sympathetically. "Pain's pretty bad, eh? I'll keep this as short as I can, then we'll give you a jab. I'll start with the easy stuff. What's your name?"

"It's still Lionel Salkind."

"Good. You're saying that a sight better than you could this time last week. How old are you?"

"Thirty-seven—unless you've had me unconscious for a few more months and not told me about it."

"Not this time. Now, I want you to think for a minute before you answer this one. I know your head hurts like hell, and I know we've bunged you full up with drugs. Try and allow for all that, and tell me, does your head feel normal?"

I tried. It didn't. My thoughts ran in swooping, random patterns, dipping away from the question and back again. I had to concentrate on every word he said, and for the first time I realized I had been like this ever since I woke up after the accident.

"No," I said at last. "My head feels funny."

"I'm not surprised. Do you think you can describe it better—give it something more than saying it feels 'funny'?"

"It reminds me of the way I feel when I speak French or German after a long time without using it. I have to grope around for what I want to say, looking for words. And when you speak to me I have to listen very hard to grasp what you're getting at."

"Good way of putting it." He scowled down at the page, then stuck the pencil up behind his ear. "One more question, then I'll talk for a while. What can you remember about your accident? Take your time, and tell it in any order you like."

I had to work hard at answering that. So long as I didn't try to pin events down closely, my memory seemed to be clear about what happened. But when I thought hard, events became confused and wandering. It was like trying to look at a very faint star. So long as you look a little away from it, your sensitive peripheral vision lets you see it. When you turn your attention to it directly, it just winks out of existence.

He showed no impatience as I went through my mental struggles, but when at last I spoke he leaned forward intently, nodding now and again. He said nothing until I described the two men who had entered the wreck and searched me and Leo for something, then he frowned and shook his head unhappily.

"That worries me. It sounds like pure hallucination from start to finish, I was hoping we wouldn't run into any of that."

"It's not hallucination. I remember it clearly, and that's just how it happened."

He shrugged. "I'm sure that's the way you remember it. The records say otherwise. The first people at the crash were a carload of farmers who saw the helicopter come down from a few fields away. They didn't search you, and they brought you straight here. Just as well that they did. Half an hour later, and we'd have been able to do nothing for you. You had a close call."

"But I'm telling you, it happened the way I said. We were searched."

"I don't want to beat that point to death—we can talk about it more later. I promised you some explanations today, and I think you're well enough to take them. But it will take a few minutes. Stop me if this gets to be too much, or if you have trouble following what I'm saying, Otherwise, let me talk."

He took a manila folder—he had been sitting on it—opened it, and started to read from it in a flat, toneless voice. The beginning was simple and unpleasant enough: my list of injuries when they logged me into the Emergency Room at Queen's Hospital Annex in Reading.

Lionel Salkind, British subject.

Crushed right leg below the knee; broken tibia and fibula, compound fracture; broken patella; crushed talus, crushed navicular, broken metatarsals.

Broken right femur, compound fracture, with severed sartorius muscle. Crushed right testicle and epididymis.

Fractured eight, ninth, tenth, and eleventh ribs, penetrating the costal pleura and piercing the right lung.

Ruptured spleen.

Damaged right kidney, and severed renal artery.

If I had been feeling sick when Sir Westcott began his catalog, I grew sicker as he went on with it.

"Don't just keep reading that," I said to him, when be showed no signs of stopping. "Tell me what you can do about it."

He waved his hand at me without looking up. "I'm keeping this as short as I can. There's a lot of messy detail for all these that don't help us at all. Let me get to the bad part. Here we are. Head injuries."

Crushed right middle and inner ear and severed pharyngo-tympanic tube.

Crushed right mastoid, sphenoid, temporal and occipital bones, with fragment penetration of right frontal, temporal, and parietal brain lobes. Crushed cuneus and precuneus. Right cerebral cortex shows numerous lesions and approximately fifty percent tissue destruction.

He coughed. "*Prognosis: terminal.*"

Then he looked at me to see my reaction. I couldn't speak, but the punch line of an old tall story would have been the thing to offer. "So what happened to you then, Bill?" "What happened to me? Why, I died, of course."

Prognosis: terminal.

If you want a phrase guaranteed to send you over the edge into lunacy, there's my candidate.

I gave a sort of hysterical titter. "What are you telling me? That I died and now I'm in Hell?"

"Nothing so sensational. Let me finish." He pulled another sheet of paper from his folder. "Your brother."

Leo Foss, United States subject. Broken pelvis. Broken lower mandible, broken humerus.

Damaged and crushed liver, lacerated pancreas, lacerated stomach.

Shattered spinal column, crushed lumbar, thoracic, and cervical vertebrae, crushed medulla, severed spinal cord in cervical region.

He looked up at me. "There's more, but it all tells the same story. *Prognosis: terminal.* For ten different reasons."

At that point he laid down his folder, pulled an apple out of his pocket, and fished about for his clasp knife. I couldn't believe my eyes. Was he going to settle in and munch one now, leaving Leo and me with our terminal prognoses while he had a mid-afternoon snack?

"You see," he said—now he was deliberately opening the knife. "I knew I had a problem within five minutes of you being brought into the hospital. I could fix your broken leg, after a fashion. You'd not walk on that ankle, but I'd have taken it off at the knee, anyway. And I could have done a halfway decent job on your ribs and lung, too. You'd have had to manage on one kidney and one ear, but there's plenty of people who do that, an' get along very well with it. Only your very close friends would ever get to know that you only had one testicle, so that didn't worry me, either. You see the problem? It was that smashed skull, and the damaged brain lobes. The right-hand side, in by the ear, that was a mess. It was all bubble-an'-squeak, no good to anybody. I might have been able to keep you alive for a couple of weeks, and that would have been it."

"It's been a month since the accident, and I'm still alive."

"Alive, and doing very well. You were in good physical shape before the crash, too, or you'd never be as far along as you are. But my other problem was your brother, Leo. He was in worse shape even than you were. With his spinal injuries and internal bleeding, he was sinking before we could even get him into the theater. I had to make a decision."

He paused, and suddenly I knew what was coming. It made me feel sick inside.

"*You killed Leo.*"

"No." He sighed. "The crash killed Leo. I saved you."

"Leo is dead. You never told me that." I was trembling.

"Because it's not true. Shut up, and listen to me." He glowered down at me. "Your brother was a hopeless case, absolutely hopeless. And you were terribly injured. I had to make a decision, but it was an easy one. Save one, or save none."

I closed my eyes. "So you killed Leo to save me."

"I did not, you jackass. Will you shut up and listen to me? You know as well as I do that you and Leo were perfect donors for each other.

There's no tissue rejection problem with identical twins. And since Madrill's work in '03, the success rate for nerve tissue regeneration has been going up every year. I did the easy work first. You have Leo's right leg, right kidney, right testicle, right inner ear, and a bone graft from his ribs. That was straightforward, and we know it will work. Once the nerve regeneration therapy is complete, you'll have full use of all those. The tricky part came later."

He took the knife he was holding and cut the apple in his hand cleanly down the middle. "If I were to put the problem in your half-baked terms, you died as much as Leo did."

"I'm here, and he isn't."

"Don't be too sure of that. Look, imagine this apple is the whole brain, and now the two halves are the left and right hemispheres. At first, I had the idea that we might be able to put all Leo's brain into your skull—a full transplant. But no one ever made one work yet, and I didn't like the odds. It was easier to be less ambitious. You lost partial segments from three main brain lobes, but you had the brain stem and the midbrain completely intact. This was what your right hemisphere looked like, if we forget the part that was damaged."

He made a few swift crosscuts with his knife, and segments of apple fell clear into the palm of his hand. He looked at them vaguely for a couple of seconds, then popped them into his mouth and ate them.

"See?" he said with his mouth full. "You lost a good part of one hemisphere, but what you had left was well-connected. People have survived head injuries in which they lost nearly this much, and had nobody around to give transplant material to them. You'd have died, but not, so to speak, by very much. And if I took parts of Leo's brain, and used them to replace the lobe segments you lost, the chances became very good. I could use undamaged parts of his skull, too, and have that as bone grafts for the smashed parts of your skull. That's what I did."

He looked pleased with himself. "And it worked—worked damned well. You're getting better all the time."

"But Leo's dead. I don't feel half like Leo, and half like myself. I'm Lionel Salkind."

"That's what you tell me—I asked you that when you first became conscious. But all it proves is that you have the verbal part of the brain under control. That's all in your hemisphere, we know that's a left hemisphere function. You feel just the way you ought to, at this stage in the recovery. Do you know what the corpus callosum is?"

"No. "

"Well, you will, for the rest of your life." He pushed the two apple segments together, then drew them apart again. "The *corpus callosum* is the part that sits between the two brain hemispheres. It acts as a sort of a bridge between them, and *pons* would be the natural Latin name for it, 'cause that means a bridge. But we got smart too late, so another bit of the brain is called the pons. But it's the corpus callosum that's the real bridge, and handles all the information transfer directly between the hemispheres. There's lots of other communication goes on, of course, through a bit called the anterior commissure, but that's mainly indirect and chemical. To make the story short, just now you're missing a corpus callosum between your brain segments and Leo's. But it'll regenerate, thanks to Madrill's treatments."

"When?"

"Ah, now there you have me. It could take three months, or it could be a couple of years. Just to complicate things a bit more, the left side of your body is mainly controlled from the right side of your brain. That's why I wanted to know if you were getting any information through that left eye. That'd give us some idea how fast regeneration of nerve tissue is going. Nothing yet?"

I closed my right eye. "Nothing. Look, are you saying that Leo's sort of alive still? I mean, if you transplanted his kidney into me you wouldn't say he was alive, would you?"

"I wouldn't; but then not many people think with their kidneys. If you want my honest opinion, yes, I think that Leo Foss is still alive, in some sense, and he's inhabiting part of your skull. At some time—don't ask me when and where, or even how—I would expect the two halves of the brain to integrate again. You'll become a single individual. And beyond that, I can't go."

He pressed a button at the end of the bed. "Now, I think you've had all the excitement that's good for you for one day. Miss Thomson will be here in a minute or two and give you an injection. If you don't mind, I'd like to sit here and watch as that takes effect."

He handed the carved-up apple to the nurse when she appeared and took the second one from his pocket. While she checked my blood pressure, pulse, and temperature (I suspect I tested worse than I had that morning) I looked at Sir Westcott and had terrible visions of those uncouth, pork-butcher hands meddling with the delicate couplings of my brain, cutting and tying and stitching.

While I watched, Sir Westcott took his open clasp knife and started absentmindedly to peel the apple. He didn't seem to look at it, and the thick fingers were as clumsy-looking as ever. But the apple peel came off magically in one beautiful regular strip, a uniform half inch wide. There was no trace of green peel left on the body of the apple, and no sign of white overcut flesh on the lengthening spiral that came off it.

By the time the injection took effect, at least one of my worries had been eased.

– 3 –

As Mark Hambourg remarked, three things are essential if you want to be a professional musician: the first requirement is good health, and the other two are the same. A performer's life is hard, and there's no way you can tell the critics that you didn't play well because you were feeling less than your best.

I had always taken health for granted, and never been really sick in my whole life. That made me a bad patient. My convalescence broke naturally into two phases: very sick, then very bored. I gradually began to regain full control of the left side of my body, but no one could tell me how fast that should happen. The operation that Sir Westcott had performed on me was experimental— as he explained, the previous subjects had been dogs, where it was much commoner to have available members of the same litter.

It may sound ridiculous to say that things could

be boring when I had to learn to control and live with a body that was more like a patchwork quilt than the standard human model. But the body was merely a nuisance rather than a real source of interest. Inside six weeks I was up and about, and had even taken the classical step in patient recovery—the "turn for the nurse." Tess Thomson handled my clumsy advance without missing a beat of my pulse, and took it for the good omen that it was.

One week more, and I was given the run of the hospital wards. Although there was plenty of evidence of imperfect body control as I hobbled, staggered and leaked (kidneys and bladder still partly out of control) along the corridors, the presence of Leo's brain segment was not apparent. Sir Westcott dismissed as "predictable and minor" most of the things that worried me.

Predictable and minor—good doctors' talk. It included incredible blinding headaches, dizziness, nausea (he blamed the ear for that, not the brain, but the distinction was a fine one to the sufferer), insomnia, sneezing fits, aphasia, weak bladder, sudden and stupefying lethargy, uncontrollable weeping, muscular spasms, and a rolling left eye. I don't know where the left eye took its orders from, but I never knew where it would be looking, or why, even though I was beginning to receive random images from it.

I poured out this whole catalog of woes to Sir Westcott. He would eat another apple and say, "Most interesting."

It went slowly. Two months after my first conversation with Sir Westcott Shaw I was ready to climb the walls. I had enough control to walk from one end of the hospital to the other without falling down, visibly twitching, or peeing myself. On the strength of that I applied (pleaded might be a better word) for a day outside.

Where would you go?

I had anticipated that question. To the Zoo. Where else?

As I mentioned earlier, it's natural to assume that anyone who performs frequently in public must be extroverted and thrive on attention. After all, applause is rightly regarded as the purest form of ego-food. I like that as much as anyone else, but once I'm offstage I have always found it hard to meet people or to feel at home among new faces. Leo was the confident and the outgoing one. I would find myself again and again in a big city, the day of an evening recital, free and with nowhere to go. Movies staled after a while, and I had no taste for museums, horse racing, or dog shows.

Zoos were another matter. Before I was twenty I was a connoisseur. Most big cities have a zoo of some kind, or at worst an aviary. I looked forward to seeing the pandas whenever I went to Washington, the snow leopards in San Diego, the giraffes at Whipsnade, the gorillas in Riyadh, springbok herd in Denver, sealions in Sydney, elephants in Tokyo, lions and tigers in Santiago, and hippopotami in Montevideo and Berlin.

My favorites, wherever I went (and the psychologists can make what they like of it) were the snakes and reptiles.

So if Sir Westcott would let me out for a day, I would go to the new London Zoo. I told him about my long-time hobby, but I didn't tell him my secondary motive. Maybe I was reluctant to admit it, even to myself. My secondary motive was fear.

Sir Westcott had given me plenty of material to read about the human brain, and I had struggled through most of it. It's surprising how fast we learn things when they apply to us personally. One message that was repeated in paper after paper was the importance of the right hemisphere of the brain for music. Even if I recovered my health completely—even if Leo and I became a single and integrated personality—the old career of concert pianist might be closed to me. I might be able to read the notes easily enough, but if the *feel* had gone no amount of technique could hide it. I was scared.

As for the technique: there is a story that was told to me when I was ten years old and attributed to Horowitz, but it's so much a part of pianistic folklore that it could have been said originally by Rachmaninov, or Liszt, or any virtuoso all the way back to Mozart and Clementi. "If I do not practice for one day I know it; if I do not practice for two days my fellow pianists know it; if I do not practice for three days everyone knows it."

I had not touched a piano for three months. I was not trained for any life other than a pianist. What was I going to do with myself from now until old age?

For an hour or two I had the wild idea that I might take Leo's job—after all, I was partly entitled to it. But it was out of the question. For one thing, he was legally dead. With two people going into the hospital, and only one coming out of it, something had to be done to make a rational record. Worse than that, though, I had no idea what Leo did for a living. He always seemed to be trotting off around the world for the U.S. State Department—a year in India, a year in Africa. But as to what he *did* there, I was as incompetent to assume that duty as he would have been to play the Brahms' Second.

That's when I got the idea that maybe my hobby could be turned into my job. If I eventually recovered sufficiently to return to the concert stage, fine. If not, over the past ten years I had built up more knowledge of snakes and reptiles than the average zookeeper. Leo and I had both been blessed with unusual memories. That might be a place to use it.

Both Sir Westcott and Tess gave me cautionary lectures before I was allowed to leave the hospital. No excitement, they said, and no exertion. Remember you are still early in your recovery, and if you feel at all dizzy sit down right where you are and ask for help. I nodded meekly—all I wanted to do was get out of there and on my way.

The weather was warm but I wore a knitted wool cap. My appearance in the mirror was something I had learned to live with. Others might balk at a tall, shambling figure, dot-and-carry-one in his walk, and with scars all over his head. Stubbly black hair was reluctantly growing to cover them, but I had a long way to go. No prizes for my appearance, unless it was in the scarecrow-of-the-year category.

It had been three years since I had last visited this zoo. I took my time, savoring each enclosure. There was a new small mammal house, and an improved environment for viewing nocturnals, with recessed red bulbs and a thermal infrared viewer on some cages.

Thursday afternoon was not a busy time. I saw two parties of schoolchildren, one policeman, and one young couple who walked arm-in-arm and never, so far as I could tell, looked at any of the animals. I dawdled through the Monkey House, then went last of all to see the reptiles. The Reptile House had been horridly renamed as the Herpetarium. Somebody had more erudition than sense.

It was highly satisfying. Crocodiles, snakes, lizards, turtles, and even a rare specimen of *Rhynchocephalia*, the tuatera lizard.

I had thought the place was deserted. So it was rather a shock when I turned from a glass cage containing a blase-looking puff adder and caught sight of a woman in a dark blue dress peering at me from the other end of the long room. She dodged quickly out of sight behind the central row of exhibits. I took a couple of steps in that direction, then my pulse began to hammer away at about twice its usual rate, I felt dizzy and nauseated, and there was no choice but to sit down on the ledge that ran in front of the cage.

Avoid all excitement, Tess had said, and I felt I had done my best. It was difficult to understand why a brief glimpse of an unremarkable—and unfamiliar—face should wipe me out so completely.

In a minute or so I was under good enough control to walk the length of the Reptile House.

The woman had disappeared. I continued through the exhibits—fine specimens of *Draco* lizards, and some unusual *Hydrophidae*, sea-snakes over seven feet long—but I felt shaken and some of my enjoyment had gone.

As I was leaving the Reptile House I saw her again. This time I had a better look. She was about thirty years old, maybe five-feet five, and a bit too thin. She walked towards me, looking sideways towards the sealions' pool as we passed and avoiding my eyes completely. Her profile was a little too sharp for beauty.

"Follow me, Leo."

The words came so softly that I wondered if they might be a fabrication of my poor battered brain. I turned, but she walked on and did not look round.

Had she really spoken? I thought of calling to her, then decided it might be very embarrassing if I had misheard. I hesitated, and trailed along after her at a respectable distance. We sauntered along, past the Monkey House, through the aviary, and finally on out to the car park. I thought for a moment that I had lost her there. She had disappeared. Then I saw that a grey van on the left had its rear doors open, and I walked hesitantly towards it as though intending to walk right past.

"In here."

The soft call would have been inaudible to someone ten yards away.

The inside was dark. I climbed up the rear step, then moved forwards on my knees onto a pile of carpets or felt matting. The door clicked to behind me. The painted-over windows allowed enough light inside for me to see the shadow of the woman, crouching in front of me. Before I could move she leaned forward, put her arms around me, and laid her head on my chest.

"Leo. Oh, Leo, thank God. I've wondered and I've prayed." Even though the voice was muffled against my coat, her accent was unmistakably American. "Thank God. I thought you were in cover, but there was no way of knowing while you were still inside that hospital."

I pulled myself away, tingling with the smell of a strangely familiar perfume.

"I'm not Leo," I said, after a second or two.

She stiffened. "Leo, Leo . . ."

"I'm not Leo. Leo is—was—" I found myself struggling to say it, almost as though I was forcing myself to acknowledge something for the first time. "Leo was killed in an accident."

My pulse was thumping again, up around a hundred and forty. Sir Westcott would give me hell if he found out—*and it wasn't my fault*. Even as I had that thought, another more peevish one crept in. It was typical that Leo, with a girl in every port, should be calling forth tears of joy and sorrow, whereas no one worried at all about what happened to me. The woman in front of me had made a snorting, incredulous sound when I said Leo was dead.

"But you can't be—" she began. Then she leaned away to the front of the van's compartment, and picked up a thing like a flashlight from the pile of rugs.

"Give me your hand." When I didn't move, she

reached out, raised my left hand, and pressed a switch on the side of the metal cylinder she was holding. Nothing at all happened, but she gave a groan of pure misery and slumped her head forward to her chest.

"It's true," she said after a few seconds. "You're not Leo. You're the brother, the twin brother. Not Leo at all."

It is never flattering to feel that you are being described as an object rather than a person. To her, I was clearly the wrong thing, no substitute for Leo. I began to feel an anger that even mastered my confusion.

"Now that you seem to know who I am, maybe you'd like to return the compliment," I said. "Who are you, and why did you ask me to follow you here? If it comes to that, how did you know I'd be here at the Zoo today?"

It was brusque, but it brought her out of her silent misery. She lifted her head and shrugged.

"I followed you here from the hospital. I thought you were Leo, and I had to talk to him. About his work."

"So why didn't you ask me back near the hospital?"

"It might not have been safe." She hesitated. "Look, we must talk. I am Valnora Warren. Leo and I worked together and we were close friends."

I leaned back on the pile of rugs and took a deep breath. If she had been close to Leo, would it be any kindness to tell her what had really happened? It would be no consolation to her to know that in a sense Leo lived on, inside me.

While I was thinking about that, another memory seemed to brush against my consciousness. I was reliving the last helicopter ride that Leo and I had made, when he told me that he needed to talk to me. There had been no time to find out why, but I could recall his worry and tension. Until I knew more about her, it seemed to me that the less I told Valnora Warren, the better.

She seemed to have herself under good control now. As our eyes became used to the dim light, I could see her peering anxiously at me, nervously rubbing her fingers along the smooth material of her dress.

"Look—Lionel, isn't it?—I know this must seem peculiar to you. Leo and I worked together, off and on, for a long time—eight years. We were very close, so I know from what he told me that you and he were even closer."

From the way she spoke, I sensed that she had been about as close to Leo as anyone could get. I remembered the way she had grabbed me when I first came into the van. I just nodded. "Leo and I were very close."

"But you didn't see each other very often, did you? I was wondering, did he ever tell you much about the work that he did?"

Her question was tentative, and I could feel a premonition building inside my head like a black thundercloud. She was too nervous. It made me aware that Leo's own emotion, that final evening, had been more than tension. He had been afraid, eager to talk to me in a way that was quite different from the usual easy familiarity that we had built up over the years.

"We talked about his work sometimes," I said. "We talked about everything we did."

"You know where he had been before he came to London?"

"He was away in the East, and on his way back to Washington."

"Do you know where in the East?" Her intensity was painful.

"No. Look here, if you want to sit and cross-examine me you'd better start by telling me what all this is about. Otherwise, the hell with it. I'll go back to the hospital."

"No. Please don't go." She was biting her lip, trying to make up her mind about something. "I shouldn't, but I'll—I'll answer some questions. Some things I just can't talk about. But you'll have to try and answer some of my questions, too."

"We'll see. I won't make any promises." (I couldn't—I had no idea what information I might have that could possibly be interesting to her.)

"All right. What do you want to know?"

"For a start, what's *that* thing?"

I pointed at the cylinder like a flashlight that was sitting on the rugs beside her.

"It's an ultraviolet lamp." She picked it up. "Leo had a small tattoo on his left wrist—invisible in ordinary light, but it would fluoresce in ultraviolet light. That's how I knew—" She paused, and looked down.

"Is that usual for people who work for the U.S. State Department?"

She hesitated again, and leaned back against the metal panel of the van. "I can't answer that. At least, I may be able to, but I'll have to call and get permission. I felt so sure that you were Leo, I didn't . . ." She seemed all set to disappear again in her trance of grief. "When you last saw him, did he tell you—"

"You find out if you can tell me what you know, then I'll tell you what I know. I don't care for all this mystery."

"I'll know what I can tell you by tomorrow." She tried to force a smile. "Could we have dinner then? If you'll do it, I promise that I'll be able to give you answers—more than I can now."

"Tomorrow?" The idea would make Sir Westcott choke on his apple, for me to be out two days in a row, but what the hell, he wasn't my keeper. "Where and when?"

"In London? Can you meet me, at, say, eight o'clock?"

"I hope so. Whereabouts?"

"How about Bertorellis, in Charlotte Street?"

"I know it. I'll meet you there, if you'll answer me one more question now."

She looked uneasy. "If I can."

"Was Leo's job a dangerous one?"

She made a noise somewhere between a laugh and a sob. "You've been leading me on. He told you, didn't he? I thought he might have, even though he wasn't supposed to. Would you answer one question for me, before you go?"

"I had my turn. What do you want to know?"

"Did he ever mention to you somebody with the initials T.P.?"

"What do they stand for?"

"I don't know—that's what I hoped you'd be able to tell me. It was somebody that I'm sure was trying to hurt him. Someone he'd heard of and I'm sure he knew rather well. But he was afraid of them. In his last message to me the tape was hard to hear, but he said that the thing he was scared of most was that T.P. would get him."

"Sorry." I shook my head and raised myself higher on my knees in the van. "I can't help you there. He never mentioned anything to me."

"Well, never mind." She gave a shaky little sort of laugh. She had come up on her knees too, as I started to open the door, and she was almost in an attitude of prayer. "It's astonishing, you look so like him. . . . Be careful when you leave here. I'll see you tomorrow night, right?" She gave another little groan when the light from outside the van fell on my face. "You look so like him . . ."

I closed the van door quietly on her misery and limped away into the late afternoon sunshine. I was sorry for her, but there wasn't a thing I could do about it. And the inside of my head was beginning to hurt badly, buzzing and whirring as though somebody had taken a power saw and was busy trimming off the rear of my skull case. Memory and speculation clashed and fought for my attention. Before Leo met me and we took our fatal ride together, he had come from Zurich. And before that, he had been doing—what? and where?

I felt terrible, dry-mouthed and panting as I reached the subway. And when I got back to the hospital, I caught hell from Tess, and then a second hell from Sir Westcott. I had arrived two hours later than I said I would. Didn't I realize that I was still a very sick man, far to sick to overtax myself like this? And didn't I know how important it was to avoid too much mental stimulation? Well, thank Heaven that the Zoo was a nice, restful place for me to visit. Tess made me a glass of warm milk.

But I ought to concentrate on quiet, peaceful activities for the next two weeks, and not let anyone disturb me. They both insisted on it.

- 4 -

When I woke the next morning I was tempted to tell Sir Westcott Shaw the whole thing. After all, how could he decide how to treat me if he didn't know what had been happening to me?

The thing that kept me silent was fear. Not the fear that he would disbelieve me and dismiss the whole thing as more mental tricks coming from my tattered brain. No, what I was afraid was that he *would* believe me, and forbid me to attend the meeting with Valnora Warren because it would overexcite me. It would, too. Every time I thought about the evening my left hand got the jitters and I had trouble swallowing. But I had to know what had been going on—and I don't just mean I *wanted* to know. I *had* to know.

The whole day would have been impossibly long but for one new factor that was added to the equation. On my morning constitutional, limping along through the interior of the hospital, I worked my way down to a basement corridor where I had never been before. Even though it was new to me, it held no particular promise or interest, and I followed it only because any change to the usual route back to my room was preferable to the same old beige corridors. The new area (I should more accurately call it the old area) was more like a junk yard than part of a hospital. I went past rooms full of old chairs, cans of paint, trolleys, gurneys, stretchers, and battered and ancient beds. There was even an old model X-ray machine in one room, crouched in the corner like a metal Cyclops, dusty and neglected. I spent five minutes fiddling with the buttons and settings on it after I had plugged it into a wall socket, but it was too seized up and arthritic in the joints even to move the position of the shielding plates.

I became bored with it after a while, and almost went on down the corridor without even looking into the next room along. But when I cracked the door open a few inches for a quick and casual glance inside, a thrill of excitement—and fear—shot through my whole body. Standing against the far wall was an old, upright piano.

The question had been staring me in the face for months, but I had managed to look the other way. There had been no piano—so far as I knew—available in the hospital. It had been possible to avoid the central issue: how much had I lost in the crash, and how much more had gone because of lack of practice?

I opened the lid, pulled over a chair, and sat at the keyboard. It was thirty seconds before I could bring myself to touch a key, and when I did my mouth was dry and my tongue felt two sizes too big.

I hit two or three timid notes. The instrument was badly out of tune, and the keys didn't strike evenly—damp had done its work. Well, so what? I took a deep breath, just like a diver standing on the high board, lifted both hands high, and plunged into the final Allegro of Schubert's Sonata in C Minor.

It was horrendous, with fistfuls of wrong notes all over the place. My left hand jumped and twitched over the bass like a demented grasshopper. I didn't care. I plowed on through every discord, and I enjoyed every note. It took me a few seconds to realize that I was getting more than a simple musical response to my playing. During every left hand run in the bass, patterns of smoke blossoms appeared as images in my left eye. They meandered up the field of view, thinning to blue and purple as they rose. If I closed my left eye they disappeared.

I switched to some of the old Czerny velocity exercises, up and down the keyboard with all the grace and elegance of a three-legged racehorse, then jumped straight into the Brahms D Minor Concerto, attacking the octave trills. While I played, regular columns of green insects came into view over the top of the piano, marching steadily to the right until they disappeared from view past the end of my nose. As I stared, the last of the moving bugs changed color, and became an unmistakable exact copy of the gold tie clip that Leo had worn in the helicopter.

Perspiration was running down my forehead and into my eyes, but I wasn't quite ready to quit.

My last effort was probably a mistake. I wanted to get a feeling for just how much coordination I could summon between my left and right hands. The C Minor Fugue, Number 4 from the *Well-Tempered Clavier*, would normally have been a fair test, but I was in poor condition and easily tired. To do Bach justice called for much more finger control and mental equilibrium than I could muster. It was a total loss. I didn't get a single visual image as I hacked and threshed my way through to the conclusion of a travesty of a performance.

When I was done, I discovered that I had wet my pants.

That ended the first Lionel Salkind post-operative recital. I slunk back to my room, thoroughly disgusted with myself and wondering if I had accidentally created a twenty-first century art form to surpass punk rock. Sonata for piano and incontinent. Serenade for tenor, flatulent, and strings. Concerto molto grosso.

I told Sir Westcott about the whole thing when he came on his rounds, and he nodded cheerfully.

"Synesthesia. Perfectly natural. Until you get some decent regeneration in the corpus callosum, there'll be referred signals like this. Look on it the way that I do—positively. The main thing is that you're beginning to get signals in from that left eye. They're bogus ones, generated on the right side and cross-switching in somehow to the left, but that's just the beginning. As I said, give it time."

"But why did I lose bladder control? That's not synesthesia, surely."

He stood up from the chair—I had progressed

to the point where I had a room with normal furniture, rather than standard hospital fixtures—and went over to the window. "You'll see a variety of physical effects before you settle down. Never mind about peeing yourself—you were doing that all the time in the first few weeks. You keep your eyes open for any kind of seizure. If you ever feel something like an epileptic fit, get to bed at once. And send for me."

Good advice, but it made certain assumptions. It's not easy to pop into bed when you're running for your life, even if there's a bed handy. Other factors loom rather larger in the list of priorities.

I felt a bit guilty when Sir Westcott left. Here was he, trying to make a whole man out of the bits and pieces that had been left over from the accident, and here was I, holding back some of the vital facts.

Rather than asking for approval to leave the hospital two days in a row, I took the coward's way out. In this case that happened to be through the kitchens, and on down the long alley known as Kitchen Lane where food delivery trucks came to drop off supplies to the hospital. I sneaked away at five o'clock, when everything was quiet, and by six I was on the train and on my way to London.

I could have saved myself all the trouble of that deception. She never came. From seven-thirty to eight-thirty I stood outside Bertorellis in a thin, summer drizzle. I didn't get particularly wet, the rain wasn't hard enough for that, but I did get slowly madder and madder. Deception at the hospital was bad enough. Wasted deception was much worse. All my sneaky behavior had been pointless.

Finally I gave up. The rain was setting in harder and the evening turning colder. I went inside, sat down at a table for one, and indulged myself. The jugged hare was excellent, and the house wine made me contemplative. I was beginning to put many things together. Leo's mood, that final afternoon. The sudden and inexplicable failure of the helicopter, listed in the accident report as "pilot error," when I knew damned well it was nothing of the sort. Valnora Warren's admission that Leo's job was not what it was portrayed to be, and, worst of all, the knowledge that Leo and I had been less close than I liked to imagine. He had his secrets.

It all made sense. From the day of our first teenage reunion, Leo had acted as the one in charge. I don't know how much was that California upbringing, and how much that tiny few minutes of seniority, but the reason didn't matter. He would see nothing unusual in having a life I knew nothing about.

There was other evidence. A week before, I had received the final probate of Leo's estate, for which I was the sole heir. That was no real surprise, with Tom and Ellen dead. But the amount he had left staggered me. Even allowing for the luck that he claimed for his stock market investments, could he have amassed such wealth as a simple government employee?

I sat there in the restaurant for three-quarters of an hour, musing over a couple of glasses of Courvoisier. When I paid the bill and left I found that the weather had turned even nastier. It was one of those drenching summer downpours that I remembered from childhood holidays in Scarborough, when the clouds swooped in low off the sea, the temperature dropped into the forties, and the whole town seemed to lock itself up for the night about eight o'clock.

Naturally, there wasn't a taxi to be seen, and the pavements were deserted. Thank goodness I had come with a hat and a raincoat.

I ducked my head low and set off at a fast walk through the slick streets, heading south before cutting through to Tottenham Court Road. I was wearing rubber-soled shoes, waterproof but treacherously slippery on the wet pavement. But it made me tread lightly and carefully, and allowed me to catch the sound of heavier footsteps behind me.

I took a quick look over my shoulder. A tall man in a tan raincoat was pacing steadily after me. The area was usually well-populated and quite safe, but the bad weather had driven everyone off the streets. With my imagination inflamed from my after-dinner speculations, I walked a little faster. I'm big enough and hefty enough to scare away most people looking for an easy mugging, but like any pianist or violinist—or anyone else who relies on uninjured hands for his living—my natural instinct was to run rather than fight. I cut east at a faster walk, heading for a busier street where people should offer some insurance. Then, at the corner, I stopped.

In the narrow street that led through to Tottenham Court Road stood a second tan-coated figure. It could have been any casual local, waiting for his girlfriend, but somehow I knew better—or perhaps Leo did. My left arm was making agitated jerking motions, and my left leg acted as though it would like to run away down the street all by itself.

I swivelled, looking for some way out. The man behind me was closer, and turning the corner after him came a blue Mercedes 450SL, gliding along at walking pace.

The left-hand side of the street was lined with small shops. I moved to stand in one of the doorways—not to hide there, because that was impossible; I wanted to protect my back and sides. The man standing on the corner had started towards me now, and the tan-coated figures were converging. They halted side by side, facing the doorway.

"All right, better make it easy for yourself," said the shorter man. In the shop window on my left was an illuminated advertisement for State Express, and the blinking light from it showed his face as a pale, asymmetrical oblong, changing from green to yellow to red. He lifted his hand and motioned to me, "Get in the car, an' we can all go nice an' easy."

He carried a dark truncheon in his left hand, and there was a flash of bright metal on his companion's closed fists.

"Come on," he repeated, when I didn't move. "If you want to stay in one piece. We ain't got all night."

There didn't seem to be much choice. I was unarmed, and still weak from my accident. The Mercedes had halted behind them, and I shrugged and stepped forward between the two of them to get to it.

I had given up—fighting never was my forte.

Leo must have had other ideas. As I came level with the shorter man, my left arm jerked sideways and thrust stiff-fingered into his midriff. As he spasmed forward, my hand flickered upwards and stabbed hard for his eyes. The fingers went fast and deep into the soft cavities, turning as they thrust. The sensation was sickening, but before I could fully respond I was pivoting hard on my left leg, spinning to the right. My closed left fist went into the tall man's larynx, then as his hand went to his throat I had seized his thumb, twisted, and jerked. I felt the bone snap and grate. My left knee came up hard into his crotch.

One second more, and I was doing my best to run down the street. It was farcical, more like a stuttering hop than a sprint. But it *was* my best. My nerves were vibrating and uncontrollable, but somewhere underneath I felt a dancing anger, a black rage that drove me along much faster than I had reason to expect or hope.

At the street corner I looked back. One man was reeling in circles, his hands to his eyes, and the other was crouched over, one hand to his throat and the other to his testicles. The only sound was the purr of the Mercedes' engine, but the car was not following me. It remained, lights off, in the road. Throughout the whole violent encounter there had been silence, nothing but the gasp for air or the snap of breaking bone.

I turned into Tottenham Court Road, then took the next left turn, and on randomly through the rainy streets of Soho. It was half an hour before my trembling subsided enough to let me venture onto the Underground, and then I sat slumped in my seat in the corner, clasping my trembling hands tightly together.

By midnight I was back at the hospital. An hour later I was shaking all over and had a fever of a hundred and three. Tess Thomson looked in on me about three o'clock—thank heaven it was her week for night shift—and had needles into me two minutes later.

It was four days before I felt back to normal. Long before that I had decided to tell the whole truth, so far as I knew it, to Sir Westcott.

I did it when I was in physiotherapy, and he had come along to see how the exercises to strengthen the left side of my body were coming along. He was particularly interested in watching movements that called for integration between right and left. I swung Indian clubs for a while, then passed a rubber ball rapidly from hand to hand, behind my back. Sir Westcott looked quite pleased—until I started to tell him about what had happened at the Zoo, and about my experience in Soho.

When I got to the end of it (even I thought it came out sounding very odd) he walked out of the room without speaking. I went on with the exercises, and in a quarter of an hour he was back.

"Pack that in for a minute," he said. "Come and sit your backside on the bench here."

I followed him to the side of the gymnasium. It was filled with the products of Sir Westcott's unique ideas for rapid physical recovery from nervous system injuries. The walls and floor were an obstacle course of mats, rubber tires, ropes, trestles, hoops, and bars, across and through which we unfortunate patients were supposed to hop, crawl, roll, swing, and stagger, under his unflinching eye.

He looked at me moodily as we sat down, rubbing at his fat jowls. It was late afternoon, and the gymnasium was deserted except for the two of us.

"I had three calls made down to Soho." He sniffed. "There was no report of a fight there on Tuesday night—nobody saw or heard a scuffle near Charlotte Street—no reports from any hospital of two men coming in with hand and eye injuries like the ones you described. All right? I'll take your word for it you had jugged hare at Bertorellis, we didn't check that. But we did call the American Embassy. There's no report of anybody called Valnora Warren in the U.S. State Department. No visitor with that name here on any sort of U.S. Government business, an' nothing on the Passport List."

"But suppose she was with one of the intelligence services?" My suspicions had blossomed further.

"Suppose she wasn't there at all?"

"She was."

"You *think* she was. I'll admit that all right, but it's not the same thing."

He lifted one fat paw, a hand with manual skills that put mine to shame. "Hold on, before you start getting excited again. We've got to face something unpleasant, Lionel, an' it's something I've been putting off, and hoping would never come up."

"She was *there*, and so were the men." Despite his good advice, I could feel my pulse pumping harder. "I'm not inventing any of this."

"Listen for a minute, then think again. Let's have

a go with Occam's razor. You've had one hell of an operation, an' there's things going on inside your head that we can't even guess at. The CAT scans look pretty good, but they don't tell us anything about your thinking. Einstein has a brain that looks no different from your Aunt Matilda's when it comes to X-rays and physiological tests."

"I know all that. But don't forget I'm looking at this from the inside—I *know* what I'm thinking."

"You don't—any more than the rest of us know what we're thinking." He snorted. "You're underestimating the human brain, my lad. The only thing we know for certain is that you've got Madrill's technique to stimulate nerve cell regeneration going on inside your head. There's an electrical storm brewing when all those little cross-connections cuddle up to each other. It's more than we can comprehend. You're going to experience perceptual anomalies, sure as I'm sitting here."

I stood up. "You've told me all that. I'm going to have synesthesia—"

"That's an easy one." He picked up an Indian club and sighted along it. "There's things a lot harder to pick up. It's easy to know there's something off when you play Mozart and get rows of green beetles crawling up your nose. But what happens when you 'see' people"—his voice put quotes around the verb—"that Leo knew? Imagining a woman that he was fond of, or people he didn't like—that'd be normal enough. But it's hard to tell a data-sorting function like that from the real thing. *That's* why I want you to take things easy. We don't want to confuse internal and external realities."

"Look, I saw a van. A grey van, with painted windows and rear doors with a black line along them. That's not part of Leo's past. I bet somebody saw it at the Zoo—it had to get into and out of the car park."

"Fine. Feel free to go and look for it, if you want to." He clumped the Indian club back hard on the floor. "If you can come back here with witnesses, and a license plate for that van, I'll eat my Sunday boots with Branston Pickle. Haven't you noticed that everything that happened to you was with no witnesses? An' a broken thumb hurts like hell, but your man didn't let out a peep. Yer see, you've no idea how cunning the human brain can be at protecting its constructs. If you talk to a man who thinks the earth is flat, or that he's Napoleon or Hitler, he'll give you a hundred good reasons why he has to be right."

He shook his head sadly and stood up. "I was hoping we could move you to outpatient status, but I think we should wait a bit longer. Let me know if anything else happens. I've got to go an' scrub."

He was a hard man to argue with, yet I still felt like Galileo as he stood down from the witness box after facing the questioning. Subdued, but unpersuaded.

" . . . but she *was* there."

Proving it might be another matter.

– 5 –

There had to be one more go-around with Sir
Westcott before I could get out of Queen's Hospital Annex. The day before my release I hung
about the top floor all morning with Tess Thomson,
waiting until there was a gap in his schedule. It
took a long time and by eleven-thirty I was feeling more and more impatient.

Tess did her best to calm me down. "Remember that blood pressure. Keep it low, or he'll want
you to stay another month."

"I'll go mad first." Apart from passes at Tess,
my only satisfaction came from the daily sessions
on the old piano down in the basement. I had
tuned it myself and ground my way through hour
after hour of left-hand exercises. The dexterity was
coming back—but it was slow. And I had the
terrible feeling that my playing had been drained
of all its emotional content.

Tess was fidgeting by the door, trying to see

through the frosted glass that led to Sir Westcott Shaw's reception area.

"You'd get used to being here after a while," she said. "Look at me, I've been in the place for four years. And I don't get to use the fancy equipment, it's the same old round of emptying bedpans."

I went over to stand next to her, and put my hand on her arm. "Tess, be serious for a minute. You've done a fantastic job looking after me, bedpans and all. How about dinner tonight? I owe you at least that, as a farewell thank-you for everything. Look." I held up my left hand and wiggled it. "See, it moves. If you hadn't made me exercise, I'd be all lopsided."

She turned around, smiling. I was always delighted when I could make her lose those frown lines on her forehead.

"Never give up, do you? What do you think my boyfriend would say?"

"Why tell him?" I had decided a month earlier that he didn't exist—he was a useful invention to keep the patients in their places.

"I don't keep secrets from him. Women are different from men; we don't like to live a double life."

"You know all my secrets—you've seen bits of me that I didn't know I had. What do you say? Dinner and dalliance?"

She stuck her tongue out at me. "I'll let you know. Later. All right?"

"When?"

"By three o'clock. I've got work to do on some of the records."

I nodded. Before I could talk restaurants the

door to the reception area opened. Sir Westcott's secretary, a plump, middle-aged woman who was rumored to also be his mistress, appeared. As she gestured me in I heard a bellow from the inner office.

"Bad mood?" I said to her.

She nodded. There was a shout from inside: "When I say the records have to be looked at, I bloody well mean it. We're a hospital, not a knacker's yard. Do you understand?"

His secretary bit her lip. The door to the inner office opened and two men in white coats came out. One of them was sweating heavily and his face was as white and shiny as bone china. His companion steered him out. Neither of them even looked at us. The secretary took a deep breath.

"We lost two patients during the night," she said softly, her hand on my arm. "He thinks it was our fault—we didn't pay enough attention to the X-rays and the drug tolerances."

"Is he right?" I automatically lowered my voice to a whisper.

"Probably not. But it always upsets him. Try not to excite him."

He seemed to me to be excited enough already. "I thought doctors didn't get emotionally involved?" I whispered to her. "They can't afford to be too subjective if a patient dies."

She managed the trace of a smile. "Not the really good ones—they're involved. HE"—you could hear the capital letters in her voice—"takes it as a personal insult from Nature when he loses a patient. Come on, let's go in. Don't mind if he's hard to deal with."

Sir Westcott was sitting at the big desk, staring blindly at a folder in front of him. His fringe of hair was sticking up wildly, and his jowls looked fatter and looser than ever. I sat down uninvited in the chair opposite and waited. Finally he grunted, closed the folder, and looked up at me.

"I know, you want to get out of here. It's too soon, and you're being a bloody fool, but that's your option."

"I'm feeling good. I'm taking up a room somebody else might need."

"That's for me to worry about." He tapped the folder. "Take a look in there if you think you're in great shape. This past week you've had fevers twice, and your blood pressure's been up and down faster than a whore's knickers. You should be taking things real easy. It's daft buggers like you that keep the undertakers in business."

As he spoke he was watching me closely, but his eyes would flicker now and again to a glass ornament on the top of the desk. Tess had told me all about it. The chair I was sitting on had sensors for pulse and blood pressure, with a display built into the far side of the paperweight. He was deliberately trying to excite me and watching for the reaction.

I sat quite still. "I'll be taking things easy. And I won't go far away. From Shepherds Bush I can be here in an hour and a half, and I'm not planning on leaving my flat much."

He took a last look at the paperweight, then nodded. "You'll do. Bugger off then, before I change my mind. And here, take this with you." He picked up a flat plastic pillbox about as big across as a ten-penny piece. "You've been moaning to Nurse Thomson about you being an experimental animal with your operation—don't deny it, I know more than you think. Well, this makes you a real experiment. The fellows over at Guy's have come up with a new drug, a synthetic neurotransmitter, right out of the lab. It still has to go through controlled tests, but they think it may damp the unstable feedback situations that we've sometimes had with Madrill's nerve regeneration treatment."

I picked up the pillbox. "How do I take this?"

"You don't—not unless you have to. You'll know a seizure's coming on if you feel like you're getting smaller and smaller. Cram a couple of these pills down, as fast as you can. They'll damp the regeneration process for a few hours. Get to a hospital."

"What if I can't reach one?"

"No problem." He grinned. "You'll be dead. An' chances are you'll only have yourself to blame. The Madrill treatment goes wild if you get too worked up and excited over something."

"Don't rub it in. I got the message." I put the pillbox into my pocket. "I'd just like to thank you for all the work—"

"Nonsense." He banged the buzzer on his desk. "Don't undo all my work, that's all. First sign of another hallucination, I want you back in here fast enough to set fire to your pants. *Verstehen?* And good luck."

Sir Westcott's secretary had given me another parting present when I checked out of the hospital: a big, four-color chart of the structure of the human brain, with views from front, back, side, top and bottom. The first thing I did in my flat was hang it in pride of place on the bedroom wall. Before I pushed in the last thumbtack I had second thoughts. Tess had agreed to dinner, but postponed it for one day. If she somehow found herself here, in the bedroom, a detailed diagram of the brain might not be the most romantic thing to find on the wall. . . .

I left it up. Maybe it would make her feel at home. I went back to the little box-room that I thought of as the study and opened the desk drawer. I reached for the colored pens, then paused. Somebody had been searching the desk. Unless my visual memory was playing me tricks—a possibility I couldn't rule out—the pens and pencils had been reversed since I last saw them.

Other things in the flat had been moved, too. That was obvious as soon as I took a good look at my clothes, CDs, and books. And I never left the piano lid open, the way it was now. Nothing seemed to be missing, though, so at last I went back, much puzzled, to the bedroom.

I took blue and red felt-tipped pens and went across to the diagram on the wall. It gave me a perverse pleasure to mark there, as closely as I knew, regions as "LEO" (blue) and "LIONEL" (red).

Now for the spooky bit. I transferred the red pen to my left hand, closed my right eye, and lifted my hand towards the diagram. Sir Westcott had suggested this experiment, but I'd only tried it once before, with no results.

No signals were coming in from my left eye now. I stood there, knowing that my left hand was moving. There was the scratch of felt tip against paper. It took a lot of self control to stand there patiently, waiting until that noise ended and my left hand stopped moving.

For the first month after I woke, the left side of my body had been almost paralyzed. Fingers and toes would move reluctantly, and they felt wooden and poorly controlled. I had been scared, but Sir Westcott had expected it. "I told you," he said, "the left half of your body takes its marching orders mostly from the right side of the brain. You're having to scramble for control right now—lots of that hemisphere was cut out. When the links to Leo's brain tissue come into action that problem will all go away."

I wiggled my fingers, willing them to move faster and easier. "How can I function with thirty percent of my brain out of action?"

"Redundancy. There's one hell of a lot of redundancy in all of us—youngsters do well even if they lose half their brain. They just rewire themselves. No trouble."

"What about adults? I'm not a youngster." I still feared that I would be a permanent cripple.

"You'll be surprised. Look, if you want to see how much Leo's active in the system without your control, there's an easy test you can do for yourself. Get a piece of paper, put a pencil in your left hand, and cover your right eye. That'll let the left hemisphere in on the action."

Trying that now in my own bedroom, there was an insane temptation to peek. Finally the pen stopped moving, and I opened my right eye. While the pen drew, I had been concentrating my attention on the functions of the brain, and how it was structured, and I expected to see something like that on the diagram—perhaps a different region marked "LIONEL." Instead, the red pen had drawn on a clear area of the diagram. Two wobbly ellipses sat there, side by side.

What were they? Not quite zeroes, or eggs—they were slightly pointed at the long ends. Lemons? A pair of lemons.

No sense there. I found that I was bathed in a cold, pouring sweat while I struggled to interpret the figures in front of me. It felt like the day in my hospital room when a nurse had brought a vase of fresh-cut red roses and placed them on the table next to me. I had begun to tremble and perspire, and Tess was forced to run in and give me an injection.

Lemons.

The hell with it. I'd have time to think on the Underground, and if I didn't leave soon I'd be late meeting Tess.

Lemon thoughts came close to spoiling the whole evening. I just couldn't get them out of my head. Tess noticed my preoccupied look after we had worked over the menu together and agreed to share a rack of lamb. Then I dithered over the wine list, not really paying attention to it, until Tess took over. She asked the wine waiter a couple of questions, and it became obvious that she knew wines better than I ever would.

"I've picked one that's underpriced and underrated," she said, as the waiter nodded respectfully and left. "I know it'll be good. Do you think you should be drinking, though? Have you had any dizziness?"

"I'm fine." I didn't mention the wine and brandy I had drunk two days before.

She looked less sure. We sat there for a minute or two without attempting conversation. As I had learned during my first conscious weeks in the hospital, a lot went on behind that broad forehead. Sir Westcott wouldn't trust his most critical cases to just anybody. Tess didn't strike like lightning, on the first encounter; she grew on you, steadily, so that after a while you worried when she was off duty and kept wondering what she was doing.

"All right, penny for your thoughts." She had been watching me closely, while I ate olives and paté. "Or are you going to sit there and brood all night without talking about it?"

I looked down at the table for something I could draw on. There were only the napkins and the cloth, and I didn't think the management would like me to sketch on those. Finally Tess helped out with a paper bag that she found in her purse.

I drew as accurately as I could (which wasn't very) and told her how they had been generated on the brain diagram.

She sat there, head to one side, studying the oval figures.

"Eggs?" she said at last, "Walnuts, lemons, balloons—they could be anything. I'd like to see the real thing. How were these placed relative to the anatomy chart?"

"I can't describe it easily. They were down on the left, in a clear area near the front view of the brain. But you'd have to see it for yourself to know how they were positioned."

"Well, I'm game for that. This could be important." She tucked the bag into her purse. "Where did you leave the diagram?"

I shrugged. "Back at my flat—hanging on the bedroom wall."

The frown lines came for a split second, then dissolved to a high-voltage smile. "That must be the worst line yet. Wouldn't it be better to offer to show me your etchings?"

She didn't discuss that any further, but she didn't make an alternative suggestion. For the rest of the dinner I felt excited, happy, and more than a little bit nervous. I had noticed when we first met for dinner that she wasn't wearing her ring, and deduced that like her boyfriend it was protection against unwanted attentions in the hospital. Tess looked at me calmly, while I drank rather more wine than I should have and made a mess of bread crumbs by working over the basket of rolls on my side of the table. For the first time since the crash (I could think of it less and less as an accident) I didn't feel embarrassed at being seen in public. Tess certainly didn't seem to care about my scars, and she knew I had a lot more than would show to the casual inspection.

In the taxi back to Shepherds Bush I worried all the way. First about what might happen, then about what might not. Brain injuries often cause other physical effects—I had read the literature Sir Westcott provided to me, and was all ready to fear the worst. And even assuming the best, there might still be mechanical problems. A good deal of interior rerouting had been done on me.

If I did have plumbing difficulties, this would be one hell of a time to find out about them.

What with one thing and another I wasn't at my mental peak when we got to the flat. I noticed that the door leading to the main hall of the building was unlocked, which it shouldn't have been. And somebody or something had knocked over and rooted through the dustbins, but that hardly seemed the sort of conversational gem to impress Tess. Maybe I didn't need to. She was much more relaxed, humming softly and taking my arm as we walked down the mews to the front door, just as though we were an old married couple.

We spent ten minutes worrying over the diagram in my bedroom, trying to puzzle some sense out of it. Tess threw out a few other possibilities for the oval shapes (eye-glasses, onions, light bulbs) but nothing useful. We sat for a few minutes looking at each other.

I was wondering what to do next when Tess went quietly out of the bedroom and back through the living room.

"Just making sure the outer door's locked," she said when she came back. "Somebody had to do it, and I'm not sure you'd ever get round to it."

She came over to where I was sitting and gave me a first kiss. It was warm, soft, and quite disconcertingly pleasant. After a few minutes I pulled myself together enough to lower the lights. I had seen myself naked in a full-length mirror, and Frankenstein's monster had less stitching.

Well, hats off to Sir Westcott. Everything seemed to be in excellent working order. I was nervous, so I didn't exactly cover myself with glory the first time, but after that with Tess's assistance everything turned into a roaring success.

"There," she said afterwards. "I knew you had nothing to worry about."

I turned my head sideways, to look down at the top of her head. "I didn't know. And I don't see how you could have."

She chuckled drowsily, running her fingers gently over the operation scars on my right side and tracing the line of subcutaneous stitching on the muscle walls. "I took a look at the latest X-rays this afternoon. I couldn't tell about the inside of your head, but all the rest of you has healed nicely. Very nicely. You're doing fine."

That would have been the right time to tell her about the crash, and my suspicions, and about the woman in the zoo and the men in the street in Soho. But her touch was soft and there seemed to be no rush. I could tell her in the morning, and see if she would believe me. I was sure she would have more faith than Sir Westcott.

It didn't work out that way.

When I woke up the sun was shining, the phone was ringing, and the bed was empty. She left a note for me on the pillow, next to my head.

Duty calls. I'm on from seven to four today. Call me tonight (if you want to).

Perhaps it was just as well. I felt terrible when I sat up, physically wiped out and certainly in no condition for the hair of the dog. I staggered to the phone, and it infuriatingly stopped ringing an instant before I picked it up.

Toast and coffee improved things somewhat, and a hot shower did even more. There were no signs of fevers or seizures, and I wondered if I should report to Sir Westcott that another step had been taken on the road to recovery. But what would I do if he wanted details? I dressed slowly, then made my way downstairs to pick up the newspapers.

It was nearly ten o'clock and the sun had moved around so that it didn't shine directly into the entrance hall. I didn't feel like going back up to turn on the stair light, so I descended into a gloom lit only by the light from the dusty window, high up in the wall.

As soon as I reached the foot of the stairs I noticed the smell. It was strong, like acetate mixed with ripe peaches. I halted, and was still trying to identify it when the floor of the entrance hall seemed to vanish from beneath my feet. I was standing on black velvet, soft and endless. I fell backwards.

"Mind his head," said a voice from behind me. Arms came from nowhere to cushion my fall. Then I was gone, down deep below the velvet surface to a place where the sun never shone.

– 6 –

"He's awake. Go get the boss on the phone."

He wasn't, though. Not if they were talking about me. He was half-asleep, with the worst hangover ever, and unable to open his eyes to face that light directly above.

Not above, I realized after a while; in front, that's where it was, and I wasn't lying down. I was sitting in a chair. There was no danger that I would fall out of it. My wrists were bound to the chair arms, and there was something murderously tight around my knees and ankles. I felt as sick as a dog. I turned my head away from the bright wall lamp and panted hard as waves of nausea ran through me.

"Here." A big hand held a cup to my mouth. "You're not as bad as you think. Drink this down an' you'll feel a sight different."

I swallowed as he tilted the cup. My mouth puckered at the bitter taste, and there was a moment when I thought it would come right back up. Then I suddenly was a lot better, improved enough physically to feel a sharp panic when I at last understood what had happened. I was completely helpless, unable to move hand or foot. Apprehension turned my mouth dry and left me unable to swallow.

I opened my eyes and peered up. The man holding the cup was tall, about my height. He was heavily built, in his early twenties at the latest. With his fresh, round face and no sign of lines or wrinkles, he could have passed as a teenager if he had been smaller. His expression as he looked at me was a mixture of wariness and curiosity.

"They're coming right over," said another voice from behind me. A second man walked forward into my field of view. "Did he drink it?'"

The newcomer was on the short side, very lightly built and dapperly dressed. His hair was greased and parted in the middle in a style that had gone out fifty years ago. I concentrated hard on their faces, looking for anything that might reassure me as to my own position. They were both unreadable.

"He drank it," said the first man. He turned the empty cup upside down. "All gone. How long before they get here?"

"Three-quarters of an hour. Zan's over in the shop, and he has to go and pick her up." He turned to look at me directly for the first time. "He'd better stay as he is—no point in taking chances."

Now that I was fully awake, I could feel the ropes around my legs cutting hard into the flesh.

Already my hands were puffed and swollen, and my ankles felt numb. The idea of being tied up for another hour like this filled me with horror.

"You're bastards, both of you," I said. "Untie me. These ropes are killing me, look at my hands."

The shorter man came forward and looked calmly down at my bonds. "Now then, mind your manners, or I'll have to ask Pudd'n here to teach you a bit more respect."

"Bugger Pudd'n, and bugger you too," I said. I was terrified, but somewhere underneath I was also furious. "You have to do something about these ropes."

The big youth came forward and bent to look at my hands. "He's right, Dixie," he said, "You've done 'em too tight, they're cutting off his circulation."

"So who cares?" Dixie looked down at me with vicious satisfaction. "He's earned it. You saw what he did to Jack an' Des. Let him hurt a bit."

"Well, yeah." Pudd'n stood there, his round face furrowed in thought. "But I think we'd better make 'em a bit looser anyway. You know the boss. You know what he'll say if there's damage before 'e gets here."

"Sod the boss. I'm not worried about him, bloody little Arab," said Dixie. But he moved forward quickly and began to loosen the knots with deft, well-kept hands. I realized that he was much older than the first impression had suggested, probably in his early sixties. It hurt when he loosened the knots, but in another thirty seconds it hurt a good deal worse. I grunted and swore as the blood began to flow back into my hands and feet.

"You're still bastards," I said shakily, when the pain was at its peak. "I've done nothing to you. What do you want?"

"You'll find out," said Dixie. They must have taken my jacket before they tied me, and now he was going through the pockets in a systematic and leisurely way. "If you've done nothing to us, then you've nothing to worry about, do you? Here, Pudd'n, take a look at this. Innocent until proved guilty, eh? Bloody likely. I reckon this proves who he is."

He had found the pillbox Sir Westcott gave me in the hospital. Now he rolled two of the blue capsules onto the palm of his hand and held them out towards Pudd'n. The big man whistled when he saw them.

"Nymphs?" he said.

"Looks like it to me," replied Dixie. He turned back to where I was sitting. "You dirty old man, you."

The pain in my hands was lessening, and I was doing my best to speed up the returning circulation by clenching and unclenching my fists.

"That's medicine," I said. "I have to have it— I only just got out of the hospital."

"I know," said Dixie. He guffawed. "Medicine, eh? That's a good 'un. You tell that to the judge, an' he'll have you back in hospital sharpish. There's only one thing that Nymphs do, an' I don't think you're a candidate for it." He had become a lot more sure of himself.

"I've no idea what you're talking about," I said. But I couldn't help wondering if there was more to the drug than Sir Westcott had bothered to tell me.

"Very good," said Dixie. His tone was sarcastic. "You've no idea, eh? So you can tell that to Zan and the boss when they get here. See if they believe it." He glanced at his watch, then at Pudd'n. "They'll be another half hour yet, you know Zan's always late. How about one more session before they get here?"

Pudd'n shrugged. "If you want to. But what about 'im? We 'ave to watch 'im."

"That's no problem. We can take him through with us."

"All right." Pudd'n came forward to stand in front of me. "Grab the back end of the chair."

I couldn't help or hinder. A bag of groceries had as much freedom of choice. The room we were in was maybe twenty feet long by fourteen across, with the windows hidden by floor-length green drapes and with a polished hardwood floor. The furniture—as much as I could see of it—was expensive and carefully matched to the wallpaper and the drapes. Pudd'n opened a pair of double doors, then I was carried, chair and all, backwards into a bigger room. This one had an open Steinway over by one wall and an old Broadwood box piano—in excellent condition, to judge from its exterior—along the wall opposite. Between the two was twenty-five feet of polished floor.

I was placed by the Steinway. Dixie remained standing in the middle of the room, and Pudd'n sat down on the piano stool.

"Ready?" he said.

Dixie nodded. "Any time."

Pudd'n began to play a Scott Joplin piece that I occasionally used as a pop encore—"Magnetic

Rag." His hands were very big—I estimated that he could span at least a twelfth—and he let his fingers do the work without much wrist movement. The tempo was a nice, medium one, just a little faster than I liked it.

"Right," said Dixie. And while I gaped, he began to dance. His face was blank with concentration as he warmed up from a delicate soft-shoe to a more complicated pattern of double-time steps. He took no more notice of me than he did of the rest of the room's furniture.

I looked back at Pudd'n. He played easily and accurately, not looking at his hands. He even seemed bored, and the second time through he added a whole series of grace notes to the right-hand melody, an *acciaccatura* to every second beat. At the end he closed with a strange anharmonic cadence that I liked rather better than the Joplin original.

"One more time," said Dixie. He was panting a little. "Take it faster."

"You start, an' I'll pick it up," said Pudd'n. He had become aware that I was watching him closely as he played. This time he showed off for my benefit, taking passages in octaves, sixths, and thirds, and adding to the chords in the bass. Like most amateurs, his right hand was better than his left, but he was pretty good. Even in my situation, I couldn't help listening critically. There were no wrong notes or fluffed chords, and the scales were nicely balanced. I didn't like his pedal timing, but he wasn't using it to cover anything, and he played with a sense of leisure, with speed to spare.

He had been gradually increasing the tempo. When he finished, with a rapid octave run upwards,

Dixie went over to one of the high-backed chairs and sat down on the edge of it. His lined face was beaded with sweat.

"That'll do," he said. "Gawd, I'm done in—you pushed it at the end there. Let's have a fag."

Pudd'n unexpectedly winked at me. "Nah, yer slowin' down, Dixie. Getting old. Ain't that right, Mister Foss?"

"You're bloody fools, both of you," I said. "Get it into your heads. *I'm not Leo Foss.*"

"You'll have to argue that one out with the boss. Want a cigarette?"

He didn't seem nearly as unfriendly as Dixie. I shook my head, and he lit a cigarette for himself and turned back to the piano. "Like music, do you?"

"Well enough." I realized he had no idea who I was. "So do you, and you're good. You've had good training."

He nodded, sucking in deep lungsful of smoke. "Too bleedin' true. Twelve bleedin' years of 'em, before I could get out an' do my own thing."

"You ran away from home?"

He shook his head. "Orphanage. Lessons every bleedin' day except Christmas, then I had to play carols for everybody else." His voice changed to falsetto. "'Now, Thomas, the Good Lord God has given you a talent. It would be shameful and wrong for you to neglect it.' They stuffed that into me with me breakfast every bleedin' day since I was four, 'til I was sixteen an' I could bugger off out of there."

A sound of a car door slamming came from outside the window. Dixie grunted and stood up.

"They're here, Pudd'n. So stow it—I don't know why you waste your time talking to him anyway."

"Calm down, Dixie." Pudd'n turned back to me. "Look, Foss, I'm goin' to give you some good advice. You don't know the boss, an' I do. Answer his questions straight, an' first time, an' you'll be glad of it in the long run. Ain't that right, Dixie?"

"Let him do what he likes," said Dixie sullenly. "I don't give a shit if he gets his head blown off." I could hear footsteps approaching in the other room. No matter what Sir Westcott wanted, I could feel my pulse beating faster and I wouldn't like to have taken any bet on my blood pressure. Pudd'n and Dixie both rose to their feet and stood waiting.

The man who entered was short, even shorter than Dixie. He was dark complexioned and swarthy, with black, straight hair and a prominent nose and chin. I placed him as Lebanese, or perhaps Egyptian. The woman who followed him was an inch or two taller, also dark haired and dark skinned, with a clear, olive complexion and fine eyes. She looked to be in her late twenties. Her nose was a classic Greek profile, well balanced by good cheekbones and a fine chin.

As she came into the room she stared at me in a strangely intense way. She did not take her eyes off me, even to look at the others when they spoke to her. In other circumstances I would have found her strongly attractive. But now . . .

The man came over and looked at me curiously. "Gave us a lot of trouble, you did. Messed up two of the boys real bad—we might have to pay yer back for that."

His voice was a surprise. It had a strong Liverpool accent—and I recognized it! He had been one of the two men in the helicopter; Scouse, the other one had called him. I took a quick look at their shoes, but—not too surprisingly—none of them wore the black leather, black-buckled footware that I could still see if I closed my eyes and thought about the crash.

I stared up at Scouse. "You've got something all wrong. I don't know what you think you're doing, but I'm sure you're making a mistake."

"D'yer think so?" He laughed, a deep chuckle of satisfaction. "No, you're the one making the mistake, Foss." He turned his head. "Did yer search him, Dixie?"

"Sure I did." Dixie scowled at me, then held forward the pillbox to Scouse. "It's not the thing we were looking for, but it proves he's Foss all right. Take a look inside—nobody would be carryin' Nymphs if he was just some ordinary person."

Scouse shot me a swift, intelligent look. "Naw—an' nor would Foss, if he had to go through Customs to bring 'em into the country. It'd be too dangerous. Use yer head, Dixie, he'd be mad to be carryin' Nymphs." He took the lid off the box and rolled a capsule into his palm. "I dunno. They sure as hell look like 'em, I'll give you that. But I'm not sure."

"They're medicine," I said. "I'm not Leo Foss, I'm Lionel Salkind, and I've just come out of hospital."

"We've heard all that," said Scouse absently. He opened the capsule with his thumb nail and poured grey-green powder into his open palm. He sniffed at it cautiously. "Here, Zan, what do you think?"

The woman took her eyes from me for a moment to take the capsule. She dipped her head and touched the tip of her tongue to the powder.

"No," she said after a few moments. Her voice was deep and musical, a fine contralto. "I do not know what this is, but I feel sure we are not dealing with Nymphs." Her words were heavily accented, and seemed to confirm her Greek appearance. "Maybe they are really medicine?"

"You'd be too *old* for them, anyway, Zan, if they were Nymphs," said Dixie nastily. Then he saw her angry look and was silent.

"Mebbe it is," said Scouse thoughtfully. I noticed that when he spoke the rest became respectfully attentive. "Mebbe it's medicine. But there's no sign of what we really want, an' that's the important thing." He leaned forward and slipped the pillbox into my shirt pocket. His eyes stared into mine, dark and unblinking. "You see the problem you've given me, do you? You might want to help me solve it. I'm sure you'll try."

"I still have no idea what you're talking about." Those bright eyes made me more nervous than anything that had happened since I recovered consciousness.

"Ah, but that's just what you'd say anyway—that's the whole trouble, isn't it? You say you're not Leo Foss, I know that. You're the twin brother, Lionel, an' it was Leo died in the crash. I know, we've heard all that."

He shot Dixie a quick look. "An' the crash was bungled bad, so we didn't have as much time as we needed there. Well, no matter, we took care of the lad who bungled that one, didn't we, Dixie? But we can't afford another mess-up. Suppose you *are* Leo, now. Then you know where the Belur Package is. An' I want to know that. An' you have to tell me. Would yer like to do it right now, an' save things getting messy?"

"I'm Lionel. Lionel Salkind." My throat was dry again. "I don't know anything about a Belur package."

"I hear you." His voice was still soft and thoughtful. "Dixie, get his shirt off. Don't untie him. Cut it away if yer have to."

Dixie took out a sheath knife. The blade was sharpened to a wicked tip, and it gleamed in the light. He cut my shirt and undershirt efficiently from top to bottom, laying the cold flat of the blade lovingly against my skin as he finished. Scouse whistled when he saw the pattern of scars on my chest and stomach.

"Been through the wars, haven't yer? Mebbe you need them pills after all. I've seen road maps with less lines on 'em than your belly. I bet you don't want more there, do yer? I can understand that. But let's do one little check before we start—just to make sure."

He nodded. Dixie took his cigarette out of his mouth and applied it without warning to my shoulder. I yelled at the pain and tried to writhe away from the red-hot ash. I couldn't move more than a few inches in any direction. Scouse nodded.

"All right. Just checking. Wouldn't be worth doing anything to yer, would it, if you'd already had a go with the Belur Package? All right, now let's have a little chat."

He pulled a chair forward and sat down facing me. I noticed that the woman was standing absolutely motionless. Her cheeks were flushed, and she was biting her lip as though under some great tension.

"Are you going to stand there and let them torture me?" I said desperately. "Can't you see they have the wrong man?"

Scouse turned to her as I spoke and saw the intense, rigid posture. He swore and stood up again. "Pudd'n, get Zan out of here and into another room. Take her downstairs."

She went without speaking, but at the door she turned and gave me a long, unfathomable look. I could tell that she didn't want to go, but she would not argue with Scouse. As soon as she was gone, he took a black case from his pocket. He removed from it a small phial and a hypodermic, and laid them on the top of the piano stool.

"That was crude with the cigarette, eh? I know." He leaned forward to look again into my eyes. "An' it left marks, an' that's never a good idea. I keep telling Dixie when he wants to have a go with the knife, there's better ways. Let me tell you what we'll be doin' instead."

He picked up the hypodermic, plunged the needle through the rubber stopper of the phial, and drew about one c.c. of clear liquid into the syringe.

"This won't leave a mark—only the needle point. What it will do is set up a stimulation to the nerves round about where we make the injection. The pain nerves, mainly. Would yer like to negotiate with me for where we make the first puncture? Yer might not believe me, but I don't get my kicks out of hurting people, not like some people here— providing I can get what I want some other way."

He had brought the needle forward to within an inch of my right thumb. I was rigid with fear. It was a scene from a nightmare, to be tortured to give up information that you didn't have. Blood from a stone. The cigarette burn on my shoulder pulsed with pain, like a promise of worse to come.

"I'm Lionel," I said desperately. "Lionel, not Leo."

"I hear you." Scouse was nodding agreeably. "An' if you *were* Lionel, an' not Leo, why there'd be no point puttin' a hard squeeze on you, would there? But how am I to know that? All I can do is make you a little proposition. You find a way to *prove* that you're Lionel Salkind, an' not Leo Foss, an' I'll stop—for the moment. I'll go away an' think things over a bit more." He turned to Pudd'n, who had come back into the room. "Do we have the report in yet on Valnora Warren?"

"Got it this morning. She didn't know anything useful."

"Mm." Scouse looked at Dixie, "She was probed right?"

"All the way to the end. Nothing."

"Right." Scouse turned back to me. "So it's up to you. If you are Leo, you know where the Belur Package is. An' I want to know. An' if you're Lionel, you'd better prove it—right now."

Prove I was Lionel. My brain wàs refusing to

function. *We* had always known the differences, known them exactly. But everybody else said we were the same—even people who knew us well. I'd never persuade Scouse with talk of a half-inch height difference, or a pound or two in weight.

My skin felt chilled, and I had broken out into a fine, all-over sweat. I thought desperately, closing my eyes to concentrate. And I saw, like a ghost image on the inner darkness, the regular lines of green marching beetles, as I had first seen them in the hospital basement. I gasped.

"How much do you know about Leo?" I burst out, straining forward in my chair.

"A fair bit—a lot less than we'd like to, obviously."

"You know his background?"

"Most of it." Scouse was frowning.

"Then I can prove to you that I'm Lionel."

"How?"

I laughed, high-pitched and nervous. "I'm a concert pianist. There's no way that Leo could fake that. Let me play that piano, and you'll see."

Scouse was frowning harder. "Foss never played the piano according to my file on him. But it could be wrong. He may have had lessons."

"Look, lessons wouldn't be enough. You have to understand the enormous difference between a good professional and an amateur. It's *huge*." Even as I spoke I worried about my own lack of recent practice. The restricted circulation in my hands for the past hour would make things worse. But I was itching to get at that piano more than I had ever wanted anything.

Scouse was shaking his head. "I don't know. I

don't think I could tell the difference between a good pianist and an average one."

"Maybe you can't. But *he* can." I jerked my head towards Pudd'n, who had been standing there scowling.

"Nobody told me you were a concert pianist," he said accusingly. "You were just 'avin' me on when you said I was good, wasn't yer?"

"No, I wasn't—you are good, and you could be a lot better. You should take it more seriously."

"Never mind that," said Scouse. "Could you, Pudd'n? Could you *really* tell if he's a professional or an amateur?"

Pudd'n was nodding his head reluctantly, "Yeah. If he's that good, I'll know it. There's things he'll not be able to fake. Nobody could."

"But if he tries faking . . ." said Dixie. He made a little upwards motion with his cigarette.

"He'll wish he hadn't," Scouse said. He nodded to Pudd'n. "All right, untie him. An' keep an eye on 'im—don't forget what happened to Des an' Jack."

When the ropes were off I lurched to my feet, hardly able to stand. I had pins and needles in my forearms, and cramps in my calves and feet. The piano stool was the right height but I fussed with it anyway, chafing at my hands and trying to relax them to get some feeling into my fingertips. I was too cold, and I put my jacket on over the sweaty, ruined shirt.

"All right, no stallin'," said Scouse.

"I'm not. My hands don't feel right yet—I was tied too tight."

"Tough. Just get on with it."

I looked at Pudd'n, who was standing impassively

beside the piano. Dixie was behind me, his sheath knife out and ready to be used if I made a wrong move.

So what should I play? It wouldn't do to handle a delicate piece that Pudd'n might play better than I would (I still suspected that all the emotion had gone from my playing). It had to be something where I could pull out all the stops and hit him with pyrotechnics. If the technical difficulties were hair-raising enough, he'd never notice that the playing was cold.

"Get going," breathed Scouse warningly. "Time's up."

I sighed, prayed that my fingers and memory wouldn't betray me, and got going. I began to play "Badinage," one of Godowsky's paraphrases of the Chopin études. All his material is horrendously difficult (the Apostle of the Left Hand, he was called a hundred years ago) and I had never dared to tackle one of his Chopin paraphrases in a public concert. But now I had to go for broke. My main worry was to get to the end without making a total hash of it. I drove along, all my attention in my fingertips.

After the final chords I took a deep breath and looked up at Pudd'n. His face was a picture.

"Well?" said Scouse. I could tell from his voice that he was impressed but not convinced. Pudd'n just stood there shaking his head. "Christ!" he said. "What was that?"

"A combination of two Chopin studies—the two in G Flat. Godowsky. He wrote fifty-three like that."

"Christ! I never heard anything like it." He

shook his head again and turned to Scouse and Dixie. "There's no way he could play like that an' be just anybody. He's a *pianist*."

"Yeah. I thought so too." Scouse looked annoyed, but not with me. I breathed a little bit easier, even though my fate was anything but clear.

"That gives me somethin' to think about," went on Scouse. He was frowning. "Damn it." He turned abruptly and began to walk towards the door. "Look after him tonight," he said over his shoulder. "I'll be back in the morning. An' don't forget to tie him, unless you want to finish up like Jack and Des."

"What about the Nymphs?" called Dixie.

Scouse turned in the doorway. "They're not Nymphs, you daft bugger. Are you deaf? They're some kind of medicine. Let him have 'em if he needs 'em. I'm going to get Zan. We've some thinking to do."

I was still sitting on the piano stool. Dixie laid the tip of his knife on the nape of my neck, pricking it just a little to add to his point. "Come on," he said.

Pudd'n was standing back warily, out of my reach. I walked meekly back to the chair and sat down.

"Not so tight this time," I said, as Pudd'n began to tighten the ropes around my forearms and legs. He nodded, but he was too experienced to allow me to create any slack as he worked.

"There," he said, and stood back. "What are we goin' to do about food for 'im, Dix? He'll be 'ere all night."

"Let him bloody well starve," said Dixie. He

looked disappointed, as though he had been hoping for some attempt at resistance. That knife of his looked well used, and not just on inanimate objects. He would like to have a go at more than my shirt.

"We can't starve 'im," said Pudd'n. "He's not Foss, he's 'is brother."

"He still did for Jack and Des, didn't he?"

"Well, yeah—but they'd have done for 'im if he 'adn't." Pudd'n looked at me. I had risen in his eyes since I sat down at the keyboard. "I could do yer eggs an' bacon. All right?"

I salivated at the thought. I was starving, and I nodded.

"Well, I'm not having anything to do with it," said Dixie. "Fuck him. He's all yours."

He strode out of the room, rapidly and light on his feet. Pudd'n hesitated, and I could see his problem. If he left me to get food, I'd be unguarded, and I had no doubt that Dixie would tell that to Scouse when he came back. I jerked my head down towards my wrists. "I can't get away, you know. You could leave me here."

He shook his head. "Not allowed to do that. If Dixie would come back . . ." He looked at the door for a second, then shrugged. "Well, only one thing for it. Hold tight."

He moved behind me, and the chair began to skate backwards over the polished floor. We went on past the room where I had awakened, and on to a long landing with deep carpeting. I heard a little grunt of effort, then I was carried, chair and all, on down the stairs. I made a mental note never to argue with Pudd'n. He was even stronger than his height and build suggested.

On the way downstairs and into the kitchen I was still trying to register everything that I saw. It seemed impossible to get away, but I couldn't afford to give up. Maybe it was Leo's influence, but my pulse was steady, my head was clear, and I have never felt more alert and sensitive.

There was little enough to see. We were in an old house, with eleven or twelve foot ceilings, thick and solid doors, and deep skirting-boards. I guessed it was late Victorian, and when we came to it the kitchen was enormous, with a great range all along one wall. The range had been converted from coal to gas, and Pudd'n set my chair next to it while he cooked about a pound of bacon and eight eggs.

"Bread an' tea?" he said. "I'm going to feed both of us. I don't want you untied."

He gave me food skillfully and quickly, cutting up everything into the right bite-sized pieces. I shook my head after the third egg and he went on to finish everything and then washed up the pans and dishes. I had some vague hope that I might reach a knife and hold it under my forearm, but I couldn't stretch my hand that far and anyway Pudd'n was watching every move I made.

"Right," he said when he was finished. "Now back upstairs. That'll be the hard bit."

He didn't call on Dixie for assistance. I could guess what the answer to that request would have been, and anyway the less I saw of Dixie, the better.

"Why not leave me down here?" I asked.

He considered it for a moment. "Don't think so,"

he said at last. "There's a lock on the music room, and none on the kitchen 'ere. We'll get yer back up there in a couple of minutes. Sit still."

We retraced our steps to the stairs and on up, Pudd'n huffing a bit but not under any apparent strain. We were at the top when Dixie appeared. He was scowling.

"Scouse called while you were feeding your face down there," he said. "He wants you to go over there tonight."

"What for? An' what about 'im?" Pudd'n laid one big hand on the top of my head.

"Don't worry about that." Dixie smiled so wide I could see the top of his dentures. "You can leave him to me."

Pudd'n shrugged. "All right. I'll leave in an hour, an' I'll hand over to you when I go."

He dragged me back along the landing and on through into the music room. All the way there I looked for a sign of anything that might be useful later. There was nothing.

"It's a big house," I said to Pudd'n, after he had moved me over near the piano and seated himself on the stool. He grunted noncommittally.

"How many bedrooms?" I went on.

He swiveled round to face me. "Look here, mate, I'm younger than you but I wasn't born yesterday. Don't try an' pump me, all right? If you're relyin' on me to tell you, you already know all about this house that you're goin' to know. Talk about something else."

I shrugged and leaned back in the chair. "All right. I was just interested, that's all. I'm surprised that you don't take piano playing more seriously. I could tell that you didn't have any trouble playing for Dixie—it didn't stretch you at all."

"Ah, he just wants easy stuff—dance tunes, mostly." He sniffed. "Fancies himself as Fred Astaire, silly old fart. He's past it. I play anythin' he asks me to, but it's not *real* music."

"So why not play real music? How are you in sight-reading and improvising?"

"I'm good—'specially improvising." His expression was interested, and he was getting into the conversation more. I didn't see how it could lead anywhere useful, but I had nothing better to do.

"I'd like to hear you," I said.

"Pick a tune." He looked positively eager. So was I. It was one thing to meet a musical thug, but natural talent is hard to find anywhere and it's intriguing when you meet it.

"How about a contemporary work?" I said. "How many late twentieth century piano pieces do you know?"

"Damn few—an' that includes *early* twentieth century as well." He struck a few sparse and dissonant chords that sounded like an extract from Webern, but not one I could place. "Hear that?" he said. "That's not music."

"So what *is* music?"

He thought for a moment. "This is." He began to play a beautifully balanced piano transcription of the first movement of the Schubert String Quintet, nodding his head with the rhythm.

After about a minute he stopped.

"Go on," I said. I was ready to hear more. "Who did the piano arrangement?"

He looked sheepish. "I did it myself, from listening to records an' all that."

"I'd like to see a copy."

"Aw, I don't bother to write much stuff down." He sniffed. "If it's any good you remember it anyway."

"Could you improvise on part of that?"

He shrugged noncommittally, and began again. This time he took only the first subject and began to carry it through a series of variations and modulations. He was soon so far away from C Major that I wondered how he was proposing ever to get back. Finally he set up a mock *fugato*, in which successive voices began to move him elegantly through the different keys. When he finally landed back in the tonic he grinned at me in triumph, ran through a flashing display of double octaves, and added a jaunty little coda. I noticed that his left hand, in spite of its less smooth movement, was perfectly agile and made the wildest jumps accurately.

"You're damned good," I said when he paused. For a few minutes I had forgotten that I was tied to an uncomfortable chair, a prisoner in a strange house with an unknown tomorrow. No denying it: Pudd'n was a better improviser than I ever was or ever would be.

He was flushed with pleasure. "Bit of all right, that, eh? It had me really goin' for a while with that fugue, but it came out not bad."

"Better than not bad. Look, if you want to try and earn an honest living, come and see me." (As I said that, it occurred to me that I wasn't going any place. See me where?) "You need some advanced training on use of the pedals, and that left hand could use some special exercises. But if you want to work at it, you could be doing this professionally in six months."

"Nah." He closed the piano lid. "I'm better off this way. Twelve years of do-re-mi practice was enough. I'm goin' to try an' learn to play that thing you did, though—just to prove I can."

He stood up. "I'll have to be off. Dixie will be up here in a minute. Take my advice, try an' act polite to 'im, even if he does come in 'ere an' start dancin' about like a bleedin' pet monkey. He gets nasty if you rub him up the wrong way—too fond of that bleedin' knife, it's goin' to finish him off one of these days."

He scratched his head. "Well, see you tomorrer. Don't get into no trouble."

I was left tied solidly in the chair, contemplating the pleasures of the evening ahead with Dancing Dixie as my companion. It was hard to work up any enthusiasm, even if I followed Pudd'n's advice and didn't get into no trouble. And I was getting awfully itchy to leave that chair.

– 7 –

Dixie had his own ideas of a pleasant evening. First he left me with the door locked for about two hours, sitting in the dark. I had plenty of time to try straightening in my chair and testing the strength of the wood. I could get about an inch of play there, far too little to do me any good, and after a while my legs and wrists were giving me hell and no amount of bending could bring my head close to them. All the knots were tied on the underside.

When Dixie finally rolled in and switched on the light, he was carrying a loaded tray of food, a flat half bottle of whiskey, and one glass.

"Still here, are you?" he said. "It's amazing how you don't get bored."

He poured himself a sizable Scotch, added water from a little jug, and sat down on the piano stool with the tray on his knee.

"What about me?" I said. "I'm absolutely starving."

Dixie stopped with the fork halfway to his mouth. "What yer talking about? Pudd'n fed you."

"No he didn't. He took me downstairs, but when we got there I was too sick to eat. I felt bad."

"Well, that's your bloody funeral, in'it?" Dixie ate the forkful of potato. "If you think you're getting any of this you'd better have another think."

I leaned back in the chair and let my head loll over to the left. "You saw the operations I've had," I said, my voice all weak and throaty. "I can't eat much at a time, but if I don't eat anything at all I get really bad. I'm not supposed to go more than three or four hours without food."

"That's your problem, then," said Dixie. "You had your chance with Pudd'n." He went on eating and drinking, but every half minute he would give me a worried and annoyed glance. I lay back, eyes half closed. I let my breathing become slowly more hoarse and labored. When he was finished he sat and fidgeted for a moment, then at last drained his glass and stood up. He left the room without speaking. I heard him going downstairs, while I strained at the chair again with the usual negative results.

He was back in five minutes with a glass of milk and a plate that held a big lump of cheddar and a thick slice of buttered fruitcake.

"Here." He put it down on my lap. "Now you can stop yer bloody grumbling."

I nodded my head towards my bound hands. "You'll have to feed me. I can't move."

"Like hell." His face turned red with anger. "I'm

not your bloody wet nurse. Hold still." He took
out his knife and held it carefully in his teeth, while
he worked the knots on my right arm loose enough
to move freely. "Now, you can work that the rest
of the way for yourself. Don't try anything, though,
or you'll wish you hadn't."

He stood about two feet away from the chair,
holding the knife lightly. I could sense from the
look in his eye that he wished I would give him
a reason to use it on me. I carefully worked at the
loosened bonds until I had my hand free, then
forced down the milk and the food. It was an
effort—Pudd'n had fed me more than I really
needed—but at last I was done.

"Right," Dixie said. "Sit still. I'm going to tie you
up again."

"Wait a minute." I fished in my shirt pocket and
took out the pillbox. "I have to take two of these."

"Well, get on an' do it."

"I have to have water," I said. He had used the
last of the little jug of water in his whiskey.

"Yer bloody moron." I thought for a moment he
was going to hit me, then he pulled back. "Why
didn't you tell me that before I went downstairs?
I'm not your bloody slave."

He stood furious for a moment, then turned and
walked out. I estimated that I had thirty clear
seconds. I took three capsules out of the box and
tugged them apart with my teeth, holding each one
in my right hand. My plan had been to drop the
powder from them into his drink, but his glass was
way out of reach, over on the piano. All I could
do was tip the contents of each capsule into the
open bottle of whiskey, then stuff the empty

containers in my pocket and give the bottle a quick shake with my thumb over the open top.

I was just finished when Dixie came back with a cup of water. He didn't even watch me take my pills, which was just as well—I'm not the world's expert on palming things. He seemed much more interested in his drink, and as I watched he poured about another inch into the glass.

"How about a drop of that for me?" I asked. I didn't want him looking too closely at what he was drinking.

"You must be kidding." He sat down in front of me and deliberately drank from the glass. "I wouldn't have given you any of that bloody lot if it wasn't for Scouse tellin' us to look after yer. He doesn't want you dead tomorrow—he has his own games to play."

As he spoke he was looking at my free right arm and touching the knife on the piano stool next to him. I realized he had deliberately left me untied, hoping I would give him an excuse to cut me. It was a bad few minutes. His face was flushed with drink but his eye still had a glassy, calculating look.

What did the drug do when it was combined with alcohol? I hoped it would be strongly sedative. Alcohol is a depressant, and the drug was supposed to damp brain activity. But what would I do if the mixture turned Dixie into a raving madman?

He finished the drink in his glass and glared at me with a fixed, cunning expression as he poured a refill. "Just you wait, you bleeder," he said suddenly. "Des was one of my best mates. I'll get you for 'im. You'll wish you'd never been born. Just you wait."

He stood up unsteadily and did a shuffling dance step over to the piano and back again. His coordination was badly off. He realized it and stood there frowning, staring at me again.

" 'Sgetting late. Better get you tied up again, an' relax." He picked up the knife and came closer. "Move wrong now, an' that'll be it. Put yer arm flat on the chair."

His eyes were blurry and blinking, but the knife was at my throat. He was still being cautious. He wound the rope one-handed around my wrist until it was too tight for me to move more than a couple of inches, and only then laid the knife aside to finish tying me.

"Not so tight," I said. "That's hurting."

He pulled viciously on the cord and made a final knot. Then he picked up the knife again and leaned close towards me. His eyes were only inches from mine, and his warm, whiskey-laden breath blew into my face.

"You'll know what hurtin' is soon." He brought the knife slowly up along my neck, drawing the tip steadily over my chin and cheek. I flinched as the point came higher, and squeezed my right eye tight shut. The sharp point was on my eyelid. I could feel the tremble in Dixie's hand transmitted through the steel to my eyeball. I sat motionless, my pulse throbbing in my throat.

Dixie moved the point horizontally along my eye, then at last drew back. "Just wait 'til Scouse has done with you. Then it'll be my turn." He straightened, and I took what felt like my first breath in minutes.

He lurched backwards to the stool, looked confusedly around him, and set off unsteadily for the door. He did not speak again as he went through, but I heard the key turn in the lock. Far gone as he might be, he remembered his orders. I waited a couple of minutes, then moved my head forward. If anything was to be done, now was the time for it. I couldn't wait too long—Pudd'n might come back. When Dixie was tying me again he must have already been feeling unsteady, and instead of tying the knots on the underside of the chair arm, as Pudd'n had been careful to do, he had taken the easier path of tying them on top, on the upper side of my wrist. And this time he had left the light on. I could get my teeth to work on them.

It seemed to take forever, gnawing and tugging at spit-covered, slippery rope until the knots began to loosen and slide open. My right hand took about ten minutes to free. Then I could work on the unseen knots below the left arm of the chair. I was impatient, and that slowed me down. It was another twenty minutes before I was able to stand up, free of the chair.

I took two slow steps towards the door, then stood shaking. For the first time in my life I had real sympathy for Hans Andersen's mermaid, the one who felt as though she was walking on sharp knives. My circulation was coming back, and at first I couldn't bear to walk. Finally I managed to stumble over to look at the door.

It was panelled, heavy oak with an embossed metal facing. The lock was massive, with a big, old-fashioned keyhole. I tried the handle for a moment, as quietly as I could, and confirmed that

Dixie had locked it when he left. Unless someone would provide me with a fire axe, that wasn't a possible way out. I went to the window and pulled back the thick drapes.

I had guessed from the trip down to the kitchen that the music room window would be twelve to fifteen feet above the ground. It was more like twenty—I didn't know how the ground sloped near the house. The window opened easily enough, to leave me staring down into a dimly-seen patch of bushes and flowers.

Too far to drop? I poised myself on the sill, inched forward slowly, and wondered if my injured leg could take the strain. I leaned out farther, holding the wooden window frame tightly in my left hand.

Too high!

I had just decided that when the traitorous fingers of my left hand relaxed and I was falling outward into the darkness, to land heavily on a rose bush and a bed of spiky flowers.

Then it was up on my feet as fast as I could, hobble around to the front of the house, and pause there to decide how to manage the next step. A Fiat stood out by the front entrance. My wishful thinking of keys in the ignition vanished quickly— I couldn't even open a car door. But standing by the front of the house in a metal rack was an old bicycle. I was on it in a second and off down the long drive, my knees coming up almost to my chin. The bike was meant for somebody a foot shorter, but I wasn't going to wait to raise the saddle. The house stood midway on a long hill, and I went swooping down dangerously fast, hugging the curb.

A police station was the logical place to go, but I was past logic. All I wanted to do was find a safe place to hide. That was the instinct to keep me going until I found my way to the Underground (Osterley Station, out near the end of the Piccadilly Line), heading back to my flat. Then I realized that wasn't a safe place any more. Instead I checked into a hotel in Knightsbridge, signed my name as Jan Dussek, went up to my room, and unravelled.

Some might call it shock—delayed terror sounds more accurate. But when I woke up it was nearly ten-thirty in the morning, and there were energetic sounds of cleaning coming from the corridor. I sat up groggily and took stock.

One jacket covering a cut and tattered shirt. One pair of trousers, smeared with mud and oil from the bicycle chain. Muddy shoes. A wallet containing about a hundred and twenty pounds. And a box of pills. With those assets I carried a strong desire to stay away from my flat. So what next? Only one hope left.

The call to Tess didn't start out well. I hadn't called her last night, as she had suggested in her note. Why not? She had stayed in and waited. . . . Her voice didn't have the warmth in it that I wanted to hear.

Well, I said . . .

I talked for at least five minutes, with an increasingly perplexed silence at the other end of the line.

"But where's the house?" she asked, when I ran out of steam. I could hear the unspoken comment that went with it: *Can you prove what you're saying?*

"Near Osterley Tube Station."

"You could find it again?"

"I think so. But I'm damned if I'm going to try. Tess, those lot are dangerous. If I go back there, I'll want a police escort. And I'm not sure they'll believe me—you know what Sir Westcott will say."

"I can guess." There was a long silence at the other end of the phone. I could visualize the frown on her forehead and the lower lip pinched between her teeth.

"Don't go back there," she said at last. "They know you got away, so they'll have made sure there are no signs left." (She believed me! I felt a huge sense of relief.) "And don't go back to your place, either. They might be watching there."

"I need clothes—I don't even have a check book on me."

"Leave that to me. I'll go to your place this afternoon."

"It's too dangerous." My hand started to shake when I thought of Dixie getting his hands on Tess. "If they're watching—"

"I won't be on my *own*, you nit. I'll ask a friendly copper to go in with me—but I'll need you to call your landlord to let me in."

"Tess, I can't let you do it. You've no idea what Scouse and his thugs are like. If they get their hands on you—"

"I'll call you late this afternoon, when I'm all done. You stay there, or go into Central London—that'll be safe enough. What's your number at the hotel?"

I argued for another minute, and got nowhere.

Tess was using the same manner on me that she reserved for uncooperative patients.

"Don't ask for me," I said, as she was about to hang up. "I'm registered as Jan Dussek."

"Who? "

"Dussek. He was a pianist back in Beethoven's time. It's the first name I could think of. Oh, another thing. The pills that Sir Westcott gave me."

"What about them?"

"Will you ask him if they're Nymphs?"

"If they're what?"

"Nymphs. I don't know what they are either. Ask him, all right?"

"I'll do it." But I could tell from her voice that my overall credibility was slumping.

I was left with the rest of the day to kill. For a while I lay on the bed in my room, thinking of Scouse and his louts and doing a slow burn. To get what they wanted, they were quite prepared to torture, kidnap, threaten, and kill. The last one wasn't a certainty, but I didn't like the way that Scouse had talked about Valnora Warren—the suggestion of past tense about it. To find out what Leo had been doing (What *had* Leo been doing?) they would crush Lionel Salkind like a beetle, casually and easily. Well, if they thought they could do that they had better think again. I was still an independent agent, and I had one resource they couldn't dream of. From now on, I wouldn't just note any actions that seemed to reflect Leo's memories or responses—I would seek them out, follow up on them, and do my best to interpret them.

My thoughts had run on haphazardly, but by the time I sat up on my bed my mind was made up. I wouldn't be totally passive, running and hiding. I would fight back and look for my own answers. I took a long, hot bath, then went out of the hotel and bought a new shirt and new pants. The day was pleasant, warm enough to encourage me to go into the City center and stroll about in the sunshine.

And it was there, while I sat on a bench in the quiet of St. James Park, that Leo with my assistance finally scored a direct hit. When I stood outside the bookstore I had something to work on. Over the hills and far away—India—flower perfumes, and secrecy, and awful sexual excitement. The strength of those feelings almost swamped me, but they also offered the direction for my next actions. By the time I went back to the hotel I knew what I had to do.

Tess's message was waiting for me there. Her house, any time after seven. She had my case and everything I needed. And a surprise.

Tess lived alone in a two-bedroom house in Henley, too big for her but kept for its garden— her pride and joy. I went in the back way, past neatly tied raspberry canes and flaming rows of salvias, on to peer in through the kitchen window and knock on the pane. Tess opened the back door and let me in without a word. She gave me a quick hug once I was inside the door, then stepped back out of reach. Her face was anxious and the frown lines were deeper than ever.

"He believes you now," she said. "I've never seen Sir Westcott look so surprised. He hates to be wrong."

"You told him everything?"

"Not at first—I knew he thought you had imagined everything, and he'd say you were giving us another tall story. So after we finished the wards I asked him right out: if he had any idea what 'Nymphs' were."

"He told you?"

"Not at first. He looked at me pop-eyed, and said he'd be buggered, and where had I heard that word? He thought there must have been a bad breach in the security system."

Tess led the way through into the living room, motioned me to the couch and seated herself on a chair opposite. Her posture said a lot. Feet neatly together, hands on knees. She didn't want me close until she got this off her chest.

"So those pills he gave me really are Nymphs," I said. "Dammit, Sir Westcott told me—"

"They're not Nymphs." Tess nodded her head towards the side table, inviting me to help myself to the coffee and sandwiches there. "He told you the truth, you have a new synthetic neurotransmitter in that pillbox. Nymphs are something different— a secret shared by the police, a few doctors, and international security. They're capsules, and they look like the ones you have—blue, usually—and they're the hottest and worst illegal drug anybody knows about. The papers haven't printed a word about them, though they must suspect that something is happening, just from the hospital reports. Sir Westcott is on some sort of blue ribbon royal panel studying the physical and mental effects— that's why he knows all about it. He gave me a choice, either I'd tell him I didn't remember a word he was going to say, or I'd be tied up in secrecy agreements for weeks."

I leaned forward. "Tess, they were all set to torture me last night. If Nymphs are a big secret, it's one that's a lot less well-kept than Sir Westcott thinks. Dixie thought those pills were Nymphs and proved I must be Leo. The crooks know all about them."

She nodded. "Sure they do, some of them. They're part of the distribution system. The drug is made somewhere in the East—India, or Afghanistan, or Pakistan—and finds its way into this country from abroad. It's synthetic, but producing it is difficult—thank Heaven. It's a derivative of Salvarsan—a dihydroxy-arsenobenzene hydrochloride, one of the old treatments for syphilis. That's too much of a mouthful for anybody, so the pills are mostly misnamed Nymphetamines—Nymphs, for short."

"But what do they do to you? They can't be like heroin or cocaine. Dixie said I'd only be using them for one thing, and he said Zan was too old for them."

"He was right." Tess sighed. "Can't you guess, with a name like that? Nymphetamines don't have much effect at all on adults. They affect children. They induce sexual desire and physical arousal responses—sensitivity, lubrication and increased blood supply for the vaginal mucous membranes— in prepubescent girls."

I sat there with my mouth hanging open. "I don't believe it. You think that people would buy those pills and give them . . ."

I didn't need to ask the question. I knew the

answer. When I was seventeen years old and on my first concert tour, I played a series of two-piano works with Duncan Casimir. He was seventy-two years old, he drank too much, and his playing was terrible, but he was still considered a grand old man of English music. I saw him when the young girls came crowding around us at the end of the concerts. He was practically drooling. And it wasn't over the ones I thought were attractive, the sixteen and seventeen year olds. He had his bloodshot old eyes on the tens and under. I'd seen the same thing a hundred times since, what old Casimir would delicately refer to as a "refined taste for slightly unripe fruit." Nymphs wouldn't lack for a market.

" . . . so your brother must have been mixed up with Nymphs, somehow," Tess saying. "Maybe he was trying to find out where they come from, or perhaps how they get to the west."

"No, that wasn't it." I leaned back without thinking, and winced when Dixie's cigarette burn pressed on the back of the settee. "That's just what Leo *wasn't* doing, I know that from last night. Dixie said I had to be Leo when he found the Nymphs, because no ordinary person would be carrying them. But Scouse saw past that. He said if they were Nymphs I wouldn't have carried them into the country with me, and anyway that's not what he was after. Leo was involved in something different—the Belur Package, whatever that is. But not with Nymphs. What else did Sir Westcott say about them?"

"Not too much. There have been four hundred reported cases in this country, with ages from seven to twelve. He thinks that the drug travels overland from Athens, and comes there either from Turkey or one of the Arab countries."

I shrugged and poured myself a cup of coffee. Neither of us knew it at the time, but Tess and I were very close to an answer. If she had asked one more simple question of Sir Westcott, we would have saved months of work, much pain and suffering, and many lives.

"I told him about you," she went on. "He's really pleased. He says that ten years ago you'd have died, and even five years ago, before the Madrill technique, you'd at best be just trying to stand up by now. As it is, the brain integration is the only big hurdle left. He did wonder a bit about the possibility of a seminal reflux from the *vas deferens* to the *epididymis*—the X-ray shows a slight residual lesion there." She laughed. "I told him I didn't know, I wasn't equipped to test for that."

With my mind still on Nymphs and the Belur Package, I hadn't been listening. It was the medical terms that caught my attention. I did a mental recap and suddenly realized what she was saying.

"Tess! You don't mean that you told Sir Westcott about us? That we'd been—that we—"

"Of course. He's your doctor." She sounded surprised. "He'll know better than we will if there was anything abnormal, anything that doesn't fit what he'd expect in a normal recovery. He asked me what happened—somehow he knew we went to dinner—and I told him."

"God. You make the other night sound like just another medical test—Intermediate Number Twenty-two, Response to Intercourse." I couldn't keep the hurt out of my voice. "I'd thought it was more than that. I'm surprised you didn't take my blood pressure and pulse afterwards."

Tess had been sitting quietly opposite me, knees together, prim and virginal in her posture. Now she stood up and came to stand directly in front of me. She was wearing a dark blue blouse that gave color to her eyes and made them seem almost violet.

"Lionel," she said softly. "Don't be a ninny." She reached out and cupped my cheek in her hand. "You've been through a medical experience wilder than any other patient I've ever heard of. You're alive, but that's only half the battle. We knew that someday you'd try to make love again, and that might be a time for difficulties—and maybe danger, too. I wanted you to be all right; and you were."

"You want the best for all your patients."

"You're more than my patient. That night was a test, sure it was, but it was a lot more than that for me. You're the hard one, not me. You never give up much of yourself, do you? Maybe Leo was the same, maybe not. But last night when you didn't call I was worried out of my head. If I called your flat once, I did it ten times. I thought you might have had a collapse, or be in pain, or all sorts of things. I even called the hospitals in the area, to see if you had checked into one."

For Tess, that was a very long speech. I sat there in silence for a few seconds. "I'm sorry," I said at last. I had to clear my throat before I could speak again. "You're right. I'm a selfish bastard, and underneath I guess I'm a prude as well."

Deep down Tess had touched another nerve. *You never give up much of yourself, do you?*

Maybe Leo was the same, maybe not. Those words stung more because I had had that thought, too. Leo gave more of himself, and more was given back in return.

I reached up to take her hands and drew her gently forward to sit by me on the couch.

"I'm sorry," I said again. "What you did was quite right. Would you tell me what else Sir Westcott told you? I promise I won't mind."

"He said that the crucial period is still ahead, no matter how well you feel now. There will be a time when the main integration of brain tissue will happen, and when it does the Madrill technique goes out of control. The information transfer will become very fast—like a hole in a dike, he said, first a trickle, then a sudden flood. When that happens you have to be somewhere quiet. You'll pass out, and you'll need good medical care."

"I've had the same sort of warning from him in person." I turned to look at her. "No point in worrying about that until it happens. But what about—you know. Did he say that it's all right for me to have sex? Am I well enough for it?"

The frown lines were gone from her forehead, "You had no pain last time, did you?"

"Did you hear me groaning?"

"Yes." Tess smiled. "But I heard me groaning, too, and I wasn't in pain."

"So everything is all right."

"I don't know." She didn't look worried, but her face wore a softer, heavy-eyed look, almost like a drowsiness. "You've had scientific training, too. You know you can't draw statistical conclusions from a single experiment. You need more data points."

"How many samples does it take?" I put my arm around her shoulder and drew her closer.

She slid forward to move her body against me. "I think that depends on you more than me."

For the first time in twenty-four hours Scouse and his gang were pushed beyond even the periphery of my attention. I hadn't realized it the first night, but Tess must have been holding part of herself in check, watching me for any signs of trouble or discomfort. Now she was willing to let herself go completely. We gave Sir Westcott's handiwork a severe test, and it passed again. I did have an after-the-fact ache in my right side, but Tess felt around it and diagnosed a simple muscle strain.

By eleven o'clock we were lying together in Tess's luxurious double bed. I knew from her breathing that she was drowsing, but for me sleep wouldn't come. A summer storm was on the way, and we lay there with the curtains open and the window cracked to let in the warm night air. The flicker of sheet lighting, far off, and an occasional distant grumble of thunder created in me the postcoital depression that Ovid attributed to all animals.

I brooded again over Tess's words. *You never give much of yourself, do you?*, and I thought of John Donne's much older ones, *Love, any devil else but you, would for a given soul give something too.*

It hurt all the more because I had suffered the same worry for years. While Leo had found ways to open himself to others, I had travelled the world cocooned in the threads of my music, protected by Bach and Mozart and Schubert. Now Tess was offering me a golden chance to change, to give in return; and I was going to turn away from it. I knew I would. Before I left the bookshop in the afternoon, I had decided. I had to chase Leo's flicker of memory, to pursue it wherever it led me. If it was unsafe for me in England, a foreign region would be no worse.

I was sweating, uneasy and weary in mind and body. I eased myself an inch away from Tess. Our bodies were sticky and closely twined, and as I moved she gave a little mutter of protest and snuggled back into the fold of my arm. Her hair tickled my chest but I did not move again. Uncertainty, misery and guilt hung over me, until finally the rain came, the air cooled, and I could drift slowly down into my own release of sleep.

— 8 —

"Keep a diary," said Sir Westcott.

"Why? I don't need one, my memory's always been good." Better than yours, I was tempted to add—Sir Westcott moved through a cloud of mislaid books, forgotten appointments, and lost umbrellas.

"Never mind how good your memory is," he replied. "Keep a diary—you'll see why in a few months."

That had been a few weeks before I was released from the hospital. I went along with his eccentric request, jotting down notes on events that I knew I'd be able to remember in detail months or years later.

Now I had the book out on my knee, drowsing through it as the plane flew steadily on through the night skies of northern India. We had left London the previous night. On the long journey east, losing hour after hour to the shifting time zones, we passed through Rome, Athens, Tehran, Bombay, and so to the final jump to Calcutta. I hoped the flight crew had taken the trip better than I had—blocked sinuses, eyes sore and gritty, and an iron filings taste in my mouth. The Persians next to me muttered to each other and puffed on a *ghalian*, passing the tube quietly from hand to hand. It didn't smell much like tobacco, but at three in the morning the stewardesses weren't worrying.

Don't think my coordination is getting any better now, I had written. *Seems to be at a plateau*. And later that day, feeling guilty about the neglect of my business manager, *Should call Mark, but it can wait a while longer*.

The entries were innocent enough, and I could remember all of them. What I could not recall, what now seemed quite wrong to me, was their tone. It was nervous and diffident, reluctant to face Sir Westcott, oddly hesitant about approaching Tess. I was beginning to understand the surgeon's flat assertion.

"It won't happen the way you're expecting. You seem to think that you'll wake up one day and feel yourself merging thoughts with your brother. But you're sitting there on the inside. There's no way a person can get an objective view of the workings of his own brain. The only way you'll see changes is by looking back at earlier behavior and comparing. Write things down. Otherwise you'll have nothing to compare it with."

It had been easy enough to do that when I was still in the hospital, with time on my hands. Recently there hadn't been a spare minute. The new idea I'd had before going over to Tess's house had been a winner.

I had to accept that the right brain hemisphere is pictorial and largely nonverbal—the medical texts had made that clear enough. That meant I was wasting my time trying to dig *messages* out of the right brain portions that came from Leo. Words were hard to get—Nymphs, Scouse, Valnora Warren, or any others. What I should be providing was picture inputs that might stimulate the right brain hemisphere and elicit a solid physical reaction from my body.

I was sure that Leo had been doing something in India. But where in India? To answer that question, Tess and I made a trip to the British Museum and looked through the picture files. It was a long job. I stared at photographs of Delhi, Madras, Lahore, Bombay, Agra, and Calcutta; and in that last city, when we came to a color picture of the *Maidan*, the big park-like rectangle at the city center, I felt a return of the vivid excitement that had hit me outside the bookstore.

Calcutta.

It was a city I had visited a couple of times on my concert tours, but never to play there. It had been a point of passage on the way back from Australia and New Zealand, little more than a hotel room near the airport. I could recall only one exchange with Leo about the place. I remarked on the poverty (which I had never been close enough to see) and he answered with a noncommittal shrug.

Now the plane was lowering flaps for landing at Dum-Dum Airport, and I still had no idea what

I expected to find here. I only knew I had to look, to learn what Leo had been doing in those hidden months before our final meeting.

It was just after dawn when we landed, with a blood-red November sun steaming up over the Bay of Bengal. The monsoon was over, and this was supposed to be the cool season, but as we stepped off the plane the humidity curled around me like a blanket. The air seemed to bleed your strength away. The walk to the terminal and the wait for baggage became a major effort.

I went straight to the new Grand Hotel on Chowringhi Road, hardly noticing the flat, wet land and the drooping coconut palms. At the hotel I went to bed, but I was too nerved up and over-tired to sleep. After an hour of tossing and turning I ran the deep bath full of rusty-colored water—a sign in the room warned me not to drink it—and stretched out to think of the day ahead.

I knew exactly one person in Calcutta: Chandra Roy; Chanter Chandra we called him, back in the old days when we had played together.

He had been a fiddle player, a child prodigy and still a fast-developing adult when he had suddenly abandoned his musical career, returned to India, and disappeared. Maybe that's too strong a term— I still had an address for him at the University of Calcutta; but he had certainly vanished from western life. I hadn't seen him for more than two years.

Chandra. As I sat on the bed and dried myself I decided to head over and see him at once. But when I was half-dressed I lay back and closed my eyes for a moment, and when I woke the room was growing dim. It was suddenly seven o'clock at night.

I was very hungry, but I didn't want to waste the rest of the evening. I took a native cab and we set off to hunt for Chandra's supposed home address, passed on to me by an oboe player before I left London.

A combination of jet lag, medication, and low blood sugar made the ride through the darkening streets curiously unreal. What I saw was always distant or distorted, the mirror of an unpleasant real world. Since the hydrological project to increase the flow of the Hooghly River, many of Calcutta's worst abominations had been removed. Now at least there was adequate drinking water. But the *bustis* were still there, the ultimate slums that formed the home for over four million people. Life in them was still below subsistence level. The cab skirted one of the bad ones. The smell of decay, excrement, and underfed humanity was like a black canker on a rose-red evening. My driver, oblivious to the dull-eyed skeleton creatures that we passed, chattered on cheerfully in a mixture of Bengali and English, telling me how the city was improving now, how things had grown better all through the nineties, and how the new century had ushered in a golden era.

"I am telling you, we will be seeing the better times. Very good better times," he said, in the curious Welsh-like Indian lilt. He swerved to avoid a legless man who was dragging himself slowly across the street. "I am seeing that you are a stranger here, and you maybe are finding this surprising. But it is so."

Chandra, according to my friend the oboe player, lived in Alipore, a southern suburb of the main city. It took more than an hour to find his house, weaving back and forth along the flat streets. The driver leaned out of the window most of the time, singing out Bengali questions to the small groups of people who stood deep in unfathomable conversation on most street corners.

We found the house at last. It was certainly big enough to notice, a great pile of rambling Edwardiana that could have been transported to Henley or Thames Ditton without seeming at all out of place. A seven foot brick wall kept it safe from prying eyes.

After a brief negotiation (my driver's hourly rate was less than I received for one second of concert playing) he agreed to eat *chuppattis* at my expense and wait for as long as I needed him— all night, if I wished it, he told me cheerfully. He was so pleased with the arrangement that I knew he believed he was overcharging me.

I was led inside by an old servant in a long, flowing robe. Chandra stood by a small table. He was almost unrecognizable. In little more than two years he had changed from a thin-faced ascetic to a roly-poly, smiling cherub. His eyes glittered with surprise and pleasure when he saw me, and that turned to a look of wonderment when he got a good look at my scarred face.

"I had read about your accident." He shook his sleek head in concern. "No one told me how serious it must have been."

In the world of music, news travels fast. Chandra must still be connected, even if he never performed.

He led the way to a sparsely furnished study. Over glasses of hot, sweet tea we sat down to talk. After playing catch-up on Chandra's activities for the past two years, I offered a version (slightly edited) of my own past six months. People were mistaking me for my brother, I said. My brother had obviously left unfinished business—I thought it was in Calcutta. It was my wish to complete it, but my knowledge of what he had been doing was limited. He had mentioned walking in the *Maidan* before he died, but nothing of business detail. I even lacked his business address.

Chandra grimaced and nibbled on a marzipan plum. A servant stood discreetly outside the door, waiting for any request for food or drink.

"You have no company name or address?" Chandra waved a plump hand. "Hopeless. You can advertise in the newspapers, perhaps. But unless he was active in the business community here I think you will find it impossible to learn much. There is more chance for anonymity in this city than anywhere else in the world. Tomorrow, if you wish, I will ask at the University. He was your twin, was he not?"

I nodded.

"Then if you have no picture of him, perhaps we could put your photograph in the papers, and ask for information."

I hesitated. "Maybe in a few days," I said at last. "Let me settle in here first, and get used to the city. There's no rush."

"Would you care to stay here, rather than in a hotel?" asked Chandra. He smiled. "The Calcutta Zoo is in Alipore—a mile or so from here."

He knew my habits. I shook my head. It had not escaped me that Chandra had made no move to show me most of his house, or to introduce me to members of his family. It was past midnight—the talk had rambled all over the world, following our mutual acquaintances—and he was beginning to yawn. "All the world passes through Calcutta," he had told me. "I do not need to travel to keep up with people." But as eldest son in a thriving family jute business, he did need his sleep. He was up these days with the sun—when he used to be ready to go to bed.

"And the violin?" I couldn't resist the question as we stood again at the front door, waiting for my driver.

For answer he held up his left hand, the fingers facing towards me. The horn-hard calluses built up by twenty years of daily playing had reverted to become soft pads of tender flesh. Forty thousand hours of practice, down the drain. He would probably never play again. As the cab took me north to the hotel, the difference between East and West ceased to be an abstraction, something that Kipling had invented for a poem. And I wondered again what the time in the Orient had done to Leo, how it had changed him inside the western exterior.

In a perverse way the meeting with Chandra cheered me up a lot. He had managed to construct a new life that did not revolve around music. If he could do it, so could I.

At 120 rupees, the three-color map of Calcutta I bought at the hotel was robbery. It was badly printed, the colors bled across the line borders, and the names were poorly spaced and hard to read. Unless I was willing to seek out a city bookstore, though, it was all that I would get.

I was afraid it would make little difference. Having come this far, I seemed to be at a dead end. It had looked to be easy when I was back in London. Leo would feed me the information I needed, somehow or other. But apart from the conviction that the *Maidan*, here in the center of Calcutta, was an important part of Leo's past, I had found nothing to guide me to a special part of the city. I wandered, map in hand, looking for some new idea, all the way from the Howrah Bridge, with its great web of cantilevered steel and its teeming cars, oxcarts, rickshaws, bicycles, trucks and people, down south as far as Alipore and the Calcutta Zoological Gardens. I spent half a day in the Zoo, marvelling at the great thirty-eight foot reticulated python that had amazed the world when Funyatti captured it live in the Sumatran jungles in '02. The zookeepers impressed me less than the animals. One of them, more foolhardy than rational, moved unprotected through an enclosure containing two splendid specimens of *Dendraspis polylepis*, black mambas that to me are the most unpredictable and dangerous of the poisonous snakes. I watched until the man came out alive.

But I found it hard to watch anything else for very long. Always, my steps drew me back to the *Maidan*. I sat there, hour after hour, looking at the white marble pile of the Victoria Memorial. It was a mixture of English and Moghul styles, and as ugly in its way as the Albert Memorial in London. I soon learned to hate it, but I went back day after day, wondering what I was doing there. Chandra twice invited me to attend University functions, and I resolutely refused both of them to sit out in that dull park and stare at that awful monument.

It was an unhappy and frustrating time. The weather was miserable, cold and windy. It wasn't until the ninth day of my vigil, when my stomach and head were both thoroughly adjusted to the change in time and diet, that the break came.

The weather turned warm and sunny. I was sitting on the same bench as usual, looking north towards Fort William. I had occupied benches that faced north, south, east and west, like a dog turning round before it can settle, but always an indefinable discomfort took me at last to a bench that looked north.

I was reading the *International Herald Tribune*, my only real link with the West. I had lost patience with the Indian radio and television in my first day, and took all my news from the paper, several days late. When I looked up, a woman was sitting on a bench across the green from me, perhaps thirty yards away.

She was very dark skinned, clearly Indian, and dressed in a green sari with flecks of yellow-gold in the long skirt. Her dark hair was drawn back from her forehead, and in the center, an inch above her eyes, I could see the glint of a single golden ornament. She was looking straight at me, her face calm and disinterested. But at the sight of her I felt myself beginning to tremble, with a wave of tension and excitement in my stomach that was too much to endure.

I stood up, looking for some reaction from her—

she still seemed to be staring straight at me. When she did not move, I began to walk slowly around the gravel footpath that bordered the small square of green.

It was perplexing enough to make my head ache and drive me dizzy. Obviously, Leo knew her. She should recognize him, and that meant she should recognize me. But I walked in front of her, almost near enough to touch, and there was no glimmer of recognition on her face. Close up, I saw that she was beautiful and young. I guessed no more than nineteen.

She had a dark, flawless complexion, and her huge dark eyes were carefully made up with a layer of kohl on the eyelids. The features were regular, with prominent cheek bones and a broad forehead. And in the center of that forehead was the thing that sent my mind reeling and spinning. The golden ornament was not the smooth metal bead that it appeared to be from across the square. It was a tiny beetle—an exact copy of the beetle that Leo wore on his tie clip at our final meeting in London Airport.

I paused in front of her, cleared my throat, and then indecision moved me on. What could I say to her? That my brother knew her, though I did not, and I wanted to ask what he had been doing in Calcutta?

As my brain dithered, my legs carried me halfway around the plot of grass, back towards my bench. Instead of sitting down again I stood and watched. After fifteen minutes—endless minutes in which she did not register my presence by a look or a blink—an older man approached her. He came slowly across from the north side of the *Maidan*, helping himself along with a black wooden cane. I found his age indeterminate, anywhere from forty to seventy, and his loose white robe made it hard to tell if his left leg was crippled by age or by injury.

He came up behind her and spoke. I heard her laugh, and she turned her head as he moved around the bench to sit next to her. As they talked together her face lost its calm appearance. She laughed again, expression alight and animated, and after a moment she patted him on the arm with a small, shapely hand. Her fingernails were lacquered a purple-red.

Another few moments, and they both stood up quickly. She took his arm and they began to walk across the park, heading northwest towards the exit. The *Maidan* had become suddenly filled with people, thousands of strollers taking a midday break from the offices in Dalhousie Square. It would be easy to lose sight of the two of them in just a couple of minutes.

I hurried after them across the grass, panting more than the effort could explain.

"Excuse me . . ." My long legs brought me close behind them. "Excuse me . . ." I had thought of nothing to say to them after those first few words. More speech turned out to be unnecessary. They paused and looked back at the sound of my voice. The woman seemed politely interested and a little puzzled. But the old man gaped up at me and rubbed a wrinkled hand across his forehead.

"Sahib Singh!" His voice quivered. It was clear

now that he was at least in his sixties—old for
Calcutta. At his words the woman gave a strange
cry, mingled disbelief and excitement. I could
see just how good-looking she was, with superb
brown eyes and white, even teeth gleaming from
a luscious mouth. Her hand went up to her
throat and she remained motionless for a
moment. Then she spoke to me in a long,
questioning sentence.

I shook my head. It sounded like Bengali, but
though I had worked hard over the past few days
to pick up a sprinkling of phrases I had nothing like enough to follow a spoken sentence.

"I'm sorry," I said. "I don't understand you. Do
you speak English?"

She gasped at my voice and stepped closer.

"Ameera!" said the old man warningly.

She reached out her hand and placed it on my
chest. I towered over both of them—neither was
more than five feet tall. She stretched up to touch
my face, while I stared down into those dark,
jewelled eyes. Less than a foot away, they showed
a hint of diffuse light in their depths, a cloudiness
behind the pupils. While I was still struggling with
the significance of that, she moved her right hand
to run it inquiringly over my nose, lips, and chin,
then fell backwards swooning into the arms of the
old man.

I was feeling dizzy, too. At that soft, careful
hand on my face, my heart leaped up to my
throat, and the rhythm, *"Over the hills and far
away,"* pulsated again inside my head.

I stood panting and helpless, watching the old
man as he held the girl. Two powerful and

conflicting urges conspired to hold me frozen: overwhelming physical desire, and the visceral urge that told me to flee and hide in the busy streets of Calcutta.

– 9 –

The house they took me to was smaller than Chandra's, but still another impressive mansion. A structure of dark-red brick, it was surrounded by the now-familiar screening wall, and the garden within was laid out with scrupulous care. The beds of sages and flowering thyme threw back at me the perfumed mix that had first hit my memory on a London street.

The old man would not (or could not) talk to me on the journey. After two or three Bengali sentences in a voice that was at once angry and deferential, he had given up on me. He had accepted my help in getting the woman Ameera out of the *Maidan*, leaving me to do most of the carrying while he shooed away inquisitive onlookers and two Calcutta policemen, but his looks at me when we came to the carriage were angry and puzzled.

The ride in the closed, horse-drawn cab was short, only a few minutes of twisting and winding up narrow back streets. I already knew Calcutta well enough to realize that the horse was a sign of wealth, not poverty—a car would have been cheaper to maintain—and the houses that we passed confirmed the impression of ample money. By the time we arrived at the big double doors and had been admitted by a man with a heavy black mustache who stood guard in a little sentry box, the woman was awake again, sighing and fluttering her long eyelashes. I got out of the carriage first, ready to try and explain my presence and coax some English-speaking member of the household into allowing me to stay. It was quite unnecessary. The guard touched his hand deferentially to his brow, bowed stiffly from the waist, and motioned me forward toward the main structure of the house.

I stood in the entrance, wondering what came next. Ameera was led away through rustling curtains of silk by an older woman who bustled out of the house as soon as we entered the double gates of weather-beaten teak. She gave me one nod, then ignored me. After a couple of minutes, the old man who had been in the *Maidan* came in behind me and gestured to another inner room.

It was a study, panelled and lined with bookcases. The wall on my left was flanked by a long sideboard bearing a dozen full decanters of different colored liquids, and heavy armchairs and coffee tables stood in precise alignment on the hardwood floor. There were no rugs—I could see what a hazard loose rugs would be to a blind woman—and there was an exact orderliness to the furniture arrangement.

The man who had led me in had abandoned me at once. I stood for a while looking at the books but that quickly proved to be a waste of time. They were all in Arabic or Hindustani script. After a futile few minutes I stepped across to the sideboard and removed the stoppers from a few of the decanters: Scotch, rum, sherry. It seemed at odds with the eastern elements of the room. I ran my hand across the smooth wood of the sideboard. Everything was spotless, no mote of dust anywhere despite the absence of occupation.

I was still standing there when Ameera returned, alone. Her color was back to normal, a rich coffee-cream with a hint of pink behind it in her cheeks. She came in confidently, skirting a coffee table and heading straight towards me. If I had not seen the telltale cloud behind her eyes in the *Maidan* I would have sworn that she had normal vision.

A couple of feet away from me she halted and spoke again in Bengali. I shook my head, then realized that was probably useless.

"I'm sorry," I said. "I don't understand."

Her shoulders slumped. "Leo-yo?" The word was musical and strangely accented. It brought the hair up on the back of my neck, and it wasn't just her use of Leo's name. I had found it, Leo's eastern contact!

"Leo-yo," she said again. "Please talk to me." Her English was precise but not fluent.

"I am Leo's brother," I said, slowly and carefully. "Not Leo. My name is Lionel."

"Brother?" Her face changed expression again, from sadness to worry and confusion. She came nearer and touched her hand up to my face. This time she was more thorough, running her fingers gently over my forehead, then back to the scars that were still lumpy patches of tissue on the back of my skull. She hissed to herself, tongue between her teeth, when she came to the patched-up bone.

"Leo-yo. You have been hurt."

"Not Leo." I took her hands gently in mine. She looked up at me patiently, her eyes wide and opalescent. "Ameera," I said. "Please believe me. I am not Leo. Leo had a brother, I am his brother." As I spoke I winced at my use of the past tense for Leo, but Ameera's English was not good enough to catch it and read its significance. Her face remained perfectly calm.

"Ameera," I went on. "I would like to talk to you. About my brother. About Leo."

The long eyelashes flickered, and the lids covered the cloudy beauty of her eyes. She was looking down, her hands running their sensitive fingers over the back of my hand and my forearm.

"I understand," she said at last. "You told me this. That there might be a time when you could not know me, you warned of hidden times. But here . . . where only we are here, after so long . . ."

Her voice trailed away sadly, and I swore under my breath. If only she could see . . . It was hard to believe that those dark orbs were unseeing. What could I do next? This was supposed to be the place where I would meet all Leo's eastern contacts—but where were they?

"Ameera, whose house is this?"

She looked surprised, her lips parting to show pearly teeth with slightly prominent canines.

"House? This house? Leo-yo, you know it. This house is your house, as it has always been—what else? We have waited for you here, waited and waited . . . Chatterji said you would not come back, you would never come back. When he saw you in the *Maidan*, he did not believe it."

I was hardly listening. *Leo's* house. I knew he had been in the east for years, and he hated living in hotels. But why had he never mentioned it to me?

"Now that you are here," Ameera was saying, "it will be a *tandoori* meal. Shamli has been told, and Chatterji will get the chutney you like. In one half of an hour it will be ready to eat."

She reached confidently across the sideboard and picked up a decanter and a glass. She removed the stopper, sniffed to make sure, and poured. It was a fine *oloroso* sherry, Leo's favorite. Should I try and explain to her again? I sipped, watched as she replaced the stopper and set the decanter back in its exact place, and caught a hint of the delicate perfume she had applied since we reached the house.

Suddenly I had a visceral understanding that she had been Leo's mistress. If I closed my eyes I saw images of dark, flawless skin beneath the modest clothes. The contours of her figure glowed with secret oils, familiar to me as no woman had ever been familiar. I took a bigger gulp of sherry.

"Ameera."

"Yes, Leo-yo?" Still she refused to accept me as myself.

"There are many books here. Where are the other books and papers in this house?"

"Many places." She was confused. "You know it. In this room, in the bedroom. There are books everywhere."

"Did you ever hear anyone talk about T.P.? As someone's name?"

"Teepee?" Her voice was bewildered, "Never. Who is Teepee?"

"I don't know—it is a bad person. How about Belur? Do you know about anything called the Belur Package?"

Now she hesitated, "Belur is a common name in the south of the country. But what is in the package?"

"I don't know." I would try Chatterji and the others, if I could find an interpreter, but I sensed that there would be no success. Leo's secrets were well-kept. He would not have told these people what he kept hidden from me.

A gong, softly struck, was sounding a low note through the house. Ameera took my empty glass from my hand and led the way towards the back of the ground floor. The table in the dining room was set for two, with gleaming Benares silver and white linen tablecloth. I sat opposite Ameera and felt enormously frustrated. I had travelled a third of the way around the world to chase a long shot. Now the long shot had come in, and I was more stymied than ever. The mysterious stranger in Calcutta had been found. He was my own brother.

The chicken *tandoori* was delicious, served with lime pickles and an array of chutneys and vegetables by silent servants whom Ameera addressed in Bengali. The effort of speaking and understanding English seemed to have tired her, and she concentrated on enjoyment of the food. Leo had been fluent in Bengali, that was obvious from the way that I was occasionally addressed in that language by the puzzled servants. As they served a dessert of banana *halva* I wondered again about the household. Leo must have managed to set it up to run separate from any business activities that he had carried on in India. It had run smoothly— at what cost I could not guess—even when he had disappeared for over six months. I had the feeling that he had left the house in the past on extended trips, and my sudden appearance was less of a surprise than I expected. I looked around me at the elegant furnishings and careful arrangement. I couldn't have set up a house to run like this in my absence, not in a million years. The old conviction that I was somehow the lesser half, a reduced version of Leo, grew stronger as the meal concluded with a demitasse of Turkish coffee, and the sun outside the window sank lower in the sky,

Afterwards Ameera led me outside, to walk in the walled garden. There was no sign of a weed anywhere. As we passed through an archway framed by climbing roses, she took my hand to lead her. I saw the new shoots that reached out to catch at our clothes and guided her clear of them. When she moved through the arch the setting sun struck directly on her face, turning it to a bronze carving.

I passed my hand across her eyes, blocking out the light, and she followed the movement of my arm with her head.

"You can see that?" I moved my hand back and forth,

Ameera smiled. "Light and dark, Leo-yo. Nothing

more. It has not changed." She reached out to take my hand as it moved in front of her. I could smell her perfume again, rosewater and jasmine. She stroked my hand.

"Your room," she said, "it was not made ready. If we had known you would be here . . . we have not even cigars for you, Chatterji will buy them tonight." She sounded upset.

"I have my room at the hotel," I said. Then I saw her face, and added: "All my clothes are there. I have nothing here with me."

"There are clothes." She turned her face again to the setting sun. "It will soon be dark. You are tired from your travel? Wait here, and I will see if the room is ready yet."

I was exhausted from tension, but before I went up to bed I wanted to look over the rooms of the house. At my request Ameera led me around the whole place. Many rooms were unlit and I had trouble following her, though she moved confidently everywhere, past huge settees in the living room and the grotesque wooden statues in a long corridor that led back to the kitchen. I realized in the first few minutes that any search of the house for evidence of Leo's activities in India would take days. But the best place to begin might well be Leo's bedroom.

The house bustled busily about us as we went through the kitchen and up the rear staircase. It was clear what was happening. The master of the household had returned. Ameera treated me just as though I were Leo, and the rest of the staff took their cue from her. Everywhere I heard polite Bengali greetings, and Ameera replied to them. She seemed to feel that Leo, for his own purposes, was choosing to speak only English, and she behaved as though it were some kind of test. She had already told me, a little proudly, that for the past six months she had been practicing English speech every day—as I had told her to.

By eleven o'clock I had seen all of the house that a lightning tour could provide, said goodnight to Chatterji (still puzzled and obeisant) and to Ameera, and was making a closer examination of Leo's bedroom. It was a huge, north-facing cavern on the second floor, with one small window that looked out over the high wall to the city beyond. Shaving equipment, towels and liquid soaps, enough for an army, were set out by a massive marble washstand, and clean clothes that smelled strongly of camphor were draped over wooden hangers. They were street clothes, and I could find no pajamas or other night attire. The room had one weak light over by the door, and another above the great bed. I could see evidence of Leo's taste in some of the fittings and in the bookcases that filled the headboard and much of the wall space. But nowhere could I find one book or paper in English, or any sign of files or recording system.

So where did Leo keep his paperwork? I yawned, and decided that had to be a question for the next morning. I washed, turned off the lights, and climbed naked into bed. It was warm in the room, and I lay covered by a single cotton sheet that smelled pleasantly of lemon and reminded me of my childhood back home in the north of England.

The headache that had been creeping up on me for the past couple of days—a mild foretaste of things to come—pushed at me, like an itch behind my eyes, and I was glad to rest my head on the pillow. Even when I fell asleep the ache remained, following me into an uneasy dream, I found myself walking through a harsh, sunlit land, all yellows and crude reds, where small lizards sunned themselves on baking rocks and fled before me as I approached. And even in sleep, I knew I was not in India.

The door of the room opened. I was hazily aware of it, wondering what was happening to throw a spear of light in across the bed. I came more fully awake with the soft rustle of clothing, dropping to the hardwood floor. After a few seconds of silence I felt hands on my shoulders and the back of my neck. I tensed and almost cried out, then suddenly relaxed as the fingers dug in to massage my tired muscles and work out their tension and fatigue.

"Leo-yo." It was a soft breath in my ear, smelling of mint and anise. I moved to sit up, then lay back beneath the pressure of her hand on my chest. Her gentle touch moved lower, exploring, pressing and rubbing and caressing.

"Lie still." There was a fragrance of oils and powder as she slipped back the sheet and moved in beside me. She slid her body across mine. She was shapely and perfumed and had a skin as soft as a peach. There were a few gentle words to me in Bengali, then she moved on to me in total silence. For a long time there was only the sound of our breathing. Ameera was in control, leading me and following me irresistibly to a sweet climax.

Perhaps I should have felt guilty, a triple cheat. I was unfaithful to Tess, taking Ameera under false pretenses, and stealing Leo's woman, all at the same time. I did feel uncomfortable—later. But as Ameera taught me something about the East that until then I had only read about, I could not feel anything but pleasure.

Her enjoyment seemed as intense as mine. Later we lay together, drowsy in companionable darkness, until she moved her hands to rub again at the muscles in my shoulders, lulling me. Again I felt her hands move all over me, caressing, renewing their acquaintance with my body, learning what her eyes could not tell her, And then, when I was very close to sleep, I heard a sound that jerked me back to wakefulness.

Ameera was weeping in the darkness, quiet and heartbroken. I could hear her trying to choke off her sobs as she moved her body away from me.

"What's wrong?" I sat up, suddenly convinced that I had committed a terrible social blunder. It was impossible to believe that I had misread the signals and forced myself on an unwilling partner. But why else would she weep?

"I did not believe you," she said at last. "You told me, and I did not believe. But it is true. You are not Leo. You are the brother."

She had moved away from the bed and was reaching down to pick up her gown. I was sitting up, but I was naked and in the darkness and the unfamiliar room I had no idea where my clothes

were. Before I could move she was at the door,
slipping away from me.

As the door closed behind her all my old
doubts and insecurities came flooding back. "Frozen Englishman," Leo had said to me once,
mocking me as we stood on the beach. "It's the
cold weather, you've got no blood in your veins.
Come on out to L.A., and maybe you'll learn the
right way to make love to a girl."

He had been joking, but it still hurt—because
I believed it.

For half an hour I lay on the bed, too depressed
even to turn on a light. My headache was back,
worse than ever. My thoughts went again and again
over the same question: What had I done, what
ineptitude so blatant that it would convince someone who wanted to believe I was Leo that I must
be someone else? In our lovemaking we had not
even spoken to each other. What had I done
wrong?

I was still in my narcissistic fit of misery and
self-pity when the door opened again. Bare feet
came padding across the floor, and the bed moved
as someone placed their weight on its edge.

"Here." Ameera's voice was only a sad whisper.
"Take this. It is yours." She pressed a sheet of
paper into my hand.

"What is it?" The darkness was total. I had the
wild idea that maybe this was the document I
sought, the thing that told me what Leo had been
doing here in India.

"I do not know," she said. "Leo gave it to us
and told us to keep it in case some day he did not
come back. I cannot see, and Chatterji cannot read

the English. He says it has writing in English. You are the brother. It tells you what must be done now."

The sheet of paper seemed to burn in my grasp. I had to get to a light, to see what it said—but even more urgent than that, I had to know something else.

"Ameera?"

"Yes?" Her voice was dull and unhappy.

"I'm sorry. For what I did. I'm sorry that I wasn't . . ." It was hard to say.

"Wasn't?" Her voice was puzzled, a couple of feet away from me on the edge of the bed.

"I'm sorry you weren't happy. I'm sorry that I failed you . . . when we made love." My voice choked in my throat. "I mean, you knew I wasn't Leo. I'm sorry for what it was I did wrong."

"Oh." Her voice sounded different, as though she had turned her head away. "No, it was not that. Not when we loved. It was . . ." Her voice faltered. "It was afterwards, when we were lying here. And I touched you. I knew then. But I do not know how to say . . ."

I felt the bed move as she stood up, and heard her bare feet as she moved towards the door.

"I cannot say it,'" she said again, and her voice sounded as though she was weeping into her gown.

"Why not? Please tell me, whatever it was."

"I cannot. I do not know the word—the English word. But I knew you were not Leo afterwards, when I touched you—there."

"Touched me?" She had touched me all over.

"Yes. He was—cut. You are not cut. I knew it then, as soon as I touched you."

The door opened and I saw a swirl of white as she glided through and out of the room.

Cut? Operation scars? I had plenty of those, but we'd had no operations, either of us, before the final crash. So what on earth was Ameera talking about?

I lay back in the bed, and suddenly understood. A strange mixture of emotions flooded over me—relief, amusement, grief, and guilt. Ameera was quite accurate. Leo had been cut. Like most American males, but unlike me, he was circumcised. Only in unusual circumstances would anyone be able to use that as a method of telling us apart.

The sheet of paper was still clutched in my hand. I wanted to read it at once, to know what it would tell me. But I was gripped by powerful and uncontrollable emotions. If I am honest, I have to say that my strongest feeling was relief. My delicate male ego had survived a major trauma. Now it was more than I could do to keep my eyes open. The headache was creeping back, pulling a band of tightness across my forehead, and my brain felt numbed. Tomorrow. I would read the paper tomorrow.

In less than a minute I was asleep. And, human sexuality being what it is, I had wildly erotic dreams—of Tess. We were making love in the middle of the *Maidan*, ignored by the hundreds of passers-by who scurried through the midday heat on their urgent but inscrutable Calcutta business.

— 10 —

I slept late and woke to a silent house. The clothes
set out by my bed fitted perfectly—no surprise
there, they obviously belonged to Leo. Downstairs
there was no sign of Ameera or of the wizened
Chatterji, but the table was set in the dining room
and a full buffet breakfast laid out in warmed
chafing dishes on the long sideboard. As I helped
myself, one of the servants peeked in through the
door that led to the kitchen, and a minute or so
later he was back with Royal Worcester teapot and
coffeepot.

Whatever I thought of Leo's habits in India,
there was no denying that he had lived like a king
here. I couldn't help comparing this with my own
travel experiences, a dreary succession of cramped
hotel rooms and warmed-over meals.

As I ate boiled guinea fowl eggs and buttered
toast I pondered again the document that Ameera
had left me in the middle of the night. My first

look, the moment that I awoke, had been doubly unrewarding. My eyes refused to focus properly, and the blurred and fuzzed image that I could see seemed to be mostly random numbers and letters. The symptoms were not a new problem—I'd encountered the same thing in the hospital—but Sir Westcott had given me stern instructions on what I had to do when it happened. No reading or concentrated eye work until the effects wore off. I was forced to sit there and wait, trying to swallow my impatience.

The food seemed to help. As I drank Darjeeling tea from a delicate porcelain cup, I took another look at the paper. Ameera had said that it was intended for me, but I felt sure she was wrong. For one thing, many of the words were written in an unfamiliar script, either Hindustani or more likely Arabic. Underneath a first paragraph of that came the cryptic "CBC, sdb 33226; Code: Redondo Beach." After that, the only words of intelligible English: "35 Amble Place, Middlesbrough, England."

My address, for the flat I kept in north Yorkshire. It was the first tie that I could relate definitely to me. For the rest, I had to have help.

The house had no telephone, or at least not one that I could find. I went outside. After a couple of false starts, my arm-waving and shouts of "Taxi-taxi" got through to the man at the little gate house. He nodded and shouted to a boy of about ten who was leaning against the wall outside the house. The lad ran off along the street and trotted back a couple of minutes later leading the way for an old blue Peugeot and its turbanned driver.

"Grand Hotel? Chowringhi?" I said.

A nod, a grin, and we were off at a sedate crawl along the crowded streets. As we chugged along it occurred to me that I would have trouble finding the house again without assistance. I handled that in the only safe way I could think of—I didn't pay the driver when I went inside the hotel, but left instructions with the English-speaking Head Porter that I might be in my room for quite a while, and if necessary he should make sure that the driver had a meal at my expense while he waited for me.

Chandra, thank Heaven, was in his office. Most of his days were spent at one or other of the family jute factories north of the city, and running him to earth there might have been difficult. He responded to my call for help with typical courtesy. I couldn't tell how inconvenient my request might be. All he would say was, "I will come at once."

While he was on the way I packed my cases in five minutes, checked out of my room in another three, and paced the lobby impatiently until he appeared. When he arrived I was trembling and my head was hurting like hell again, but Chandra was as unflappable as ever.

He took the page from me and studied it in silence for a couple of minutes. When he looked up his smooth face was puzzled.

"Can you understand it?" I asked.

He shrugged. "The words? Certainly. But before I can tell what they mean I think we ought to take a look at this." He tapped the sheet where the coded message appeared. "This part is clear enough. 'CBC' is the Central Bank of Calcutta, and I imagine this is simply the number of the Safety Deposit Box, and the code that we need to access it."

"And the other messages?"

"I do not know about the English address. But the message here says that in the absence of Mr. Singh, household decisions are all to be made by Ameera, and that all bills are to be sent to the Central Bank of Calcutta for payment." Chandra arched an eyebrow at me. "Do you know of the woman Ameera?"

"Yes." It seemed to be time to tell Chandra more about everything, if he had time to listen. "Can you get what is in this safety deposit box?"

"I don't see why not. But what am I to do with it?"

"Bring it with you to a house near here. The driver outside can give you directions how to get to it."

Chandra looked at me again, but apparently decided to let further questions wait. We parted, and as the driver puttered his way back to the house I wondered again what I was going to do next. No matter what was in Leo's safety deposit, I couldn't see how it would take me any closer to the mystery of T.P. or the Belur Package.

Ameera was still missing. I spent the time until Chandra arrived looking again at the papers in the study, and confirming my intent to call Sir Westcott as soon as I could. Something was worse inside my head, and I had to know what it was.

I went upstairs to the bedroom and ran cold water over my hands and forehead. When I came down again Chandra was there, talking rapidly in Bengali to Chatterji. He had a package of papers under his arm.

"I think we must talk in private," he said, and

I led the way through to the study. His look suggested that I had to provide some explanations. I poured a brandy for each of us—Chandra, like me, had a good musician's digestion—then told him everything I knew. His look changed slowly from skepticism to intrigue.

"You are two people now? Lionel and Leo? It is a tale from Hindu myth, Parmara and Peruma." Chandra tapped the package he was holding. "Leo has a sense of humor, too. Did you know that this house is owned by a Mr. Singh?"

"Chatterji—the man you were talking to—called me Singh when first he saw me."

"That was Leo's joke. 'Singh' means 'lion'—just the same as Leo and Lionel do. This was Leo's house, and according to these papers, you now own it and all its contents." Chandra gave me an odd look. "*All* its contents. And that means you now have the responsibility for looking after them. Goods and people."

"People! How many people? This house seems to be full of them."

"Eight, according to Chatterji." Chandra tapped the package again. "If you have worries about the cost of supporting them, this will reassure you. The assets that 'Mr. Singh' holds in the Central Bank of Calcutta are considerable. But there is one other complication."

Chandra paused, and the look on his face told me I wouldn't like what was coming.

"I don't see how it could get much more complicated," I said. "Eight servants and a house—I've never owned as much as a dog kennel before."

He coughed. "Perhaps not. How much do you

know of the Code of Manu—the forms of marriage ceremony that are practiced here?"

"I've never heard of it."

"It is the old code that enumerates the permitted forms of marriage. There were eight of them, but these days only two are still in use. There is the *Brahma*, the approved form, and there is the *Asura*, which is a form of purchase of the bride by the bridegroom. It has been officially banned, but is still in use. These documents show that your brother, under the name of Singh, went through the *Asura* form of ceremony with a woman who was brought here from Bihar."

I knew what was coming.

"Ameera?"

"That is correct." Chandra didn't look either surprised or shocked. "This may be a complication."

I admired his gift for understatement. It seemed like a time for another brandy, though I was still not sure what drink might do to my aching head.

"Any other bombshells in that package? We might as well get the whole thing over at once."

"No bombshell, but it seems that your brother went to extraordinary measures to keep this house and his financial affairs in this city a secret. There are bank statements here, both deposits and withdrawals, but the deposits are always money orders rather than checks, and the withdrawals are always via another local bank—hard to trace back here. What do you think your brother was doing?"

What indeed? I shook my head, then wished I hadn't. "That's what I'm here to find out—if I can. These other things, the house and Ameera, they certainly make things more difficult. Is there anything else at all in that package? So far I've heard nothing but trouble."

"A list." Chandra puffed out his full cheeks. "It is of places and people, but they mean nothing to me. I looked again when you told me of the men who pursued your brother, but I see none of their names here. Perhaps you will be able to find some clue that I cannot see."

As he spoke, I heard voices outside the study. A few seconds later Ameera moved to the doorway and stood there, turning her head from side to side. She clearly knew we were in the room but she was not sure where we were sitting. I stood up and moved to take her hand. As our fingers met I instinctively drew my thumb gently across her palm. She gasped, and I felt a tingle through my scalp. Somehow I knew it had been Leo's gesture of greeting to her. I led Ameera across the room to settle in an armchair next to me.

Chandra was frowning as he took a close look at her. Instead of his usual polite greeting he gabbled a quick question in Bengali. Ameera gave him a terse answer. He nodded and spoke again, and after a brief questioning frown she rose and left the room. I marvelled again at the easy way she navigated through the furniture, knowing precisely where each chair and table was placed.

"Another little problem," said Chandra as soon as Ameera had left. I winced. "She has gone to have tea served to us. I thought it better to talk without her here."

I looked at him warily. "What now?"

"You seem to know little of Indian women. We

are a race that matures early, and we marry young." He smiled. "Think of me as the exception that proves the rule, all right? As soon as I saw Ameera I thought that she must be much younger than you realized, so I asked her age."

"Nineteen?" I said hopefully.

"Fourteen." Chandra leaned back in his chair. "Illegal, of course, but not at all uncommon. It does mean that an Indian court will take Ameera's side should there be any argument as to rights. We must assume that your brother was sleeping with her, I suppose?"

He was diplomatically looking away from me.

"I suppose so." My voice sounded hoarse and (to me, at any rate) full of guilt.

"I will leave any discussion of that between the two of you." Chandra stood up. "If there are financial matters that I can help you with, of course I'll be happy to do my best. For the rest, I suspect that the arrangements in this house may be settled better without me."

"What about your tea?" I said stupidly.

"Some other time." Chandra grinned, and something in his look took me back five years, to the days when he was the biggest Romeo on the concert circuit—and that was saying something.

"Cheer up, Lionel. Responsibilities sometimes have their compensations. The ladies of India are not without their charms. Do not forget that."

He left.

Fourteen, I kept thinking. *Fourteen*.

As Chandra left I wondered about the Indian penalties for statutory rape.

❖   ❖   ❖

Chandra had left the package of papers on the chair. I picked it up and was sorting through it when Ameera came back with a young boy in tow. As he poured tea and then left, she came to sit on the arm of my chair.

"Your friend has gone," she said happily. (How did she know?) "Why did he ask for tea and then leave without drinking it? That is very impolite."

"He is a very busy man. His work called. I should not have asked for his help."

"But I am glad he has gone," she went on illogically. "I prefer to be alone." She snuggled closer to me on the chair arm.

I cleared my throat and wriggled on the leather cushion. "Ameera, I really need your help. Did Leo ever talk to you about his business—about his work?"

Ameera's look of satisfaction and pleasure was replaced by a wary expression.

"Sometimes. Sometimes we talked. But he did not want his work here—he said this was his— 'hideaway'?"

"Hideaway. A place where he could feel safe."

"Hideaway. Where we could be close." She reached out and ran her fingers softly over my cheek and forehead. "He was safe here. He said that he could keep us all safe if he did not talk about his work. But sometimes, when he was tired or sad, he would talk."

"That's good. I'm going to look through the papers that Chandra brought from the bank, and perhaps I'm going to ask you about things I find there. Not about the money—Chandra can tell me about that. Damnation!"

Ameera smiled. "You sound the same as Leo-yo—he would say that. What is wrong?"

"I might need to ask Chandra questions, and there's no telephone here."

"But there is! There is a special one, down in the pantry. Lee-yo used it only two times. But you can use it when you want to."

A hidden phone, used only in emergencies. When we were still in our early twenties, Leo and I had talked about setting up our own secret hideouts, places where we could say and do whatever we liked without anyone bothering us. To me that had been just dreaming, building our castles in Spain. But my brother had done it, from foundations to battlements.

And what else had he done? I took the sheet of names and places from the packet of papers.

Ameera snuggled closer, her breath warm against my cheek. "What does it say there, Lee-yo-nel?"

I saw what Chandra's problem had been with the list. Leo had created a jumble of names, places and descriptions. But I believed I could see more than anyone else—Leo and I always thought the same way, and now we were in some sense one person. I ran my eye over them quickly. Promising. For example, there was a line about halfway down the first page. It stood out to my eye like a beacon. "B.P. Get from Cut. 026411, take with 0433 to Ri., contact 277 + double bl."

It was the sort of entry that I expected from him. Leo would not keep elaborate notes—why should he, when we shared the same accurate memory? He would only bother with numbers and addresses, and maybe a couple of names when he wasn't sure of them. It was a reasonable bet that B.P. would be the Belur Package. But what about the rest of it? I needed help.

"Ameera, did Leo mention somebody or somewhere that began with C-U-T? It is something in his notes here."

"Yes." Was the expression in her voice relief? It certainly sounded like it. "I think he went to Cuttack, he had to do something there. I am sure of it. When he was last here in Calcutta, he went to Cuttack."

"Where is that? Do you know how to get there?"

"You can go there by the new railway. It is not far—two hours from here, on the coast in Orissa."

"Do you know who he went to see there? Maybe a man called Belur?"

"I do not know. Maybe."

"How about something that begins with R-I? A place or a person."

"I do not know." It seemed to me that there was now an evasiveness in her answer. "It could be Riang, or Riga in Assam. They are far away from here."

I realized that I was being irrational, asking a blind fourteen-year-old girl for details of Indian geography. Ameera could help only if she recalled something particular that Leo had said or done.

"Ameera, did Leo ever tell you about his work in America? Who he worked for, or what he was doing in India?"

There were tears welling from the dark eyes. I felt ashamed at what I was doing to her.

"No, Leo-yo-nel. If he told anyone, would it not be his own brother, when the brother was from one egg? Did he not tell you?"

"No. He did not tell me."

And that was the curse of it. Leo hadn't told me, and he was having trouble telling me now.

"Ameera, I will go tomorrow to Cuttack. Do you know where the man lives that Leo went to see?"

"Some company. A company that makes—what is the word?—computings? Things that are used for calculations." It seemed to me that there was definite relief in her voice. "Lee-yo-nel, if you go there, to Cuttack, can I come with you? I can speak the language—it is Oriya spoken there—and I want to help you. I cannot help you if I stay here in the house."

It seemed to me that I could easily find somebody there to act as an interpreter—but even if I couldn't, I didn't want Ameera with me. I had no idea what we'd be finding.

"No!" I spoke more loudly than I had intended. "I do not know what might happen there. Definitely not."

Ameera did not speak; but the tears that welled silently from those dark eyes were more persuasive than any words. I swore under my breath, and most of it was directed at the right half of my brain. But some of it went to the prurient fantasies that were conjured as I put an arm around Ameera to comfort her.

"Hello? Operator, what in God's name is happening on this line? I can hear four other people speaking."

"One moment more, sir, you will be connected."

I stood in the dark of the pantry, sweating and swearing. For twenty minutes I had been struggling to get a connection through to Sir Westcott at the Queen's Hospital Annex in Reading. The lines were full of chattering monkeys and dolphin-like squeaks and chirps, and every few minutes the line went entirely dead.

"Hello?"

"Hello, hello?" I felt like a character in a P.G. Wodehouse short story. "Hello, hello, hello."

"No need to shout like that—I'm not deaf. What do you want?"

Thank God. It was the familiar grumbling voice. "Sir Westcott, this is Lionel Salkind. I'm calling because I'm having trouble—trouble inside my head."

"What do you expect, if you go piddling off all over the globe? You ought to be back here, where we can keep an eye on you."

He didn't seem at all worried. It was a huge relief just to hear that gruff complaint.

"So what's your symptoms? Something new?"

The line had that built-in quarter-second delay that indicated it was being sent via satellite transmission.

"I think so. I've been getting bad headaches, and sometimes I don't seem to have the proper control over the things I'm doing."

"Join the club. Look, is that all? 'Course you're getting bad headaches—didn't you read that stuff I gave you when you left? You're gettin' atrophy of the Schwann cells now they've done their stuff, an' the axons are beginning their main growth. That's what the Madrill treatment is all about. Read the bloody reports—why do you think I gave 'em to you?"

I felt like an idiot—the papers he had given me were still sitting in my suitcase. In the excitement of leaving for India I hadn't given them a thought, and it had certainly not occurred to me that they might be useful to tell me what was going on inside my head.

"D'yer read the papers out there?" Sir Westcott's voice had taken on a new tone. "I don't think this would be in 'em anyway. I hate to say it, but I owe you an apology. Remember you told me about somebody called Valnora Warren?"

"What about her?"

"She's dead. They fished her out of the Cherwell four days ago—dead a couple of weeks. An' she'd been beaten to death before she was put in the water. Can you hear me?"

"I hear you. Do they know who did it?"

"If they do, they're not telling." Sir Westcott sounded grim. "Watch your step out there—I've put in too much work on you to have it buggered up by some bunch of gangsters."

"I'll be careful." I had just got the closest I would ever get to an expression of concern for my welfare from Sir Westcott.

"Another thing while we're at it. Remember tellin' me that your thug friends thought you were carrying Nymphs?"

"I'll never forget it."

"Well, I did a bit more checking with the police here about where the drug is coming from. It gets to England from Athens, like I told Tess. But it's manufactured a lot further East—somewhere like India. An' Calcutta is one of the biggest centers for use of Nymphs. So keep your eyes peeled for that while you're there."

I didn't say anything—it seemed to me I had more than enough problems, without throwing Nymphs into the act.

"Anyway, are you ready to come on back home yet?" he went on. "Tess seems to have been worrying about you. Beats me why."

"Tell her I'm fine." I drew in a deep breath. "I wanted to ask you another thing—not about me this time, and not about Nymphs either. There's somebody here with an eye problem, and I think it's caused by childhood ulcers that have scarred the cornea. Can it be operated on?"

"If you're right about the cause of the problem, it should be easy enough. How old is the patient?"

"A teenager. A girl."

I don't think that I imagined the sniff over the phone. It was easy to visualize him, scowling into the set on his desk. He seemed to be a thought reader for my guilty conscience.

"Aye. A girl, you say? Well, a patient is a patient. If you bring her here, I'd see what we could do for her. But watch what you're playing at. No point in fixing up her eyes if the next thing you know Tess is scratching 'em out. Behave yourself out there— you know damn well Tess is too good for you. Don't you try—"

The line chose that moment to die completely. I was left standing sweating in the cool of the dark pantry, cursing India in general and its telephone company in particular. Upstairs, the gong was sounding. Ahead lay another evening with Ameera, and whatever went with that thought.

Damnation.

I climbed slowly up the stairs. Leo had got me

into all this, completely against my will. It seemed only fair that he ought to be doing a lot more to get me out of it, and I had no doubt at all that the secret of the Belur Package lay in the city of Cuttack. But although Leo's notes and Ameera's recollection both pointed in that direction, together with a deep instinctive feeling that perhaps came from my brother, I had no sensation of accomplishment or progress.

What I felt, like a tightness in my gut, was powerful foreboding.

– 11 –

When the brain tissue is cut, as for example in the separation of the hemispheres via severing of the corpus callosum, the damaged nerve cells will not normally regenerate. Although the axons of each cell can produce new sprouts, which could in principle connect anew to the target cells, this sprouting is short-lived. It lasts for only a few days, and it does not produce the needed links to the neuron target cells.

Instead, glial cells proliferate in the damaged region, producing a tangle that blocks neurons as they seek to regenerate axons. The solution to this problem, developed first by Madrill in his groundbreaking work at the turn of the century, is via the Schwann cells—the nonneuronal cells that are present and which can serve to direct axon regrowth in peripheral nerves.

The Madrill treatment inhibits the growth of glial cells in the damaged area, and stimulates the *growth of Schwann cells that normally will not be present in the brain. It is the later atrophy and disappearance of the Schwann cells that causes the patient considerable early discomfort, though later possible side effects of the tissue regeneration process are in fact far more serious in their potential consequences . . .*

I rubbed at my tired eyes and leaned back in my seat. This was supposed to be an air-conditioned first-class carriage, but I was sweltering, perspiration running down my forehead. The countryside outside was flying by at more than a hundred and fifty miles an hour, a dizzying blur of green in the long cutting; but the more substantial dizziness was inside my head.

And what I was going through, if the paper in front of me was to be believed, was a mild foretaste of what I had coming in another week or two. That was a depressing thought. Already I seemed to be absorbing words from the page one at a time, poked into my head through a small hole using a rusty nail end. I forced myself to read on—hard going as it was, this was the first paper from Sir Westcott where I could understand even a fraction of what the author was trying to say.

Following the full growth of the axons, and their attachment to the target cells within the brain, the final and most sensitive phase of the Madrill treatment begins. With the mechanical connection complete, it is now necessary for the brain to resume its information processing functions. Although these might appear to be routine, it has been observed that in over thirty percent of the cases where the Madrill treatment has been used, an unstable feedback in the regrown area leads to a variety of psychoses, many of them leading to terminal dysfunctions . . .

Very nice. The bad bit was still to come, and there was a one in three chance that I wouldn't come out of the other side. "Terminal dysfunction"—pleasant medical double-talk for madness and death. The odds were a lot worse than Sir Westcott had led me to believe.

So what could I do about it?

Not a thing.

I gave up my efforts to understand the next section of the paper, which was a long discussion of methods used with enzyme injections by the Armenian Academy of Sciences. Instead I looked across the carriage table.

Ameera was painting her nails there, calmly and contentedly. The heat in the compartment didn't seem to trouble her at all. I couldn't see how she could fix her nails without being able to see what she was up to, but the purple-red lacquer went on steadily and smoothly. Her sense of the position of one hand relative to the other was almost beyond belief.

Somehow—perhaps I moved in my seat—she knew that my eyes were on her.

"How much longer, Lee-yo-nel?"

"Half an hour, if the train is on time."

She nodded happily. To Ameera, this whole trip was nothing but pleasure and excitement, an extended school picnic. For the tenth time in two days, I wondered just what sort of friend Chandra thought he was. Instead of agreeing with me that Ameera's presence in Cuttack would be a total disaster, he had sided with her from the beginning.

"How will you talk to people if you are alone there?" he asked. "Cuttack is not like Calcutta, where many people speak English."

(As I later discovered, Chandra was not telling the truth—many people spoke English in each place. But he was being at his most Indian, helping Ameera to get her way from pure perversity.)

I had argued the point with them, insisting that I would do much better to hire an interpreter when I needed one. Verbal persuasion by Chandra during the day, and more powerful arguments by Ameera at night, had beaten me. I sat and looked at her, at the gorgeous dusky skin and midnight hair, and wondered how I had held out for so long. The odds against me had been overwhelming.

My original plan, to head for Cuttack the day I learned of its existence, had fallen apart as soon as I tried to act. I had made no allowance for the Indian sense of pace. Even the train tickets took twenty-four hours to arrive at the house.

While Chandra and Chatterji made arrangements for our trip I spent long impatient hours in the little pantry, pitting my wits against the vagaries of the Indian telephone system.

The telephone number that I was asking about for someone in Cuttack? No, sir. It did not exist. A difficult operator insisted that it could not exist, had never existed—perhaps I was reading it wrongly to him? An hour of argument and re-calling to Cuttack revealed the existence of a second exchange, in the same province but not within the town.

I called the new exchange.

Triumph! The number had been listed for a Mr. Belur. But it had been taken out of use four months ago, and there was no new listing for that Belur. Computer companies in the same area where Mr. Belur had lived? Of course, sir, they would try to check it for me, but I had to remember that this was not the way that the directory was organized . . . the chance of success was small . . . the difficulty was very great . . .

I longed for an outstretched hand into which I could drop a little silver, but that time-tested method would have to wait until we got to Cuttack. All I could do from a distance was establish the names of half a dozen candidate companies that might possibly be connected with the vanished Belur. Unless they, like he, had disappeared in the past few months.

Patience, Chandra told me. Patience is all in India.

Patience. I had to learn my own limitations. When we finally reached Cuttack and could begin our search, I was forced to revise my ideas about Ameera's usefulness. She could wheedle cooperation and information out of the least obliging public servants. I could get nothing from them at all.

Cuttack was one of the Indian government's new development areas. In the past ten years there had been a huge effort to set up advanced technology there—fiber optics, microprocessors, vapor deposition methods, and hyper-bubble memories. The plants were scattered like white rectangular play-blocks over the brown and green hillocks that lay west of the main city.

Taxis were hard to come by. Ameera snagged one at the railway station while a horde of noisy travellers shouted at the porters and each other, and we set off on our search. Since we looked at Leo's notes together I had been through every emotion, but now that we had reached Cuttack my spirits had plummeted. The chances of tracking down Belur had to be low. Only Ameera's bubbling enthusiasm kept me going.

Computek was our first stop (all the companies we visited had shunned Indian names in favor of pseudo-American ones). The taxi waited while Ameera and I went in through the paint-peeling door.

Nothing there—not even evidence of technology development. The staff were suspicious. Were we perhaps inspectors from the Government over in New Delhi? Ameera soothed their fears, but we gained no useful information. The pattern was repeated at Info-systems Design, Electro-mesh, 4-D Systems, Compu-controls, and Autodyne. I was ready to give up when we came to the shabby grey building on top of a hill eight miles outside the town, and I read the frayed wooden sign that announced the presence of Bio-Electronic Systems.

"Belur?" said the man. He was all white teeth and cuffs, center-part hair, and oleaginous voice; the very model of a modern manager. "Rustum Belur?"

Ameera squeezed my arm—she knew how despondent I had been getting. I nodded. "I think that would be him. But as I understand it, he is no longer with your company?"

The man across the polished desk smiled and

offered me an Indian cigarette. I had learned to
refuse those on my first day in Calcutta. I shook
my head.

"No longer with us?'" He blew out a cloud of
poisonous smoke. "That is certainly one way to put
it, I suppose. He is not with anyone, eh? Not with
anyone we can talk to."

"Did he leave the area?"

"I should jolly well say so." He coughed. "Jolly
well say so. He is dead, you see—Rustum Belur
was killed, four months ago. Most sad." He smiled
cheerfully. "Most sad indeed. A nice man."

I sat there gaping, unable to think of anything
at all to say. *There goes another one!* would not
have been a socially acceptable utterance. Ameera
helped out.

"Mr. Belur—how was he killed?"

Mr. Srinivasa stood up from his seat and went
across to the window. "You see that building down
the hill, where the cables run from over to our
left? That is one of our laboratories. One night,
Rustum Belur must have taken a short cut to his
home—under the cable. Most irregular, of course,
and we have told our employees not to do it."
He shrugged. "They will not listen—not my fault,
you understand? He must have slipped and fallen
across the high-voltage line. *Srritt.*" He rippled
his hand through the air. "Twenty thousand volts.
A deadly charge.

"We found him the following morning." There
was a cheerful gusto to his voice. "Fried like a
maro fish. Jolly bad luck, eh?"

"Did he leave a family?" That seemed the only
avenue left to us.

"Alas, no," said Srinivasa happily. "He was not a person to mix well—not like you or me, eh?" He gave a knowing nod towards Ameera. "Mind you, he was a very intelligent man, and his visitors came from many places. But it was all work—nothing for a social life. You knew his work, eh?"

"A little." I was ready to leave, but as I started to straighten up in my chair my body twisted to one side and dropped me heavily back to a sitting position. Srinivasa looked at me oddly.

"Are you feeling all right, Mr. Salkind?"

"Yes." I played for time to regain control. "I was wondering just what work Mr. Belur was doing when he died. I had lost touch with him in the past year or two."

"More of the same." Srinivasa shrugged, but I detected in his manner that the question was not to his taste. "He was still working on the electronics-biologic interface, as he had for years. Always the claim that his big advance would be here soon. It never came."

"The Belur Package?"

"He called it that to you?" He stubbed out his half-inch-long cigarette butt and happily accepted a new one from my packet, bought especially for our interviews. "Always the same talk, eh, always about the introsomatic chips? Jolly hard worker, but not too practical."

I looked around us, at the evidence of past success and recent failure. It was a fair bet that Belur— "jolly hard worker" and much-visited scientist—had been the sparkplug for Bio-Electronic Systems. When he died, the operation had begun to run downhill. And Srinivasa found it hard to face that fact, like any manager who imagined the success of an organization was really his success.

"Do you have notes regarding the Belur Package?" It was my last hope, and a slim one.

"He did not keep good notes." Srinivasa shook his head disapprovingly. "A good worker, but his habits were strange. Here late at night, then away all the next morning—jolly hard to run a lab efficiently, eh, when people will not keep regular work hours? He insisted that most of his work was better done at home."

"He kept a lab there?"

"Not a real lab. It was in his house, equipped like a lab, but not you understand a real lab." The expansive gesture around him at the clutter of dusty equipment suggested that Belur's humble home efforts could not compare with the magnificence of our present surroundings. "Even though he was very rich," he added after a second or two.

There was new irritation in his voice. An employee who was not merely of irregular habits, but rich enough to be independent, was a hard cross for a manager to bear.

"Do you think we could visit his house?" I asked. As I spoke, my stomach seemed to seethe and rise inside me. I thought for a moment that I would be sick on the spot. What was Leo trying to tell me now?

Srinivasa did not notice. He was too busy registering disdain at my request. "If you really want to, I do not see why not. It would of course take a little time to get there"—wasted time, his manner implied—"and I am afraid we are too busy here to arrange transportation."

"We have our own driver," said Ameera. She was much more successful than I at squelching objections. "If you could tell us how to get there . . ."

It was easy to see why Rustum Belur might have taken a short cut to his home. The road went around the hill in a long, winding spiral, so that half a mile on the ground, under the power cable, was stretched to more than five. As we drove steadily around the hillside, Ameera shook her head firmly.

"Very bad man. I did not like his smell."

"You think he is evil?"

"Not evil. Stupid. He had plenty of time to come with us if he wanted to. And he could show us Belur's workplace."

But not, I suspected, tell us anything useful about it. Belur's work was beyond Srinivasa's comprehension. And beyond mine. What had he been doing?

"What are intro-so-mat-ic chips?" Ameera's words echoed my thoughts. "He said Belur was making them."

"I never heard of them. But 'chips' are what they put into computers, to control their programs."

And I'll bet my last penny that Leo could tell me more about them, if only we could find a way to tap his memories. I thought that, but I didn't mention that to Ameera.

Belur's wealth was obvious as soon as we came into sight of his house. Most of the buildings that we had passed were no more than shacks. This one was a thirty-room monstrosity, a wood and cement structure that must have been there long before the industrial park grew up around it. We drove towards it along a road of hard-packed dirt—probably impassable in the rainy season, but now as firm as concrete.

"Wait here for us." The man nodded. Indian taxi drivers were very good at patient waiting.

We were on the eastern side of the hill, towards the town of Cuttack, and the bulk of the house stood high between us and the setting sun. I saw Ameera shiver a little as we moved into the deep shadow.

"What is the house like, Lee-yo-nel?"

I suppressed my own gut urge to go back to the car. The house wasn't inviting, but I had come too far to back off because of some vague uneasiness. Anyway, I felt that I already knew the layout of this house.

"It's big—very big. The place that Belur worked is near the back of the building. We have to go down a long corridor, then up a staircase." The words came out instinctively, yet I was convinced that the description was correct.

We moved to the open front door, Ameera clutching hard on my arm. "Slowly, Lee-yo. Let me know where we are going."

She felt the door to her left, then ran her hand slowly along the wooden panels inside the house.

While she studied that, I took another look around us. According to Srinivasa, the house was being looked after by two housekeepers until Belur's family decided what to do with it. But there had been no sign of people, inside the house or out. That was less surprising to me here than it would have been in Europe. I had already learned the tendency of Indian staff to disappear from their duties for long periods on mysterious errands of their own.

"Anyone at home?"

The wooden walls and floor echoed back my voice and made me feel slightly ridiculous. With Ameera following methodically behind me, touching and listening, I led the way along the uncarpeted corridor. The whole house was unnaturally silent, and with the sun already low in the sky the windows off to our left threw long, enigmatic shadows over the scanty furniture. The house had not been sold, but someone had done a good job of helping themselves to the fixtures. Marks in the deep carpets told of chairs and tables that had been moved recently from the main rooms.

We had reached the end of the corridor. Ahead lay a long staircase, curving around one hundred and eighty degrees to the upper floor. I started up hesitantly, Ameera still one step behind and holding to my sleeve. But there was no doubt at all in my mind: Belur's lab was straight ahead, past the first bedroom, just before the room with all the musical instruments. That knowledge was built-in, a legacy from Leo's past.

Halfway up the stairs I paused. Ameera, right behind me, bumped her breasts softly into my back.

"Why do you stop here, Lee-yo-nel? This is not the end of the staircase—the sounds tell me that."

"I don't know." My uneasiness was increasing. "Ameera, it's getting dark. Maybe we should come back here and look around tomorrow, when there is more light."

"You cannot see here? Is there not the electricity, for lighting?"

There was a switch on the wall, at the turn in the staircase. I moved forward and pressed it down. Unshaded electric bulbs in wall brackets threw a shadowy illumination along the stairs. Instead of easing, my sensation of discomfort increased. I stood, half a dozen steps from the upper landing, and looked around us.

"Lee-yo-nel, what is that?"

My ears were less sensitive than Ameera's. It took me a couple of seconds to register what I was hearing. From somewhere ahead of us, on the upper landing, came faint musical sounds. It was the playing of a piano, just a little out of tune.

I glanced around at the deserted staircase and lower floor, then moved silently to the top of the stairs. Ameera, always graceful and light-footed, was half a pace behind.

"Lee-yo-nel, who is playing?" Her words were a soft breath, just audible in my ear.

I didn't answer. My hands were trembling, and the sound of my own breathing was loud inside my head. Twenty-five years of piano playing had given me at least one talent. Different pianists each have their own stylistic foibles, as unique and recognizable as a signature. I could recognize the masters, old or new, from a few seconds of their playing. Gieseking or Gould, Horowitz or Hellman, Schnabel or Serkin—every one put a personal imprint on the music, unmistakable and undisguisable.

And the sounds that came from the next room along the landing? I was on the brink of certainty long before I looked in through the half-open door.

The glittering runs and trills in the right hand and the bravura octaves and tremolos—they carried me back a month in time.

The pianist was playing in the evening gloom, his massive back towards us. As I was already moving away to seek an escape along the landing and down the stairs, he swivelled on the piano stool and looked directly at the door.

"Well, it's about time you got here," he said. "Where've you been the past few weeks? We've been sitting around in this place too bleedin' long." It was Pudd'n. The familiar voice merely confirmed my earlier recognition of a distinctive piano style.

I spun around, pushing Ameera ahead of me, wondering how fast we could tackle the stairs together without falling. But before we had taken one step, a loud slamming noise came from downstairs.

"Hear that?" called Pudd'n from behind us. He had moved from piano stool to doorway. "Don't go running off now, it won't do no good an' you might get hurt. You know old Dixie. He gets excited real easy."

Ameera and I had reached the top of the stairs. I looked down along the smooth spiral of the banisters. The front door of the house had been closed. On the lowest step, with his head tilted up towards us and a broad grin on his face, stood Dixie.

The light from the unshaded staircase bulbs reflected as a silver glimmer from the gun in his left hand.

– 12 –

My first instinct was to run. But where could I go?

Dixie controlled the stairs, Pudd'n was a formidable presence behind us. In any case, I would not leave Ameera to face those two alone.

While we stood there, Dixie advanced warily and came to within about nine feet of us: too far away for any attempt at manual combat, even if I had possessed the talent and taste for it.

I took Ameera's hand firmly in mine and led her towards the music room. Pudd'n retreated warily before us. Whatever our harmless appearance, neither man was taking any chances. Dixie kept a safe three paces behind us.

"Lee-yo-nel!" Ameera's voice was frightened.

I squeezed her hand with an assurance I did not feel. "It's all right. Stay next to me, and don't move quickly."

Dixie circled us until we were facing each other. The gun had been transferred to his right hand,

and he was training it alternately on me, then on Ameera.

"Back up, and sit down." He lifted the gun until the open barrel pointed a dark circle straight into my right eye. "On the settee. No funny moves, or you get it."

As soon we were sitting side by side on the settee, Dixie came around behind us and put the gun against the back of my head. My scalp shivered at the cold touch. We sat perfectly still while Pudd'n came forward and frisked us.

"Sit tight, Missie, I'm not trying to get fresh," he said apologetically to Ameera as he ran his hands gently along her breasts, armpits, and thighs. "They're both clean, Dix. Not even a penknife."

Dixie gave a high-pitched laugh of relief. "Pity, really. Two bloody weeks we've waited here for you. That deserves something from both of us." He moved the gun away from my head, while I shivered at the venom and triumph in his voice. "An' I owe you a good one. That stuff you poisoned me with had me puking for two days. You'll pay for that before I'm done with yer."

Pudd'n went back to sit on the piano stool, while Dixie again circled to stand in front of us.

"How did you know where to look for me?" I said.

As I spoke I looked around the room and wondered about our driver. How long would he wait before he decided that something was wrong? Hours, at the least—we had been that long with Srinivasa.

"Use your loaf, man." Pudd'n turned back to face the keyboard. "You left a trail a mile wide gettin' to India. Scouse couldn't believe it when he found you'd bought a ticket as Lionel Salkind—he was sure you'd have some other fake passport. An' once he knew you were goin' to Calcutta, it was obvious you'd be coming back here."

"I've never been here before in my life."

"Yer, pull the other one," said Dixie nastily. "We know you were here for sure. Belur told us that months ago, before he croaked."

He wiped his sleeve across his nose and stared curiously at Ameera. "Anyway, what's wrong with her? Why's she starin' at me like that?"

"She's not staring. Ameera is nearly blind. She isn't seeing you at all."

"You kidding me?" Dixie stepped a little closer and peered hard at Ameera, looking into her eyes. "Hey, kid. How old are you anyway?"

"I am fourteen years old." Her voice was husky, and she was trembling a little. Her head turned slowly from side to side, like a hypnotized animal. "Lee-yo-nel, who are these?"

"Fourteen!" Dixie turned his head to give Pudd'n a brief glare of triumph. "See, I was right about the Nymphs as well. He's like all you bloody musicians, screws anything that lets yer."

"You're an old poof, Dix—you're just jealous of my good looks," said Pudd'n. His voice was good-natured, and the relief in both men's expressions was obvious. Waiting for our arrival must have been boring and nerve-racking. "Relax a bit, can't you? We've got 'im now, an' that's what counts. Who cares if he's got her on Nymphs or not? That's their business."

Instead of more talk, Pudd'n expressed their

jubilation differently. He started to play. His choice was "Les Fastes," one of Couperin's masterpieces, and Pudd'n picked the riotous passage that the composer described as "the jugglers, acrobats, and tumblers, with bears and monkeys." Dixie had to keep his gun trained on us, but I noticed that his feet automatically went into a little back-and-forth shuffle with the music, like dancing in place—no doubt which Couperin group he belonged in.

"Like that?" said Pudd'n to me as he finished.

"Pretty good. You've been practicing hard since I last saw you. But it's supposed to be in C Minor, you know. You put it up a tone."

"Don't make much odds on this bleedin' thing." Pudd'n crashed his left hand flat on the keyboard. "It's all way out of tune, flat as hell. But you're right about the practice. There was bugger all else to do around this place until you got here."

He ran a fast chromatic scale up three octaves.

"Never mind all that," said Dixie. If it wasn't music you could dance to, he wasn't interested. "Let's get 'em through into the back."

He nodded his head towards the door. "Come on, you two, on yer feet." He leered. "I didn't know there'd be two of you, but I've got a nice little love nest for you back there. Real cozy."

The gun couldn't be argued with. Pudd'n led us along the corridor, then down another staircase that took us below ground level. Dixie, bringing up the rear, must have noticed my glance towards the front of the house before we started downwards.

"Don't waste your time wonderin' about old

Gunga Din," he said. "I dumped a handful of
rupees on him, an' he'll be back at the station by
now looking for his next fare."

That ended any hopes I might have had about
our driver.

We came to the bottom of the stairs, where a
solid door led through into a small, windowless
room. The heavy padlock and metal frame suggested that the place had been created originally
as a store for valuables, probably tea and spices
as well as family papers. Broad shelves ran along
three walls, and the only furniture was a chair,
table, and narrow bed. Seated upon the latter, and
rising casually to her feet as we entered, was Zan.
It only needed Scouse to make the London cast
complete.

"You're a cool one," said Dixie. "Didn't you hear
the noise? He could have been shootin' me an'
Pudd'n full of holes for all the help you were."

"No such luck." Even before she spoke, the
animosity between Zan and Dixie was obvious. It
seemed to crackle between them, a field of hate
and contempt. Two boring weeks, cooped up in
each other's company, had changed smoldering
dislike to active rage.

It was the first hopeful sign since we had
entered the house. I remembered how Scouse had
sent Zan out of the room when they started to
torture me. If she was no more than Scouse's
mistress, dragged into this thing against her will,
she might be ready to make the break from them.

Her first act was promising. Ignoring Dixie's
curses, she stepped forward to Ameera and took
her hand.

"This is an added factor." Her husky voice was thoughtful. "Where did she come from?"

Dixie shrugged. "Ask Casanova there. She's his bit of stuff."

Zan flashed him a look of loathing. If she was Scouse's mistress, he had chosen fire over comfort. "You simple-minded fool. Can't you see what a complication this introduces? We know his background, where he came from and who might look for him. What about her? Where is her family?"

Dixie had flushed at her tone. "How the fuck am I supposed to know where her family is? She come in the door with him, right, an' we've never seen her before, right? I don't know who she is, but you don't need to be a mind reader to know who's screwing who—just look at 'em. If her family don't mind that, they're not likely to be worryin' when she's not home by teatime. Why don't you use *your* bloody loaf, instead of tellin' me I'm stupid."

"Steady on now." Pudd'n used a carefully neutral tone. "The main thing is, we've got him. That's what Scouse told us to do, an' we've done it. Zan, why don't you get him on the phone, sharpish, an' tell him? You an' Dixie can't afford to be fightin'— we've all got work to do."

Zan looked at him thoughtfully. Her eyes were shielded by heavy lids, and it was hard to know how she reacted to his comments.

"Did you search them?" she said at last.

"Yeah," said Dixie.

"No," said Pudd'n. "I mean, all I did was look for weapons. You mean papers an' other stuff, don't you, Zan?"

"Naturally." Again her look at Dixie held only contempt. "If we come seven thousand miles to seek the Belur Package, we ought at least to look for it. I would be surprised if he is carrying it on him, but we cannot rule that out."

"But we know he doesn't have it," objected Dixie, "or he wouldn't ever have come back here."

"Logical, but not necessarily true." Zan stepped forward to Ameera. "Dixie, you keep them both covered." She began to search Ameera carefully and unhurriedly, exploring each item of clothing down to skin level, while Pudd'n did the same thing to me.

"Here's something," he said after a few minutes. "Look, it's got the old Belur phone number on it."

He was holding the paper that Leo had left for me, with its cryptic message. If they could read any more out of it than we could, good luck to them. First Pudd'n puzzled over it, then the other two each had their turn.

"Arabic, is it?" said Dixie. "Can't Scouse read that for us when he gets here?"

Zan shook her elegant head. Something about her gave me shivers, but I couldn't be sure whether the feeling was pleasant or unpleasant. All I could say for certain was that when she brushed against me as she was searching Ameera, a tingling wave had run like cold water up my spine.

"Scouse speaks Arabic, but he never learned to read it or write it," she said.

"We don't need Scouse." Dixie nodded his head at me. "Not with 'im here to do the work for us. Give me an hour with him, alone, and I'll get you a translation."

"No." Zan moved to stand in front of him and they stood, eye to eye.

Dixie was the first to flinch. "All right, let's see what Scouse has to say about that," he grumbled, and moved away. "When are you going to call him, anyway?"

"Now. He should be able to take an overnight flight and be here by noon tomorrow." Zan set off purposively towards the door, pausing only to give first me and then Ameera a strange and speculative look. Again I felt the vibration up my spine.

"What about these two?" said Pudd'n.

"They can stay here." She turned in the doorway and slapped her hand against the jamb. "You checked this place out properly, didn't you? No way they could break out of it?"

"The door's metal lined, and the walls are concrete block," said Pudd'n. "They're safe enough, but there's no lavatory. And no food. We didn't expect two of them—what do we do with her?"

"We'll worry about that after I've called Scouse." Zan and Dixie left. Their relationship had not improved during the last interchange, and they carefully avoided looking at each other. After an apologetic glance at the narrow bed, and a shrug of his heavy shoulders, Pudd'n followed them out.

The door boomed shut with a clang of finality, and a second later the light went out. The switch must be outside the room.

This time, Scouse's mob was taking no chances.

The darkness was harder on me than on Ameera. To her, a light haze had simply become darker haze. We groped our way forward for a few seconds until we located the bed, then while I sat uselessly on it Ameera explored the room using her hands, feet, tongue and nose.

She had slipped off her shoes. I heard her padding around quietly, sniffing curiously in one place, rubbing her hand or foot against the floor or wall in another. At last she came back to where I lay and snuggled beside me on the bed.

"No good?" I said. Somehow it seemed right to whisper, even though there was no one to overhear us.

"It is no good." Ameera moved closer to me. "It is solid, the way that the man said. Lee-yo-nel, what will they do with us?"

"They will let you go—maybe tomorrow." I tried to sound confident. "But they want to keep me here and ask me questions about Belur."

"But you do not know about Mr. Belur."

"They don't believe that."

"What will they do to you?"

Burn me with cigarette ends. Beat me to death and then stick me in the river, the way they had handled Valnora Warren. Torture me to learn my secrets, and then fry me to a crisp on a high-voltage wire, the way they had treated Rustum Belur.

"Lee-yo-nel?" Ameera interrupted my gloomy introspection. "Why did the man with the scratchy voice say that you were using the Nymphs with me? That is not true. I am a full-grown-up woman, not a child."

"Eh? How do you know about Nymphs?"

"Everyone here—every girl in India—knows about them. Lee-yo said that most of the nymph-et-a-mine tablets for the whole world are made near Calcutta. But why do the men here say that you use Nymphs?"

"Ameera, you shouldn't be thinking about that sort of thing." I lifted myself higher on the bed. "People who use this drug are sick—sick in their minds. Let's talk about something else."

"Lee-yo-nel!" Her body jerked against me. "How can you say that the Nymphs are bad? What is wrong with them?"

"Everything. They make little girls want sex." I didn't want to talk about it, but Ameera would not change the subject.

"How can it be right," I went on, "when men drug children and force them to have sex? It's wrong, and it must be stopped."

Ameera was silent against me for a long time, then she sighed. "Lee-yo-nel, you do not understand anything. You think I am blind, but you see less. My sister will marry next year. I will give her a wedding gift of Nymphs."

"You will do *what*?" I wondered if the Madrill treatment was making my brains into mush. "Ameera, you are insane even to think of that. What will her husband say?"

"He will never know." Ameera's voice was angry now. "You do not understand our ways—Lee-yo was the same. My sister is ten years old. The new laws say she is a child, and she is too young, but my father says she is not too young. He wants a rich husband for her, and she will find one only if she marries soon. So she will marry. Without the Nymphs, she will have soreness, and bad hurt, and bleeding, and bad fear. Her wedding night will be all pain, as it was pain to me. I was married at ten,

and widow at twelve. All the nights then were fear
and pain."

She was weeping against my chest. I suspected
that the tears were not for herself, they were for
all the young girls of India. I stroked her hair
gently, and waited. She had never made such a long
speech to me before.

"We will not need Nymphs when the men are
changed," she said at last. "Lee-yo-nel, you are not
like this, I know it. But four years ago, I would
have starved to get those Nymphs you tell me are
so bad."

She was silent for many minutes. At last her
regular breathing told me that she had fallen
asleep. I lay awake beside her, wondering what
tomorrow might bring. No matter what I had told
Ameera, I was sure that they would not let her
go either. To leave this house alive, we would have
to escape from it.

How?

My head was aching again, but I dared not lose
time in sleep. The room we lay in was silent as a
grave. As the night wore on I reviewed again and
again what we had seen of the house, what I knew
of Pudd'n, Dixie, Zan and Ameera, and how I
might put that knowledge together to free us. It
was slim pickings, but after a couple of hours I
could see only one hope.

Reluctantly, I woke Ameera. We whispered for
many minutes, huddled close in the unrelenting
darkness.

– 13 –

"What time is it?"

My eyes wouldn't focus and my head was bursting, but when the door to our little room creaked open and the overhead light went on, that was the only question my lips could frame. A lot depended on the answer.

"Just after midnight," said Pudd'n's voice. His broad and amiable face was better to wake up to than Dixie's vicious leer. "Eyes open now. Zan's talked to Scouse, an' she needs a few words with you."

He may have looked friendly, but the gun in his great hand told a different story. Ameera and I sat up wearily. I blinked and squinted at the unshaded light, a single forty-watt bulb in the multisocket bracket.

"Couldn't it wait until morning? We need to get some sleep."

"We want to finish this before morning," said

Zan. She was standing in the doorway, just behind Pudd'n, and despite the hour she looked fresh and alert. She had changed from blouse and skirt to a clinging purple robe that hugged her figure and showed off her clear olive complexion, and her eyes and lips were freshly made up. She moved forward to stand in front of Pudd'n, always slightly to the side so that we were covered by the gun.

I touched Ameera on her arm. She sat up on the bed and swung her bare feet lightly to the floor.

"Please. I must go to the lavatory. Now."

Zan and Pudd'n looked at each other. "Take her," said Zan after a moment.

"What, me?" protested Pudd'n. "She's a woman, you oughter do it."

Zan shook her head. "I have to talk to Salkind— Scouse's orders. You can leave me the gun, if you're worried about him getting awkward."

"An' what about me? You know we're not supposed to be unarmed."

Zan looked from Pudd'n's great frame to Ameera's five-foot nothing, and gave a slow and lovely smile. "Pudd'n, if she beats you up I'll look after the wounds myself."

Pudd'n was not amused. He handed the gun to Zan, stepped forward, and took Ameera by the hand. "Come on, Missie. Let's get you taken care of an' back here. Hey, Zan, Dixie ought to bring her back. You know I've got to get stuff ready for Scouse. I'll be up all night as it is."

Zan frowned. "I suppose so. Tell him to bring food for these two when he comes."

"Yeah." Pudd'n grinned at me. "He'll love doin'

that. Don't worry, I'll keep an eye on him an' make sure he doesn't try an' poison yer."

Zan waited until he was out of the room and the door had been closed before she spoke.

"I think I have a surprise for you. Scouse believes your story."

"It's not a story."

"He believes that Leo Foss is dead, that you are his brother, and that you truly do not know where the Belur Package was left. Why would you come back here, he argues, unless you were trying to find the Belur Package?"

"Full marks for Scouse. So far he's spot on."

Zan nodded thoughtfully and leaned forward. "But he knows there must be more. First, you know that the package exists."

"Damn it, your bunch told me that, back in London."

She ignored the interruption. "Obviously, you also know the value of the package. And in order for you to come here, you must have received information about where to come. Leo must have told you that. Perhaps at the time of the helicopter crash? That detail is less important. Scouse wants to offer you a deal. We will pool the information, yours and ours, and look for the package together. You will share in the profits from its sale."

"What makes you think that I have more information?" This conversation was not going the way that I had planned. Instead of convincing Zan to break with the gang, I was being recruited myself.

"When you left England, you disappeared for two weeks. You could have been travelling around India, but Scouse is convinced that you actually went to Leo's house, the one we have never been able to locate."

I felt a surge of satisfaction. At least one of my brother's plans had worked out as he intended. His hideaway was still hidden.

"You're making an awful lot of assumptions."

"Scouse is an awfully intelligent man. Somewhere in that house there will be the evidence to show what your brother did with the Belur Package. He is convinced of that. You realize that the chips are worth hundreds of millions, and that we can hold a secret auction for them once we have them? So which is it to be—prompt cooperation, or agony for you and the girl until you agree to take us to the house?" She licked at her full lips and shivered a little as she spoke.

"Not much of a choice, is it?" I tried to sound calm. "But I'll have to think about it for an hour or two."

"No." She shook her head firmly, as cool as though we were discussing the choice of dishes for a lunch menu. "You will decide at once. You were left here alone long enough to think about this situation. Decide *now*."

She slapped her hand firmly on her thigh, and as she did so Ameera reappeared in the doorway with Dixie scowling behind her. He had no gun, but his knife blade was poised a couple of inches from her kidneys.

I sighed, and stood up slowly. Ameera and I could have used another few minutes alone, but that would be denied to us.

"All right. I know when I'm beaten. We'll cooperate with you. But let's do it upstairs, away from this damned room, and you can give us some food. We're starving down here."

I moved forward, slowly enough so that Dixie wouldn't get the wrong idea, and stood in the middle of the room a step away from Ameera. Dixie and Zan moved to cover my back, knife and gun both ready for use.

"When can I start walking?" I asked, and as I spoke I lowered my hands a few inches towards my pockets.

"Stop that," barked Dixie. "Get them hands up above your head, where we can see what you're doin' with 'em."

"Oh, take it easy." I looked over my shoulder at him. My pulse was up about a hundred and fifty, but some detached corner of my intellect controlled my actions and made them smooth and precise. "You know we're not armed. What do you think we're going to do, fly away?"

As I spoke I followed his orders and raised my arms high over my head. The light fixture was directly above me.

Now or never! Don't stop to think about consequences. As my right hand went up I slid the short length of bedspring out of my sleeve and thrust it up hard into one of the empty light sockets in the ceiling bracket.

There was a sputter of hot sparks onto the back of my neck, and a tingling shock through the cloth that protected my hand. Then all the lights went out.

I had used the last moment before darkness came to fix my attention on Ameera's position. As Dixie swore behind me, I grabbed her hand in mine and squeezed it hard. We had agreed that neither one of us would speak unless we were absolutely forced to. She turned and we began to run back along the corridor, as I allowed myself to be drawn in whatever direction she chose.

There was a flash as the gun went off behind us, and a shrill scream of fear from Dixie—I could see his point of view, he wasn't holding the pistol. Then Ameera hissed "Stairs," at me, and we were staggering up the long flight as fast as we could go. We had removed our shoes before Zan and Pudd'n arrived, so our run made little noise. One of my big fears was that Pudd'n would be waiting for us on the ground floor.

A turn, a mad dash scraping along the wall of a corridor, and then we were moving down another staircase. Another one of my fears was ready to be tested—it seemed certain to me that Belur's lab would be on its own circuit, even if everything else in the house came through a single fuse. We might have to face the danger of a lighted corridor.

We came safely past that area. All the lab lights must have been turned off.

The dusty glass panel in the front door gave me my first sense of position. As Ameera ran towards it and halted, gasping and shivering two feet from the threshold, I squeezed her hand again.

"Me now, Ameera," I panted—my first words since we had left the cellar. "Let me get past and open the door."

Unlocked. Thank God for that. Dixie and Pudd'n had expected no surprises coming from outside. We slipped through as quietly as we could, and were suddenly together in the cool, moonlit midnight.

Ameera and I had made no plans past that point. In the gloom of the cellar it had seemed to need a miracle to take us this far. But now we needed another one to help us to the railway station.

This time I was the leader. We scurried around the big house, panting and frantic, our feet cut by the sharp stones and gravel. Surely the gang would have rented a car to get to and from the station? I couldn't see Dixie doing much walking.

"Is there, Lee-yo-nel?" gasped Ameera. It was doubly hard for her, not able to look for the ways we might get away.

"Here, on this side of the house." I led her to the shiny Toyota and opened the driver's door.

Useless. There was no ignition key, and although Leo might have been up to hot-wiring the engine I knew it was beyond me. I left the door open and ran on farther around the house, guiding Ameera to run along the softer grass.

The second car was old and battered, a relic of the eighties, and it looked as though it would never see thirty miles an hour again. But to me it looked better than a Rolls—the key was sitting in the ignition, and the car was already pointing in the correct direction, towards Cuttack.

"Here. Inside." I helped Ameera through the door and she lay down on the back seat. "If I am not back in a couple of minutes, don't stay here. Get out and go, anywhere away from the house. Wait for daylight. When you meet people, show them your railway ticket and ask to be taken to the station."

"Lee-yo-nel! Where are you going?"

"The other car is much faster—they will catch

us easily. I must fix it so they cannot drive after us. It will take only a moment."

"Lee-yo-nel!" Her cry was low-pitched, and she kept her head low on the seat.

I dashed back towards the other car, looking around me in the moonlight for something to put it out of action. The only thing remotely useful was a garden fork that stood upright against the wall. I felt the tines. With my weight behind it there was a pretty good chance it would slice through a tire.

The windows to my left suddenly came alight. That had been much too quick—either the fuse box was close to the cellar where we had been imprisoned, or there was an auxiliary circuit for some of the ground floor lights. I lined up the fork with the right front tire and leaned hard into it.

I had done my best, but I was too slow and too out of shape. While I was just getting started, the side door of the house opened and Dixie came running at me. He was still holding his knife. To my terrified eyes, the gleaming blade looked about four feet long.

Dixie was moving fast and crouching forward. His lower lip was drawn down to show his bottom teeth, and I could hear his strained breathing even when he was ten yards away. No matter what Zan's instructions might have been, Dixie was holding the knife as though injury to me was more important than capture.

The garden fork was getting nowhere—it's not easy to pierce a rubber tire. As Dixie ran in at me I leaned back against the body of the car. My left hand raised the fork, and I sent it with one vicious underarm thrust up into his chest. It seemed like the instinctive action of a trained killer.

I saw the tines go in just below the line of his collarbone. They missed the ribs and drove deep into his chest cavity. He gasped and staggered backwards, but long before he reached the ground I had turned and was running back to the other car. Even if we were followed to the station, we had to get away from this house.

Too late.

Before I had taken five steps I heard the grating whine of an old starter motor. The engine of the car ahead misfired a couple of times, then caught and revved up hard. There was a horrible grinding of gears.

Had Ameera somehow started the car, ready for me? I knew that was a ridiculous idea, but it was the only thing I could think of.

The lights of the car came on. I could see the shape of a woman in the driver's seat—but it was not Ameera. It was Zan. There was another moan of gears, then the car jerked into motion and was off along the drive. I ran after it. The back door handle was close to my hand. Four more steps would have done it, but Zan found second gear and the car accelerated away from me, helped by the long hill that led down towards Cuttack.

And was that Ameera, sitting up in the back seat? I could not be sure. But surely she would do something, interfere with the driver to let me catch up with them . . .

The car was a black, noisy dot on the road. I groaned and turned back towards the Toyota. Dixie was leaning against it now, watching the other car

vanish into the darkness. Somehow he had managed to stand up, the fork still buried deep in his
chest. He was bracing both hands above the tines,
trying to ease them free. A trickle of dark blood
had run from each round hole and made a long
stain down his shirt. Still he worked at the tines,
delicately and single-mindedly.

I felt sick at the sight. But Dixie might have the
keys to the Toyota, and that car was my only hope.
As I approached him he stood upright, away from
the car, and bent forward in an amazing effort to
reach for his knife. It was lying on the ground a
few feet in front of him. He leaned down, grunted,
and toppled sideways into a thick bush. The fork
still impaled his chest.

"Dixie." I leaned over him. There was no time
for caution. "I'll try not to hurt you worse, but I'm
going to search you. Where are the car keys?"

The bush he lay in was like a sweet-smelling
viburnum. The heavy, snowball-shaped blossoms
obscured his legs and trunk but left his face grinning up at me in the moonlight. Blood was oozing out of his mouth, up past the loosened lower
dentures and onto his chin. He was trying to speak,
but at first there was only a bloodied gargle from
his throat.

I knelt by him, the sap and nectar of crushed
blossoms damp on my pants. "Where are the keys,
Dixie? I'll get help for you as soon as I reach
Cuttack."

He did not speak. As I watched, his hands came
up again to the fork and began to push the tines,
easing them away from his body.

I tried again. "Dixie, if the pain's too bad to talk,

try and nod your head. Do you hear me? Car keys—I have to have them."

He glared up at me in hatred. "Not pain. Got implant. Bloody bastard." The grunted words were barely intelligible.

I was lifting and turning him as gently as I could while I patted the pockets of his coat and trousers. His only sounds were grunts of rage, and he made weak efforts to interfere with my actions. Impatience made my fingers clumsy, and I fumbled and fumed in the darkness, my nostrils full of the scent of blood and flower blossom.

The bunch of keys was in a little leather pouch in his left-hand coat pocket. As I took them out he made a mighty effort to sit up and grabbed for my hand.

"Bloody fool. Bloody fool." A film of blood made his neck and chin look black in the dim light. "T-Tippy—Tippy got. Worst of any. Serve you right. Bastard. Serve you right. T—T—"

Tippy. T.P.?—Leo's bogeyman? There was no time to waste—at any moment Pudd'n could appear from inside the house. But I had to know what he was saying about Tippy.

"What about Tippy? What do you mean, Tippy got?"

He was lying back again, eyes like black pools. I shook him. "Dixie. What about Tippy?"

He smiled again, a death's-head mask of triumph. "Real treat for Tippy—bloody fool, you. Serve you right." The old eyes were glazing, filming into darkness. He seemed quite immune to pain, supported by his hatred.

Another door slammed inside the house. I had

to go, no matter what other information Dixie's brain might hold. I ran for the car. By the time I had the Toyota's engine running another outside light had been switched on. I didn't wait to see who it might be. Rather than reversing I accelerated forward and drove on screaming tires right around the house and onto the road. The moonlight had been growing steadily brighter. Cuttack lay in front of me, a faint sprinkle of yellow lights. I took the car up to ninety and snaked it down the dusty ribbon of road that led towards the city center. If there was anything in my way, God help both of us.

The eight mile trip to the station was done in a few minutes. I screeched to a halt by the entrance, abandoned the car in the middle of the road, and ran towards the platforms. Cuttack Station was like a miniature version of Howrah Station in Calcutta. There were the same hundreds of people apparently living in the station, eating, drinking, and talking, even though it was one o'clock in the morning. I pushed my way rudely through them, looking for anyone in an official's uniform. As usual, none could be found. The people near me looked curiously at my stockinged feet and dust-fouled clothes, stained with blood, sap, and pollen.

"Train to Calcutta," I called desperately. "Where is the train to Calcutta?"

The sleeping and eating multitude stirred uneasily at my call, but there was no reply. I was heading towards the other side of the tracks when a tall, angular man wearing a Sikh turban stepped in front of me.

"Calcutta? Do you want to buy a ticket?"

"I have a ticket already. When is the next train?"

Without the chance of selling me a ticket he showed much less interest. There was a shrug, a turning of the head, and an arm waved casually along the northern line.

"You just missed the last one for tonight—see its lights there? Now it is necessary to wait for the morning service: six o'clock, arrival time nine-thirty. Do you need accommodation to sleep while you wait—or a place for food or entertainment? I can provide you with all."

I shook his hand away from my arm. Nine-thirty in Calcutta. I could do a lot better than that by road. The Toyota had nearly a full tank, and according to Chandra there were good highways all down the east coast of India.

I had stuck the pouch with the car keys in it into my pocket. Now I took it out again. Was I in any condition to drive? My head was pounding, and the station around me was reeling and rolling. Zan seemed like the best of the bunch, but even when I had permitted wild thoughts that she might help us I never considered revealing to her the location of Leo's hideaway. Ameera might think Zan was now on our side. If she followed my instructions and headed straight for home, Zan would be with her.

What should I do now? Wait for the train, or try it by car?

I had no choice at all. I discovered that in the next thirty seconds. The pouch containing the keys held more than I had realized. It also had space for paper money and for a driver's license.

As I opened it Zan's handsome face stared up at me, her expression stern and wooden in a Motor Vehicle Department mug shot.

Xantippe Gerakis, said the caption. Twenty-nine years old, height 1.7 meters.

It took a few seconds before I could make the connections. Xantippe; like the wife of Socrates, in keeping with her Greek appearance. But I had been following my ears and thinking of her as Zan. She was *Xan*.

Xantippe. Xan-Tippe. Zan-Tippy. Zan-TP.

The names ran like electric shocks through my brain. I recalled Zan's expression when she talked of torture for me and Ameera if we would not cooperate. And now I could interpret that strange look of excitement on her face when Dixie burned my arm back in London. Scouse had sent her away before they tortured me more—not because she hated inflicting pain, but because she was much too fond of it.

I stood in Cuttack Station and shivered.

Telephone.

It took me two frantic minutes to locate one, and ten more to battle my way through a sleepy night operator to the Calcutta number I wanted.

Chandra was not home. At one in the morning it could be business or pleasure, and I had no possible way to track him down. I left my message with a sleepy and alarmed servant, who seemed to speak just enough English to misunderstand every other word, and half a minute later I was back in the Toyota and bracing myself for a wild and exhausting drive to Calcutta.

"Regular hours and lots of sleep. Otherwise,

there'll be trouble." Sir Westcott had driven the message in as I was leaving the hospital.

Yes, sir.

I didn't disagree with his prescription. Following it was another matter.

– 14 –

Cuttack to Calcutta: 205 miles as the crow flies, 300 by road. The Indian traffic police apparently all went off duty at dusk. On the empty highways I pushed the car up to over a hundred, gritting my teeth at the scream of the over-revved engine. Even then I was passed a couple of times, once by a lunatic in a Ferrari and once by an old Rolls-Royce Silver Wraith that breathed past me like a moonlit ghost.

I reached the suburbs of Calcutta in less than four hours, then was slowed to a crawl by dawn traffic. As the sun came up like a smoky red ball, great lines of carts and bicycles crept out to clog the roads ahead.

Before I reached Howrah I had faint hopes of arriving before the night train. That prospect disappeared as I merged into the sluggish sea of commuters. It was seven o'clock and full light before I jerked the Toyota to a halt by the old double gates of the house and hobbled inside. Running on sharp gravel and six hours of driving without shoes had left my right foot raw and blistered.

No sign of Chandra's car—but perhaps he had received my message and come over by taxi.

And no mustachioed guard in the little sentry box. That was the first oddity. He was always there, unless he was sent on some errand.

I resisted the urge to run straight into the house. Leo's training was at work, as it had been working for me during our escape from Belur's house. At the open front door I forced myself to stand still for several minutes, listening.

Had I beaten Zan and Ameera in the trip from Cuttack? Surely not—the train would make the trip in little more than three hours. So perhaps they had not headed here at all. Maybe Zan had gone to meet Scouse and taken Ameera with her.

Dead silence. In my days there the house had *never* been empty, never silent. It would be quiet like this only if all the servants had been sent away.

I stole inside, shaking with tension and fatigue. The house was peaceful and spotlessly clean in the morning sunlight. Everything normal—except for that unprecedented and uncanny quiet. At the foot of the stairs I paused, uncertain where to go next. The silence was broken for the first time. A soft, spine-chilling noise came faintly from above me. Someone was crying—not crying, it was more like an animal moaning, faint and broken.

Ameera.

I ran up the stairs, forgetting the need for caution. She lay spreadeagled on the big bed in my room, face down and near naked. As I came closer to her I saw that she was tied, hands and feet, and that bandages covered her mouth.

I bent to remove the gag and felt the first moment of relief. She was here, she was alive, and she seemed to be unharmed. The strips of cloth that stretched her arms and legs towards the corners of the bed were tight-knotted and cut deep into her wrists, but her face and body were unmarked. When I struggled to undo the bonds she turned a tear-streaked face towards me.

"Lee-yo-nel?"

"I'm here. It's all right."

I finally had her wrists free, slid my hand reassuringly along her bare back, and moved down to tackle the ankles. Before I could touch her legs and feet she writhed and gave a warning cry.

In my haste to remove the gag I had not bothered to look closely at her legs. The curtains of the room were drawn, and in the dim light she had seemed to be wearing a pair of light slippers, purple-red in color and extending upwards only an inch or so from the bottom of her feet. Now I was seeing them more closely.

No slippers; her feet were bare. The skin had been flayed from the soles in neat half-inch strips. I could see how the first shallow cut had been made on the hard skin of the heel, before a uniform band was peeled off and run across the exquisitely tender area on the ball of the foot, all the way to the delicate toes. The operation had been carried out with diabolical skill. Zan must have taken several hours to do it. By now the bleeding had stopped, but a clear lymph was seeping from the stripped surfaces and oozing onto the bed sheet. As I touched her ankle, Ameera cried out in anticipation.

"Lee-yo-nel! No!"

I put my hand lightly on the back of her head. "It's all right, Ameera. I see it. I won't touch your feet."

As I bent to work on the knots my fatigue was washed away by an enormous and overwhelming rage. Much of it was directed toward myself. My curiosity about Leo's past had led directly to Ameera's torture. If I had been content to lie low in England, there were a dozen places where Scouse would never have found me . . .

A noise downstairs jerked me upright. Leo took over. I spun around, ready to kill without warning if it was Xantippe coming back for Ameera. When soft footsteps came up the stairs I moved silently to the doorway, poised for action.

One hard chop to the side of the neck . . .

A sleek head poked in through the door. I pulled back my hand at the last moment.

"Chandra!"

He turned swiftly to stare at me. "What is all this, Lionel? Messages in the middle of the night, frightening my man out of his negligible wits. What has become of that famous English *sangfroid*? What is happening here?"

As he spoke he turned to stare at Ameera on the bed. She had moved to bring her tortured feet clear of the sheet. Chandra's eyes, quicker than mine, saw at once what had been done to her. He went across to the window and drew back the curtains with one rapid and angry motion.

"Who did this?"

"The same people who have been pursuing me. They were waiting for us in Cuttack."

"And they followed you here?"

"My fault." I nodded my head towards Ameera. "We have to get her to a hospital." At Chandra's voice she had tried to wrap the bedsheet around her, but the pain from her feet was too great to permit the movement. Chandra questioned her briefly in Bengali, his voice calm and reassuring, and she made a brave attempt to smile before she replied. He asked her another question, then nodded at me.

"No hospital. We are agreed on that. The care she would get for this injury is no better there than we can bring to her here, and she would like to be among friends."

"But she must have a doctor." I looked at the raw wounds, and shuddered again.

"Of course. I will arrange for that immediately." Chandra was already moving towards the door, his smooth face determined and angry. "Leave all those arrangements to me. You stay here with Ameera. Do you think that they might come back here?"

Ameera gave a frightened little cry, and I moved to take her hand in both of mine.

"I don't know. If they do, then God help them."

He paused in the doorway. "God is fickle. Sometimes he chooses to help the wrong group. You are not Superman, Lionel. And you are exhausted. I think a little help from the Calcutta police would not be out of place here. I will call them."

He seemed to be taking over, and that felt like a good idea to me. He was right, I was worn out and running on nerves. I went downstairs with him and locked the doors of the house as he left. We wanted fair warning of visitors, welcome or unwelcome.

Ameera was lying flat on the bed when I went back upstairs. She shivered as I came into the room.

"Lee-yo-nel?"

"Try and lie quiet. Chandra will be here soon with the doctor."

"Will she come back?"

"She will not dare. Ameera, I am sorry. I should not have left you alone in the car. It was my fault."

There was no reply for several minutes, and I wondered if after her ordeal a natural emotional exhaustion had taken over. Finally she sighed and turned towards me as I sat on the edge of the bed.

"Lee-yo-nel, it was my fault. All of it. I am afraid to tell you this, but I did not speak the truth to you. About Lee-yo, and where he went."

"You told me he went to Cuttack—that was true." My brain was too dulled to go beyond the obvious. I wriggled my stiff and aching shoulders. "I should not have taken you there with me. Even when you wanted to go, I should have refused."

"Not Cuttack, Lee-yo-nel." Her voice was trembling. "I knew he had been there, and come back safely. It was the other place, the place that he was afraid to go. The place that he did not come back from."

I grunted and sat up straighter. "After Cuttack? You said that you did not know anywhere else that he went."

"I was lying to you." The tears came rolling down the dark cheeks. "I was afraid that you would be hurt, too. If we went to Cuttack, I thought that would be safe. Lee-yo went to see Belur there, and he was all right. But he never came back from Riyadh."

"Riyadh?" A flash of ocher sands and cool green dimness skimmed through my mind, a level below conscious memory. "Ameera, why did he go there? Was that the 'R-I' that I saw in his notes?"

"I do not know." The tears were coming faster now. "After he came from Cuttack, he left again at once. I do not know why he went to Riyadh— but I think that she knows. Lee-yo-nel, I did not want to tell her. But the hurt was so much, and she said she would keep hurting until I told. I had to tell. I said he went to Riyadh."

I looked down at her flayed and naked feet. "Ameera, anyone would have told. I am proud of you that you took so much hurt before you spoke."

"But I did not." She rubbed a knuckle at her tearstained eyes and sat up a little on the sheet. "I am not brave. I told her quickly, as soon as the hurt was bad. I thought she would stop then, but she kept on for a long time. Lee-yo-nel, why would she do that to me? I had told her everything."

I knew, but I did not want Ameera to know. Zan had been seeking information; when she had it she should logically have left the house at once. If she stayed, it was only for the pleasure of tormenting a helpless victim. Sadism is not rare, but it is unusual to find it given full leash.

Xantippe had known I might be on the way here, or have telephoned from Cuttack. Only a consuming urge to torture and torment had kept her so long at the house.

And if time had not been short, so that she could linger as long as she chose with Ameera? . . .

I went to the window and stared out. Instead of Calcutta, the city of Riyadh now seemed to spread its towers and minarets before me, the jewel of the Arabian Peninsula, a modern miracle of science that bloomed in the desert. I had been there many times, to play in the pinnacled concert hall and underwater theaters, making music for the idlest rich of the world.

Now I had to go there again; in pursuit of an unknown goal, following a woman who frightened me more than any wicked witch of childhood stories.

For Ameera's sake, I would be on the first airplane that could take me.

A gigantic bookcase, and beyond it the chair of a Titan. I blinked, blinked again, and screwed up my eyes against the sunlight. In the distance, over at the limit of vision, a dark-edged monster crouched forward over a colossal bed. There were sounds, the pizzicato plucking of strings over unresolving harmonies. An automatic filing system in my head identified the *Bhairava* raga, with its symbolism of waking dawn and reverence for the new day. The *vina* played on, its notes clean and soothing. My eyes closed.

And opened, to a room filled with uniformed figures, shrilling and gesturing to each other with insectoid precision and rapidity of movement. They were gathered around a bed, and I heard the *sforzando* command of a single voice demanding silence for the sleeper there.

I blinked once more. When my eyes opened again the group of figures had suddenly shrunk to two. They were wearing the uniform of the Calcutta police, standing solemn guard by the bed where Ameera lay. She was silent, her face open and innocent in sleep. Heavy bandages swaddled her feet.

"Any better now?" It was Chandra, sitting quietly by my side.

I shivered and took a deep breath. "I'm all right. How's Ameera? I guess I fell asleep for a while. Boy." I shivered. "Weird dreams."

"You have a right to them. Ameera told me what the two of you went through in Cuttack. Her condition?" He shrugged. "As well as can be expected. There is mental injury as well as physical. The woman—Xantippe?—said she was helping you. Ameera trusted her, they came back here, Ameera sent the servants away. Then—" he shrugged. "You know what she did next."

I shuddered from head to foot and looked more closely at Ameera. "At least she is sleeping. When I first arrived she was hysterical."

"It is more shock than sleep. When you passed out—"

"Me?" I stared at him.

"You do not remember it? You let me in, came up here, and fell over into that chair. That was four hours ago." He stared at me as I turned away from him. "Now then, what do you think you are up to?"

He grabbed me by the arm as I began to stagger off towards the door. I shook off his grip.

"Got to get to Riyadh." My voice was a thick-tongued mumble. "Next plane."

"Not yet." Chandra had taken my arm again,

and this time his grip was firmer, holding hard enough to hurt. "You want to pursue Ameera's tormentors? Very good; I commend the intention. But before you think of doing that, you must know of some other matters. You realize that they are murderers?"

"They killed Rustum Belur, and I think they killed a woman called Valnora Warren."

"It comes closer to home than that. When Ameera told the servants here to leave, one of them refused to go. Xantippe asked to speak with him privately, downstairs." Chandra lowered his voice to a whisper, glancing at Ameera. "When the police arrived they searched the whole house as part of their routine work. Mr. Chatterji was found in the pantry. Dead. He had been stabbed, many times."

He followed my look. "She does not know. There will be a time for such news. Not yet. It was enough effort, after the treatment of her injuries and after the police were finished here, to ease her into sleep. We talked about many things. We have surprisingly much in common, and Ameera has an excellent mind. But she could not rest, for all our talk, until we came to music. It worked where words could not."

"That was you? Playing the ragas?"

Chandra smiled, and there was a flash of the old, superconfident prodigy. "For my sins. The instrument was not in great condition, and the technique is rusty—but she did not complain. I know the music of Bihar, the folk tunes and the festival dances of her native area. I think that I played well. Perhaps there is still more to life than jute."

"But your fingers—I saw them last week. They were not in shape to play."

"Indeed?" This time the smile was different, a sad glint of oriental resignation. "Now you mention it, I think I noticed."

He held up his left hand. The soft fingertips were bloodied and torn from the pressure of the *vina's* seven thin strings.

"It was in a good cause. My suffering was nothing compared to hers. And now she is asleep, peacefully, without drugs."

He looked at his watch, and I realized that it was late afternoon. He had spent the whole day here. "Chandra, what about your work? I've already taken more of your time than a friend should ask."

"Assume that I do this for Ameera—not for a *feringhee* with no sense. Do you still talk of running off to Riyadh, now that you know what may face you there? Your enemies have more knowledge and more resources, and they are ruthless. How will you know what to do there?"

"How did I know what to do in Calcutta?" Despite the logic of his argument, my resolve was strengthening. "Chandra, there are other factors involved here. Earlier today, you were playing the *Bhairava* raga for Ameera. Correct?"

"True enough. What of it?"

"I recognized that piece."

"So? It is famous enough."

I shook my head. "To you. But I don't know Hindu music at all. Yet I recognized it. Don't you see what that means? I'm getting some of Leo's memories. I was told this would happen, and it has started."

He pouted and shrugged his chubby shoulders. "That is excellent. But if you stay here longer, you will receive more memories. Why not wait until you know exactly where to go, and what you are doing? There will be risks in Riyadh, but here you will be safe."

"That's not the whole story." I was stammering, and cursed myself for my lack of control. "I'm getting Leo's memories, and they will help—that's the good news. But I'm also getting flashes of sensory distortion. When I was first waking up here everything seemed out of proportion and the time scale went crazy. If I'm going to follow Scouse and Xantippe to Riyadh, I'll have to do it soon. The doctors warned me to watch for those symptoms. A few days from now I'll be in no condition to chase Zan, Scouse, the Belur Package or anything else."

I paused. My manner was much too emotional to persuade Chandra. Perhaps it was the sight of Ameera, a tiny child-figure with her bandaged feet and rope-cut wrists, that upset me so.

"I must go now," I said at last. "Time is short. If I can find a charter jet at Dum-Dum Airport and leave tonight, there's a chance that I can be in Riyadh before Zan or Scouse."

Chandra was behaving oddly, too. At my last sentence his face had twisted into a scowl, and now he was shaking his head violently.

"Before you think of going within a thousand miles of that —that woman, you must know one other thing. *She expects you to follow*. Can you not see the danger? She plans to trap you in Riyadh. Look at this, and then tell me if you wish to be in that city when she is there."

He had gone over to the window sill and picked up a sheet of paper. "Here." He held it forward. "A message, Lionel—for you alone."

I stared down at the thick, creamy notepaper. A white rose from the front garden had been pinned in the middle of the sheet. Above it sat an imprint in lipstick, a vermilion mouth shaped to kiss, and written beside those full lips were six words in dark red ink: *durch Blut und Eisen, te inveniam.*

Chandra was watching me closely. "There is no doubt who the message is intended for, and I assume that there is no need for me to translate it. Do you know why she did this?"

"Durch Blut und Eisen, te inveniam—*through blood and iron, I'll seek you out.*" I muttered the words, while the full red lips seemed to glow at me from the paper. I struggled to control my voice. "It's Zan, following Scouse's orders. I'm sure he wants to make sure I don't follow them. Psychological pressure. He wants me too frightened to go on to Riyadh."

And he's doing pretty damned well, I felt like adding.

Chandra nodded over to the bed, where Ameera was still sleeping soundly. "So why didn't Xantippe kill Ameera, as well as Chatterji? Then you could not have followed."

"She couldn't be sure I didn't know it anyway." I thought of Ameera, and a chill certainty grinned within my mind. "And *she* wants me to follow— never mind what Scouse wants, Zan has her own desires. I know how she looked at me in Belur's house. Ameera has just whetted her appetite. She missed her chance with me twice now, once in London and once in Cuttack. Third time lucky."

Chandra gave a nod of relief. "It is settled then. You will stay here."

"No." The red lips were smiling at me above the rose. "I'm going. Chandra, I'm going tonight. I won't let those bastards win. If they get away with this, Ameera suffered and Chatterji died for nothing."

He was staring at me, wide-eyed. "But Ameera—" he began, then paused. "You are right. Revenge is a universal emotion. It should be ours."

He was heading for the door. "Be ready quickly. Let me take care of Ameera, and do not worry about this house. If there is a charter jet of any kind at the airport tonight, you have my word that it will be yours."

– 15 –

Calcutta had been easy: all the time in the world to wander the city while I waited for some kind of subliminal clue from Leo to lead me to his contacts. But in Riyadh I would have only a few hours before Scouse and his bullyboys came after me.

Right.

Calcutta had been, at least to my knowledge, quite safe. But Riyadh would hold a crew of known killers, waiting for the next chance to slice fillets from my delicate flesh.

No denying it.

I had a personal friend in Calcutta, a man who was willing to drop his work at a moment's notice and come to help me. In Riyadh I had no close friend.

Absolutely true.

Beyond question, Chandra was perfectly logical. He had made all these, and a thousand other arguments, in the hours before I flew out of Calcutta. And yet, despite everything, I was right. On to the Arabian Peninsula and Riyadh, as soon as the plane could take me, and never mind every argument that a subtle, devious, and devoted Indian mind could conjure to hold me in Calcutta. That was the way to go.

I was right, and Chandra was wrong.

He didn't have all the feelings that lay behind the cold facts.

I spoke maybe a hundred words of Arabic, picked up in travels from Morocco to Iraq, but I felt at home in Riyadh. The city fitted my inner self. My first concert there had been back in '88, when I was only nineteen years old. I had played the obligatory Tchaikovsky Number One in the brand-new concert hall, before a vast (and, I suspect, mystified) audience who had been dragged in from the streets for the inaugural concerts. Most of them were receiving their first taste of western music. That was the year the king decided to import European culture. Between the movements I had sensed a dignified and baffled silence.

That bizarre first exposure led to a genuine love for the city and its hospitable *Najdi* population. Over the past eighteen years I had taken engagements there whenever they were offered to me. Apart from anything else it allowed me to follow the fantastic change from desert to garden as ten billion gallons per day of fresh water gushed in from Dammam on the Persian Gulf.

Not only that, Riyadh had the best zoo in the whole world. The new Tokyo Zoo was the only competitor, but Tokyo didn't have those hushed deserts to the north and west, less than a day's drive away, where I could struggle mentally with tough nuts like the *Hammerklavier*, and decide how I was going to play them that night.

So here I was, maybe half a day ahead of the killer pack. But how was I going to take the next step? Scouse and Xantippe must have some idea where Leo had been heading, but I didn't. Yet I had to get the Belur Package—and keep them from getting it while I stayed in one piece.

A nice problem.

My chartered plane had arrived at the airport north of the city at midnight. I hired a car, parked it at the exit to the rental area, wandered back into the arrival area, and settled down to wait. Each time that any plane with a stop in Calcutta came in to land, I went over to watch the passengers arrive in the lounge. And every couple of hours I risked leaving my inconspicuous post for ten minutes, to wolf down a sandwich or go to the bathroom. Naps were taken when I knew there was no flight due in the next hour.

Dawn at last. The passengers who straggled off in the chill morning light were paste-white and red-eyed, shuffling zombies sifting the piles of luggage for missing bags. In half an hour the last of them was leaving. An age until midday. Then I stretched, yawned, and dozed through a long afternoon. The glow of a fine evening streamed in through the high lounge windows, and finally the hush of desert night, lulling the activity in the airport. I had to prop my eyes open, and the lure of a hotel bed grew stronger and stronger. I went to the rest room, washed and shaved, and came back to my seat. Midnight again; cramps in my legs and back; imagined insults and bloodcurdling oaths from Sir Westcott about the way I was abusing my body. Worse aches as the second night wore on.

If my analysis of the situation were wrong, I was in for an uncomfortable couple of weeks.

Anywhere else but in an airport I would have been conspicuous, but here I was surrounded by dozens of weary passengers waiting for their flight, the one that had been delayed in London, Rome, Athens, Bombay, Moscow, Baghdad, Jakarta, or Sydney.

There was plenty of time for thinking, about Leo, Nymphs, and Ameera. I did a negligible amount of it. Other factors were taking over. The latest signs of sensory distortion had begun in Calcutta, when I was overtired after the drive from Cuttack. Now they came sweeping back, *con brio*, during the long hours of solitary waiting.

The towers of the flash distillation plants that took piped seawater from the Persian Gulf and turned it to drinking water and valuable solid minerals lay ten miles east of the airport. By day they had appeared to me like new temples to Allah, dazzling white spires and metal skeleton mosques rearing their heads four hundred feet above the desert while the watchful German engineers sat in the control rooms at their summit, infidel *muezzin* flooding the plain below with water instead of the call to prayer. Now, as midnight approached, the warning navigation lights on each tower glowed in the night, red eyes in the desert. They crept steadily closer until they peered in at me from outside the glass windows of the lounge, glowing tigers ten times my height. I was a homunculus in the dust beneath their paws as they pressed against the fragile panes.

I forced myself to look away, to concentrate on my hands in front of my face. This was what Sir Westcott had warned about back in Reading. I struggled to recall his fat, scowling jowls and brusque orders.

If you feel like you're getting smaller and smaller, cram a couple of these pills down as fast as you can . . . get to a hospital . . .

Inside my head, the nerve cells were sprouting their long, threadlike axons, reaching out to couple and reconnect with a billion neighbors. The slow work of regeneration had been going on for months, but no results could come until near the end. As the neurons finally locked in to their matrix of shared pathways, information would begin to flow through the new lines: a tiny trickle at first, then suddenly a mind-breaking flood, a trillion items of data transfer between the lobes of my brain and Leo's. When the flood came, I ought to be a patient at peace in some quiet hospital ward of a London suburb—not a stiff-limbed hollow-eyed ghost in a foreign airport lounge.

I heaved myself to my feet and picked up the little bag of necessities I had brought with me from Calcutta. If I drove carefully it was less than half an hour in the rented car to Riyadh's Yaghut Hospital. I had been there six years ago for a gamma globulin shot, when the hepatitis epidemic was running wild through the Middle East. There would be no traffic at this hour—it was almost three A.M.

Before I had taken two steps, there was a shimmer of green lights behind me. The big screen that provided arrivals information in Arabic and English was flickering again. Terminating passengers from the Manila-London flight were now clearing Immigration; intermediate stop: Calcutta.

I moved back to my favorite spot, a balcony above the main concourse. Passengers would look around them, but they seldom looked up.

If Pudd'n hadn't been there, I would have missed them completely. Scouse was wearing flowing white robes to the manner born, and Zan, two paces behind, wore no makeup and the concealing black veil and gown of the *chador*. Their dark complexions matched those of the crowd, and they both blended well with the homecoming Riyadh businessmen and their wives. Zan had even adopted the slow, hip-swaying walk that looked so attractive in the women of the town.

But not old Pudd'n. He was half a head too tall and a hundred pounds too heavy. He wore a robe, but it didn't help a bit. It was too short. Size twelve shoes and six inches of grey trouserleg were visible below the white hem, and his face was flushed and rosy as he carried their three bulky suitcases.

All three of them were looking around suspiciously and I was afraid that they might somehow catch sight of me. I kept well hidden behind a pillar in the lounge as they headed for the exit and piled into a taxi.

The dawn was just a glimmer in the eastern sky, but already there was a good deal of traffic on the road from the airport. I moved my rented car out onto the access road a few hundred yards behind

them, and kept my distance. I had assumed that
they would go first to a hotel, and catch up on
missing sleep; then I could do the same, close
enough to track their movements. But as soon as
we came to the Medina Highway that led around
the city to the west, the orange taxi left the road
to Riyadh.

I followed.

The volume of traffic was picking up rapidly.
Trucks and cars roared and reeled about me, and
their sizes changed as I looked at them. In most
cities of the world I would have been arrested at
once for wild driving; here I didn't stand out from
the crowd. Put a sober Saudi citizen behind the
wheel, and he becomes so macho that a new word
is needed to describe his behavior. To yield right
of way is unthinkable, and traffic lights are an insult
to driving prowess. The flowerbeds that stood in
the middle of the broad double roadway were
scored by tire tracks, and in ten miles I saw three
wrecks.

Soon we were passing the vast grounds of the
old royal palace of Nasiriya, where the zoo was now
housed, and still we were heading resolutely west.
Finally, a mile beyond the palace, we took the
southbound exit and were in the most expensive
suburb.

It was full dawn when the taxi pulled to a halt
in front of a pink concrete house, pseudo-Moorish
in design. Elaborate fountains played in the front
garden. Three hundred billion petrodollars a year
allowed the Arabs to indulge all their old fantasies about running water.

The road was busy, broad and curving, and lined

with expensive parked cars. Houses along it were widely separated—more like imitation palaces than conventional western dwellings. I cruised slowly past with the traffic, parked a quarter of a mile farther on behind a big crimson Cadillac, and waited. Scouse, Zan and Pudd'n had emerged from their cab and entered the arch that led to the front garden.

It seemed I was in for another long wait. At the airport I had at least had food, drink, and some comfort. Here I was cramped in the front seat of a small car, watching the sun rise behind me and already feeling those desert rays at work on the metal roof. I passed the time trying to work out in my head exactly where I was in Riyadh. A mile from the Nasiriya palace put me quite a way from the city center.

The inside of the car grew steadily hotter. I was thirsty as well as dizzy, and knew that I would have to leave within another hour, whatever happened, or I would be too far gone to get to a hotel under my own steam. When I opened the car windows for air, tiny midges swarmed in and attacked my face and arms. I closed them again, started the engine, and turned the air-conditioning up to full blast. After a few minutes more I cruised a couple of hundred yards farther along the road, turned the car, and drove slowly back past the house.

Come on out, dammit. They *had* to come out, I knew that—their suitcases were still in the waiting taxi. The taxi driver was in no hurry. An import like all the rest of the Saudi work force, he was dozing in his seat, mouth open, black face peaceful. The midges didn't seem to trouble him at all.

What in God's name were they up to in there? Torturing the residents, if Zan had her way.

Their reappearance took me by surprise. I was leaning forward, adjusting the fan setting, and when I looked up they were back in the taxi. A fat man in a dark suit was leaning to talk to them through the open window. He waved his farewell.

Mansouri. The name came into my mind as I was putting the car into gear and easing forward to follow them. It was hard to be invisible in broad daylight, and I was obliged to keep well behind until we were into the crowded city center, near the line of the old west wall. After that it was a fight to keep them in view in the swarming traffic. I lost them for a minute, and when I saw them again they were outside the taxi and about to enter the Intercontinental Hotel. Zan had abandoned her *chador* in favor of a smart green blouse and skirt, long enough for modesty.

I gave them a couple of minutes free while I parked my car. This was a tricky bit. I had to allow them long enough to be out of the lobby before I went in there myself, but not too long to be forgotten by the staff.

"Remember the lady in the green dress who just came in?" I asked the man behind the desk in reception.

He was perhaps thirty years of age, with the eyes of an old man. They looked at me without any expression at all.

"I'm very interested in her." I slipped a hundred pound note across the counter and it disappeared. "I know you're not supposed to tell me her room number—but if you could call my room, and let

me know when she comes again into the lobby . . ."
I held up another note, but didn't hand it to him.

He didn't seem surprised. After a few years in
a major hotel, he must have seen it all. There was
a minimal nod of the head and he handed me my
room key. His hand looked about three feet long.
As soon as I got up to my room I drank a glass
of cold water and swallowed one of Sir Westcott's
blue pills. As I did so I wondered who the hell
Mansouri was, and how Leo knew him.

The bed in my room cried out to me to come
and lie down on it, but I had lost half a day that
way when I first arrived in Calcutta. The next few
hours, when Scouse and Zan would be sleeping,
were all the margin that I had. Their faces when
they stood outside the hotel had not been those
of happy and successful hunters. It was clear that
Leo's contact in Riyadh had not been at Mansouri's
house, and for the moment Scouse was stalled; but
I knew he would be seeking the trail of the Belur
Package again before nightfall.

By then, I had to be ahead of them. (By nightfall
I would be ahead of them—but not in the sense
that I intended.)

I turned on the cold shower and stood under
it for ten minutes, until the chill had seeped in
from my skin to the middle of my solar plexus.
Then I changed clothes and left the hotel. Too bad
if Zan wasn't in a sleeping mood and decided to
go for a stroll as well.

I had less worries about Scouse. He must have
been travelling for three days straight, and he
looked the way that I felt.

In the taxi to the British Embassy, I tried one more time to shuffle the pieces. Every way I turned them, they came up one tantalizing fragment short. There was Leo, picking up the Belur Package and skipping Cuttack one step ahead of Scouse and his thugs. Rustum Belur had been less fortunate—but he had not told them where Leo had gone underground in Calcutta.

I tried to reconstruct Leo's pattern of moves. What would I have done next? Wait a few days, then try to get out of India and back to the United States.

Success at first. I reach Riyadh safely, without being tracked there; but then I find out that Scouse has the routes through Europe covered. And I have to get to Washington. People must be told what I've discovered.

It felt right so far. What next?

Think!

Leave the package in Riyadh. Where?

That's the missing piece. Find the package, and you'll also find out what it's used for.

Think!

Back through Europe with a false passport. Meet brother in London, tell him where I've left it in case I don't make it to Washington.

Give him the message: the missing package has been hidden—Where?

Memories not my own, not fully accessible. They sat there on the brink of recall. My head was full up, spurting random thoughts, everything but the one I needed. Sweating in the back of the taxi, all the old wounds waking; every stitch of Sir Westcott's delicate needlework stung and burned with a touch of nitric acid. Kidneys, testicles, right leg, rib cage, eye, ear and skull conspired to torture me, until I sat mindless, gripping the cool plastic of the seat.

I was panting and shivering like a fevered animal. My brain was overloading and the feeling terrified me. Unless I could relax, it would *spill*, ooze its melting grey matter out of my ears and down my neck.

I fumbled in my coat pocket and swallowed another blue tablet—to hell with any glass of water—and looked at my watch. We were approaching the British Embassy, but already twenty-five precious minutes had passed since I had left the hotel. I was banking on at most six safe hours; after that Zan and Scouse would be ready to try something else.

The embassy lay southwest of the city center, in an area that had once been the most prosperous part of the town. Now it was just a little past its peak, with the hint of genteel and decaying opulence that exactly matched the British influence in this part of the world. I had made a point of dropping in on each visit to Saudi Arabia. Usually my main contact was the Cultural Attaché, but today the Science Attaché was my best hope.

I left the taxi waiting at the main gate. The embassy grounds occupied almost ten acres of sculptured gardens, and the slow walk past the military guards and along a cool, shrub-lined pathway did me good. By the time that I was sitting in the inner lobby and accepting the ritual offer of hot tea, the world was regaining some stability.

The little red-haired man who finally wandered out to meet me looked vaguely familiar. He stood in front of me and frowned, one hand fiddling with the side of his scrubby mustache.

"I say. Aren't you Lionel Salkind?" He shook my hand vigorously. "We didn't know you were coming here to play this month—looks like somebody slipped up in getting the word out."

"I'm not here for concerts." Apparently most of the world hadn't noticed that I had been smashed to pieces and out of circulation for six months. So much for fame.

"I'm here on other business," I said.

"Pity. I'm Cyril Meecham. We met a year ago, when you played the Diabelli what-not, and then that thing with Parkinson. You remember it?"

That thing with Parkinson. I remembered all right, and he had put it very well.

Last year I had given a small private concert at the embassy, and the chargé-d'affaires, Parkinson, fancied himself as a violinist. I played the Beethoven Diabelli Variations, then together we tackled the Spring Sonata, Opus 24. The scherzo movement wore him out, and in the final rondo we went slower and slower, limping across the finish line, roughly together, after the longest last movement in musical memory. I remembered it all right.

"Mind you," Meecham was saying. "I liked the concert we had with that other pianist, Schub, a lot better. Somehow seemed to be a lot more *tuneful*, if you know what I mean." He sensed a possible lack of tact in his remarks, and waved an arm towards his office. "But come on in, and tell me what we can do for you. I'm surprised you're not talking to Draper and the chaps in Culture."

"I need some information about science." I followed him into a panelled office with an oar hung prominently along one wall, and we settled down into creaking, leather-covered armchairs. "At least, I think it's science. Can you tell me what *introsomatic* chips are?"

"Mm. See what you mean." He stroked at his mustache again. "Can't see you getting too much out of old Draper and his culture-vultures on that one. Introsomatic chips, eh? I could find you some papers on them, let you read all you want to. Mind you, some of that stuff's hard going."

"I don't need details—just the general idea. And I'm in rather a hurry for another appointment." I looked at my watch. One hour since I left the hotel.

He was nodding vaguely. "Of course, of course. Well, the idea's simple-enough. You know what a pacemaker is, don't you, for heartbeat control? The introsomatic chips take it a step farther. You take a chip with a whole lot of integrated circuits on it, and you preprogram it with stored programs. Then you add a bunch of sensors to it—little ones. And you implant it into the body, bung it in wherever it's right for that type of chip. *Intro– somatic* chips, see?—means it's computing equipment *inside* the *body*. The sensors measure various physical stuff—you know, pulse, temperature, ion concentrations, things like that—then the program calculates a signal to be sent to the nervous system. Sort of an override to the natural control signal."

"And what does it do?" I was getting ideas about the Belur Package, and why there was such interest in it.

"Well. That all depends on what the implant is programmed for." He was looking at me as though only an idiot would ask such a question. "You see, it's completely flexible. Any procedure can be programmed in, and so long as the sensors and the output signals are right you could in principle control any body function any way you like. That's just the *theory*, you understand. In practice, they're still fiddling around on the research. Maybe we'll have something really useful in five or ten years."

"What can they do with it now?"

"Oh, the easy stuff." From the look on his face, I sensed that he was at the limits of his real knowledge. "You can get an implant that controls some of the peristaltic actions in the digestive system—for people who have trouble in the small and large intestine. And of course, the heart pacemakers are a lot better now; they respond to adrenaline and hormonal levels in the blood."

He leaned forward. "Look here, old fellow, d'you mind if I ask why you're so interested in all this? I mean, it's a long way from bashing out the old Rachmaninov. What are you up to?"

I hesitated. Danger might come from unlikely places, but I just couldn't see Cyril Meecham as the instrument of evil.

"I think somebody has made implants a lot more sophisticated than any that have been done before. He was an Indian named Belur, and I'm pretty sure he made a prototype set maybe a year or two ago."

(The mental image of Dixie, garden fork deep in his chest, blood welling up over stained lower dentures. No signs of a death agony. *"Not pain. Got implant. Bloody bastard."*)

"The prototypes could be implanted to override pain signals, wherever they came from in the body. But more recently Belur made a new set of introsomatic implants, with different functions. I don't know what the newer ones do—but my brother was trying to get them from India to America when he was killed in an accident. I'm convinced that he had to leave them here, in Riyadh. And I'm trying to find out where."

"Hmm. Sorry about your brother." Now he looked intrigued, and his condolences were no more than a bow to propriety. "Haven't seen anything about these newer implants in the journals. Mind you, we're not exactly at the center of scientific action out here. I don't know how to help you. Do you have any idea at all where your brother was staying when he was here in Riyadh?"

"I don't know. If I give you a street address, is there any way that you can tell me who lives there?" I caught his look. "I don't want to go there myself, in case he shouldn't have been there—Leo was always one for the ladies."

His frown disappeared. "Aren't we all when we get half a chance?" He winked and pushed a memo pad across to me. "Jot down an address, and I'll pop over to civics and run a check for you. Push the buzzer if you want more tea."

In the minutes he was away I had time to look at my watch twenty times and to ponder again Big Brother Leo's activities. The more that I followed his tracks, the more I understood our relationship. The contrasts between my hard-working and well-planned life (concert tours fixed a year in advance) and his wild continent-hopping flights were apparent on the surface—even extreme; but underneath there were deep similarities. The difference was only this: where I dreamed and imagined, he carried thought to action.

We were identical twins, with all the genetic correspondence that implied. If I allowed my thoughts to range unfettered, and forced myself to follow after them, I would arrive close to Leo's destinations. The thoughts were easy; the hard part was to dare to act them out.

"Aren't we all when we get half a chance?" We are, but some of us find it difficult to know a chance when it stares us in the face.

The clock on his desk ticked on. If he didn't hurry, my chances might be reduced to zero. I was at the point of leaving the office to look for him when he hurried back in. His pleasant look had been transformed to one of anger and suspicion.

"Look, I don't know what your game is here, but I want to tell you that I don't care for it."

"No game—I told you the truth. You checked that address?"

"Too bloody true I checked it. If my brother went there I think I'd disown him. That street address is the *Maison Drogue*. The man who lives there is Abdi Mansouri. He's an ex-Iranian—and he's the biggest drug dealer in the Middle East. Millions a week in illegal narcotics, and nobody willing to lift a finger against him."

He slammed the directory he was holding down on the desk. "I'm giving you the benefit of the doubt for the moment, but you'd better have an awfully good explanation—or the Embassy Police will need a few words with you."

My suspicions were turning one by one to certainties. I held up my hands to soothe Cyril Meecham. "I'll explain what's been happening—everything. But it will take a couple of minutes."

He just glared at me.

"My brother was working for the American government, as some sort of freelance agent." I spoke fast, and my mental fingers were crossed. I knew Leo, and my explanation was the only acceptable one that fitted his personality and moral code.

"He was in an undercover position, investigating organized crime in the East, and particularly the way that illegal drugs get from India to the West. He had been tracking something called Nymphs, a new drug, trying to see what route was being used for shipment—I think he realized they were coming through Riyadh."

I paused. At the mention of Nymphs, Cyril Meecham's face had turned white. He might not be a senior instrument of evil, but I would bet my Brahms that he knew more than somewhat about the use of Nymphs. Young Cyril had his own guilty secrets.

"I think my brother must have been in touch with this man, Mansouri," I went on. "And he pretended that he was in the drug business himself. He had been working with a bunch of drug dealers in England, trying to see how their

operations were run. Did you ever hear of somebody called Scouse—head of an English gang who
imports drugs? He's a sort of Liverpool Arab,
speaks English and Arabic."

Not too surprisingly, Meecham shook his head
vigorously. He didn't want that association at all.

"Never heard of him."

"He thought my brother was a dealer in Nymphs.
But then they heard of something that looked like
a much bigger deal. They both went after it, but my
brother Leo beat Scouse's group to it. He escaped
with it from India and came here. If anyone did
manage to trace him, they would assume that he had
brought the goods to show to Abdi Mansouri. But
he didn't go to Mansouri. I confirmed that this
morning. He went somewhere else, and hid the
package he had with him."

While I was speaking, Meecham had been leaf-
ing through a fat binding of computer listings. He
looked up at me, his face now skeptical and wary.

"I hear what you say, but I don't believe it. You
said that your brother was here six months ago,
right? There's no sign of any Salkind entering or
leaving this country during that period."

"His name was Foss—we were raised separately.
And he could have been here travelling under a
false name," I added, as he looked again at the
listing and shook his head.

"No Foss in here." He slammed the directory
shut again. "Look, Mr. Salkind, I'm doing my best
to give you the benefit of the doubt—but it's not
easy. I've never heard such a bloody weird story
in my life. You don't want the Science Attaché, you
want the flying carpets department." His freckled

face was turning redder. "As for the false name idea, we keep close tabs on all travellers with British passports travelling into and out of this country. There's no way he'd get in with a false name and a false passport, and we'd not know it and record it."

"He wouldn't be here on a British passport. I didn't mention it, but he's a naturalized American, born in England. So that list of yours—"

I paused. Cyril Meecham had sat down hard in his chair. He was glaring at me with the old reserved-for-hopeless-idiots expression.

"An American? A bloody *American*? Why the hell didn't you tell me that to start with?" His bushy eyebrows were stretching upwards towards his carroty hairline, and his voice went higher and higher. "Your brother is an American. All right. But then why waste my time with questions I can't answer?"

He stood up again.

"Mr. Salkind, you're in the wrong place. Did it never occur to you that you'll do a damned sight better to take your tale of undoubted woe to where it belongs—to the *American* bloody embassy?"

– 16 –

I must have sat there gaping at him for half a minute. What Cyril Meecham said was so obviously right and rational that I couldn't understand why it had to be told to me.

Imagine what I would do in Leo's place, then carry it to action. Reasonable enough—but I had been too stupid or too exhausted to allow for undeniable real differences in our backgrounds.

On every trip to a foreign capital I made a habit of visiting the local embassy. They would give me good free advice on hotels, restaurants, and local tourist traps and rip-offs, and if I ever ran into trouble with the locals the embassy staff knew me and were ready to bail me out. Leo would probably follow my pattern abroad—but as an American citizen he would check in with the U.S. embassies.

Cyril Meecham let me use the phone before I left. The snake-eyed receptionist at the hotel

238

confirmed that the young lady I was so interested in had not yet left her room—did I want to leave a message for her? I thought of Zan's full red lips, of her agate eyes measuring my body as I sat on the bed in Belur's house.

No thank you, no message; *definitely* no message.

But keep an eye open for her. I would call again later.

Hurry.

I emerged from the British Embassy into the full heat of early afternoon. Even this late in the year the sun turned everything to a shimmer of baked air. The southwest part of the city had been built before the sprinklers and abundant supply of fresh water turned Riyadh to a riot of lush garden greenery. There was still dust here, dust and lung-crippling clouds of photochemical smog from cars and trucks.

My taxi driver didn't need any urging to drive fast—he wanted to find some shaded spot where the long wait for a passenger was more tolerable. We made the usual death-defying run through the network of narrow one-way streets and broad boulevards.

The American Embassy stood only a block from the old palace of Nasiriya. There was my real stamping ground, inside the palace walls where the original royal zoo had been extended to provide well-designed habitats for every beast that walked or swam the earth or ocean. The aquarium held a dozen fresh and salt water pools, hundreds of yards long, where the visitor could find everything from humpback whales to Lake

Baikal seals. Lions prowled the pseudosavannah, and polar bears fished live cod from deep, icy waters. The estimates to create the new zoo ranged from hundreds of millions to billions, and its maintenance called for a permanent working staff of two hundred people.

It was a zoophile's paradise. Perhaps it said most about my lack of social graces that I had been to the Riyadh Zoo half a dozen times, but this would be my first visit to the U.S. Embassy.

Again I told the taxi driver to wait, and walked down the shaded avenue that separated zoo and embassy. A chorus of roars, barks and grunts came from the enclosures to my left; feeding time. I had the sudden heart-stopping desire to turn that way, go on through the zoo gate instead of into the embassy, back to the familiar world that I had inhabited before the accident. This wasn't me at all, running from beautiful sadists in a frantic search for who-knows-what. I was cut out for the quiet life.

But I'm so close, I can't stop now. Keep going.

Whose thought was that?

I went on towards the embassy, past the lines of beggars that not even Riyadh's gigantic wealth had been able to eliminate. An honorable calling. Sightless, armless, legless, they sat head down against the walls, shaded by shrubs that grew along the tops. Two little metal bowls stood in front of each man.

I hardly glanced at them, even when one rose suddenly from almost beneath my feet and scuffled away along the street with his empty bowls tucked away under a withered left arm. That was my mistake, and I would pay for it later, but my attention was all on the moving digits of my watch.

Three o'clock. Despite my instructions to the driver to hurry, two and a half hours had now passed since I left the Intercontinental.

Time runs, the clock will strike, the devil will come . . . If I couldn't track down the Belur Package by six, I had to get back to the hotel and follow Zan and Scouse in their next move.

The embassy entrance lay a little off Beggars' Row in a narrow cul-de-sac. A blind brick wall closed off the end, with a coffee shop on the right-hand side and the big double doors of the embassy on the left. Marine guards stood just within the gates, by a huge sign in English and Arabic announcing that beyond this point lay the sovereign soil of the United States. A much smaller sign warned visitors that the embassy closed at four-thirty, and all non-U.S. nationals had to be outside by then. My time was squeezing down, tighter and tighter. And I was feeling ghastly, wondering how long I could last before I just toppled over into the dirt. I needed to get some food and drink into me.

Coffee. Go in there, into the shop on the right.

I actually took a couple of steps in that direction, then halted and stared at the bottle-green shop window. Coffee? I rubbed at my aching eyes. Nice to have some, but this was the worst time in the world to look for it. Afterwards, when I was done in the embassy—the place should still be open at four-thirty. I turned back to the embassy gates.

Some bright ideas just don't work out the way they ought to. In the next two hours I talked to fourteen embassy staff, not counting the two young Marines who started me on my rounds. Science Attaché, Commercial Attaché, Counsellor, First and Second Secretary, Military Attaché—they were all very polite and totally uncommunicative.

Leo Foss? No, we didn't know about the accident—very sorry to hear it, he came by the embassy now and again. Very sharp man, knew exactly how the natives operate.

The last time? Well, let's check the file here. Over a year ago. No, we haven't seen anything of him since then.

Easy to see you're his brother—older brother, I suppose? Leave a package here six months ago? What kind of package? No, we didn't see it—who would he have left it with? Never heard of anything like that in this department.

It was clear that Leo had not been a person greatly popular at the embassy. For one thing, he was much too fluent in Arabic to let the staff there feel at ease. What did you do with an odd fellow who knew more about the country and its people than you did? Two of the men I saw recognized me as Lionel Salkind, pianist, and tried to steer the conversation towards music and away from the dull matter of my brother. Was I planning any concerts here soon? Riyadh needed more western influence. There were some ICA funds available if I was interested . . .

I squirmed free, went to the next Attaché, asked the same questions.

Nothing. Not a nibble. Four-thirty came, and I

was quietly shown to the main exit. Come again when you are in Riyadh. Let us know in advance, and we'll make sure that we have a recital in the embassy. Sorry to hear about your brother . . .

I was standing by the double gates again, going through the rituals of a polite farewell. My head was an inferno. As the doors swung to behind me I leaned against one of the pillars and damned the American Embassy and all its staff to perdition. *Over a year ago.* So Leo had not come here on his last trip. He had been—where?

I walked to the end of the cul-de-sac and looked around me. Beggars' Row was empty now, the crippled line of human wreckage melted away in the late afternoon sun. Beyond the chest-high wall across the main avenue, feeding time at the Zoo was over and the whole street was quiet now. I turned and looked back toward the embassy. In the two hours that I had been inside the sun had swung through thirty degrees in the sky, to throw a harsh light onto the front of the coffee shop. A faded beige awning had been moved out to shield the exposed window. Across the top ran a line of Arabic lettering, and lower down there was a crude oil painting of a tall glass with two bright green fruit being squeezed into it . . .

I was hurrying back to the embassy, hammering frantically on the big double doors. Was it already too late?

One of the doors cracked open a few inches.

"We're closed until eight o'clock tomorrow." It was one of the young Marines.

"I know. The coffee shop there—what's it called?" He stared at me. "Called? I don't know the

Arabic, but in English all the people here call it 'The Limes.' See the sign?"

The Limes. Not zeroes, eggs, lemons, balloons or walnuts—Leo had drawn limes. Two of them, staring back at me in vivid green from the sun-bleached awning.

As I walked across to the open door I glanced again at my watch. Four forty-five. I was too excited to notice that the taxi left waiting for me in the avenue was no longer there.

Close up, the wrinkles showed. The door of the coffee shop was beginning to shed its blistered green paint and the letters of the menu just inside were faded by sunlight. Within, the bench-lined room was cool and dim. The awning and thick green window glass cut off most of the sun, so my eyes took a few seconds to adjust.

"You wanta ha-lunch, sir-ha?" A waiter, thin and ancient, stood at the door and addressed me in his idea of English—he must have seen me coming over from the American embassy.

I nodded. "Coffee. Lots of it. And do you have pastry or sweet cakes?" My blood sugar badly needed a boost.

"Ha-past-ery. Sa-weatcakes? Yes." The forehead wrinkled in perplexity and he scurried away through a door in the back. What would come back was anybody's guess.

I would have guessed wrong. What came back was a small, barrel-shaped woman with a cheerful, wrinkled face and a generous Jewish nose. She took two steps into the room, put her hands on her hips and glared at me.

"Sweet cakes, eh? I ought to 'ave known it. Leo, you are very bad man. When you die you go to 'ell for sure. Why you playin' games with me an' poor old Fazil?"

Narjes The name came as another random impulse in my mind, accompanied by a feeling of warmth and affection.

She came close, wrapped her arms about me, and hugged hard enough to make my tender ribs creak. Over her shoulder she shouted a brusque order to the waiter, who hurried in and placed sweetened coffee in front of me, together with a big plate of powdered sugar biscuits. Then she scowled at me as I took a life-restoring gulp of hot coffee and crammed two of the biscuits into my mouth.

"You come 'ere an' eat like pig, eh? An' you think Rabiyah still like you, mebbe? What you think she bin doin' while you gone, sit 'ere an' wait? She 'as other men want 'er, all time. You think she want to stay an' 'ang aroun' upstairs for you?"

My left eye suddenly winked at her as I was cramming two more biscuits into my mouth. She reached out a tobacco-stained finger and thumb and pinched a fold of my cheek affectionately.

"Leo, you are bad bastard. I tell 'er, don' think about 'im, he cocking leg over woman someplace else, like 'orny bastard. I warn Rabiyah, but she stupid. Me, I know what you are like."

When I sat and stared at her, my mouth still full, she shook her head. "Where you been this time? You look 'orrible. An' why you sit there like an old goat? Why you not talkin' to me?"

**Rabiyah. Pale skin, untouched by the sun;

*luscious body, the breasts and hips too heavy for western tastes. Notice how the lecherous eyes follow her at Embassy parties. Watch her laugh, a pink, meaty tongue quivering between even white teeth.***

I cleared my throat and spoke in a hoarse voice. "I'm feeling horrible, Narjes—even worse than I look. But I need to see Rabiyah quickly. Where is she?"

"Where you think she is? It still afternoon, right? She sleepin', like other girls. Don' you try an' see 'er—she need rest. She's working woman. She got work to do tonight." Narjes shook a finger at me. "You 'orrible man, Leo, I tol' Rabiyah that whole lots of time. You want to see 'er now? O.K. You pay like rest of men pay."

The package. She has it. Rabiyah has the package.

I reached into my jacket, pulled out my wallet, and dropped a fat bundle of *riyals* next to the tray of sweets. Narjes looked at them and her brown face twisted with rage.

"What the 'ell that? Leo, you try to make me real angry, eh? You doin' it. You better learn now, you never try offer money again. Or I call an' we get Tughril come in 'ere an' throw you out on your skinny ass, an' I tell Rabiyah how bad you insult me, an' you never get see 'er anymore. You hear?" She jerked her head at me imperiously. "Come on. You follow me, an' keep your big mouth *shut*. We got girls sleep up here."

She led the way through the back door of the shop and turned left up a broad staircase. On the upper landing the building changed character completely. The old, fly-specked look of the lower floor was replaced by wall-hung carpets, brass lanterns hung from the pink and gold ceiling, and thick curtains that cut off all outside light from the windows. We walked over the thick pile of a gorgeous Baluchi rug, quietly past a row of closed doors. Narjes stopped at the fourth one along.

"In here. If she got brain at all she tell you bugger off an' don' come back. An' whatever you do, *don' make no noise*. We got people try to sleep—me too 'til you give Fazil hard time down there."

She opened the door without knocking and pushed me inside. The room was completely dark. I had a sudden moment of terror and total disorientation.

Arriving in the middle of the night. Afraid. Mansouri and Scouse on my trail, afraid to wait until dawn to go across to the Embassy. Sanctuary, the safety of this room, this house . . .

"Who is that?" The voice from in front of me was a sleep-edged murmur.

I moved forward until I was at the end of the bed.

"Narjes?" There was a sound of creaking bedsprings, then a thick curtain on my left opened a crack. Evening sunlight streamed in. The girl on the broad bed gave a little mutter of complaint and shielded her eyes with one hand. Her skin had the pale fineness that goes only with true burnished-copper hair, and her figure defeated the modest intention of the green nightdress.

She yawned, squinted up at me through half-open blue eyes. A sudden gasp, and she lifted herself from the pile of thick pillows.

"Leo! When did you get here? Narjes didn't tell me you were in Riyadh."

"She didn't know until a few minutes ago." A true enough statement. I had already made the decision that this was not the time to explain that I was Lionel, not Leo. If somebody realized that for themselves, fair enough. I knew of only one infallible way to prove I was not Leo, and that worked only with someone like Ameera, who knew him inside out, in intimate detail. But as I learned more of my brother's past, the number of people with access to that mode of identification seemed to be growing rapidly.

"I'm just passing through Riyadh," I went on. "But I had to see you. Rabiyah, do you remember I had a package with me last time I was here?"

"Package?" The big blue eyes were still sleepy, but at least they were wide open and looking at me with a puzzled expression.

My spirits sank to a new low. This was my last hope. If Rabiyah didn't have the Belur Package, I had run out of all ideas on where to look for it. I might as well give up, go back to the hotel and let Zan carve me up into little pieces.

"Some kind of package," I said desperately. "Don't you remember? I came here late at night."

"I remember that." She stretched and gave me a smile and a long-lashed look. "You'll come back tonight, and see me when I feel awake?—I'm tired out."

Instead of waiting for a reply, she stretched backward to the little bedside table and opened the drawer.

"You come in the middle of the night, and ask

me to save things, and run away without even a goodbye," she grumbled. "Why don't you bring me nice presents? This is all you left last time. But no package."

It was flat, less than a quarter of an inch thick and smaller than a matchbox. The surface was a dull grey, like slate, and one end was marked with a ribbed pattern. I put my thumbnail in the indentation and pressed. The thin plastic moved stiffly away. Inside were a score of paper-thin wafers, each one resting snugly in its own holder. Tiny beads of silver glinted along the upper edges. Each introsomatic chip weighed only a fraction of an ounce.

Still safe. Have to get them to Washington. Don't wait.

Silver beads flashed and winked as I turned the little box. I could not take my eyes away. All at once I knew what the wafers did, knew why they could not go to Scouse or to Mansouri, knew what forces had driven Leo and me this far. This had to be put into the hands of responsible people. Would the American Embassy open its doors tonight, even though it was officially closed?

I knew the answer to that. They would not open when Leo arrived here late at night and needed a safe place. Rabiyah had been the only refuge before he had to make his run for Zurich and London.

Thoughts buzzed through my head like drunken bees, staggering and turning in wild collision. The tiny silver beads in my hand went out of focus, then appeared again as a double line. Memory came in surges.

Follow the drugs to the source, back from Athens to Riyadh to Calcutta to Singapore. Scouse— Mansouri—Radha—Drisco. The hint of something more than Nymphs . . . follow it west . . . take the package . . . to the Embassy . . . to the Limes . . . to England.

A jumbled vision of my other self turning from the girl at the El Al desk in London Airport. Of myself seeing myself . . . of myself, seeing myself, seeing myself . . .

Rabiyah saved me from the endless loop down into the depths. Her hand had rubbed affectionately at my knee, then climbed like a knowing animal towards more sensitive areas. I jerked at her touch and the movement dragged me back to the present.

The slanting sunlight winked off the tiny box in my hand. For this, at least four people had died.

"You'll come back later?" Rabiyah was running her hand gently along my thigh. "I'm tired now— O.K.?"

Her eyes closed. I patted her on the arm, stooped to kiss her lightly on the pale forehead, and caressed a rounded breast.

"Later. As soon as I have this lot in a safe place." I meant it. No criticism from me of Leo's tastes.

She smiled drowsily and released the curtain she had been holding, so that the room was once again in total darkness. I closed the lid of the little box and slipped it into the pocket of my jacket. It took both hands and a lot of blind groping to get me back to the door.

Narjes had disappeared. Like the young women, she normally slept through the afternoon. There was no sound from any of the rooms as I slipped back across the thick carpet and down the curving staircase.

The old waiter had deserted the coffee shop, to leave a solitary customer quietly sipping tea and staring out of the bottle-green window. Not much light came in now, even though the sun was shining past the awning. I looked at my watch. Six-thirty. If I could get no response from the American Embassy, the best bet was a direct run to the airport. My luggage could be forfeit, but the avaricious porter watching for Zan would wait in vain for his second hundred pounds.

I stepped towards the door, peering out at the empty street. Twenty yards and a massive pair of doors lay between me and the inside of the American Embassy. So near, so far. Leo must have stood here in this same spot, wondering how much time he had. His trail was well hid, but was it good enough? Had someone already followed him here?

While I watched the Embassy, the man on my left had set down his cup and pushed the loose headdress back from his face. He turned to look at me for the first time. I returned his glance casually. Then we both froze. His arms unfolded from the loose sleeves of his robe. He was holding a gun in his right hand, and the brown eyes were gleaming.

"How about that!" There was a little smile on his lips. "I sit wondering what's keeping you so long in the Embassy—an' you're upstairs here, screwing your brains out. You're a cool one, I'll say that for you."

It was Scouse.

A cool one. He was wrong about that. So near, so far. I was ready to sit down on the tiled floor and weep.

- 17 -

"Outside."

Scouse jerked his head towards the door, but the gun held its aim at the center of my chest. He moved close behind me as I went into the street, near enough to frustrate any attempt at a sidestep along the wall, too far away for a backward kick or lunge.

"Turn left and head for the main avenue." The joking tone had disappeared from his voice. "Make any funny move an' you get it. Treated you too bloody easy, we did, but that's all finished. Where's Belur's bag of tricks?"

"I don't know." The flat box in my pocket seemed to bulge outward, shouting to be noticed.

The gun in his hand clicked to automatic setting, the trigger half-depressed by the pressure of his index finger. He grunted. "I don't believe you. You were too keen to get to Riyadh to play innocent now. Where is it?"

I didn't answer. I couldn't answer. The sudden sunlight set up a tornado of images inside my head. Twisted beaches; a long run down a ski slope steeper and faster than anything I had ever dreamed of; flickering candles on a restaurant table, with unfamiliar Spanish music playing in the background.

The street came into focus, shifted, swam about me. After an indeterminate period of lost control I came back to reality and found we had walked along the little cul-de-sac and were standing now on the corner of the avenue.

"Left here." Scouse still kept his distance, eight feet behind me. "All right. You've been asking for it—Des, an' Jack, an' then poor bloody Dixie. I gave you the chance to go easy—even gave you the chance to come in on it with us. Now you'll go hard, an' to hell with you. Here comes your friend."

The sun had gone down behind the wall on our left, and the light in the avenue was fading fast. Towards us through the early dusk came a green Fiat with tinted windows. It crept along in low gear at no more than five miles an hour, and halted ten yards away.

"You should see her with a cigarette lighter," said Scouse. "An' she does things with a spoke from a bike wheel that you wouldn't believe. I can't stand to watch 'em. But you'll see it first hand. I mean, for as long as you can see anything."

The car door opened, and Xantippe got out. She looked more beautiful than ever in a green pantsuit and open-toed sandals. Instead of a handbag she was carrying a flat leather case about ten inches by five. Twenty feet away from me she halted.

"Got him easy as wink," said Scouse cheerfully. "Now he's all yours. Where do we start?"

Xantippe moved closer, so that she was only two paces in front of me.

"No closer," warned Scouse. "We know he's dangerous."

She nodded, but her eyes never left mine. A flush of color was creeping into her cheeks, highlighting the exotic bone structure, and the look she gave me was erotic, the unfocused stare of sexual arousal. Her tanned fingers stroked the leather instrument case.

"At Mansouri's house—it will be quiet there." Her voice was soft and husky.

Scouse had edged around to my left, keeping close to the wall until he was standing next to Zan. Where she was all unconcealed excitement, he was as cold and analytical as one of Belur's computer chips. I looked hopelessly up and down the street. A tall figure was slowly approaching us. Pudd'n. No help from that quarter. Even if he didn't approve of torture, he wouldn't have the nerve to argue with Scouse. Not when Zan was there to punish disobedience.

"Want to tell us where it is now, an' deprive Zan of a night's fun?" asked Scouse.

I shook my head, while Zan frowned at him in outrage. "You *promised* this," she said.

"Yeah—but that was before you an' Dix screwed things up in Cuttack."

He nodded his head towards the car. "Go on, Salkind, get in there. In the back. Pudd'n can drive us."

The gun couldn't be argued with. I took two

paces towards the Fiat. Then there was a sudden angry hissing from behind Scouse, and he flinched and spun around as something cold touched the back of his neck.

It was seven o'clock. Accurate to the second under the control of the German engineering staff, Riyadh's evening irrigation system had turned itself on. A sprinkler had been set up to water the line of shrubs that grew along the top of the long wall. The first drops of clear water jetted out into the avenue and caught Scouse where he stood.

It took him only a second to realize what was happening. In a fraction of that time I was running to my right, towards the chest-high wall that separated the avenue from the grounds of the Riyadh Zoo.

I didn't wait to see what lay on the other side. As I went over headfirst, four shots crackled out from behind me. I felt a tug in my left calf and a hard blow on my left heel. Then I was landing hard on my forearms and right shoulder, and rolling across baked earth and prickly scrub. A patch of gravel stripped the skin from the back of my left hand. I rolled, and rolled again.

Scouse would find the wall too high to lean over and shoot at me—but Pudd'n could do it, if he had a gun. I scrambled to my feet and ran diagonally to the right, towards the shelter of a wooden fence. Something was badly wrong with my left leg, there was a searing, stretching pain with every step. As I reached the fence I heard curses from behind me, and the scrabbling of shoes against the outside wall of the zoo.

It was the irony of ironies. The Riyadh Zoo was

one of my favorite places in all the world, a spot where the architecture of the old Nasiriya Palace had been blended with the special needs of the world's animals, to create a magical Arabian Nights atmosphere. In the past I had always felt rushed for time. A concert or a plane trip was only a few hours away. Now I could look forward to the whole night here—if I was clever or lucky enough to avoid Zan, Scouse and Pudd'n.

How did my chances look? As I headed deeper into the Zoo I made my checklist.

I was unarmed; they had at least one gun, plus other weapons in Zan's case. There were three of them; I was alone. I was exhausted, brain-damaged, and hallucinating; they were rested from a day's sleep. I had a bullet wound in my leg—blood was trickling down now into my left shoe, leaving a trail they would find easy to follow; they were fit, and Pudd'n at least was as strong as a bull.

A hopeless situation. I knew it, but I dared not admit it.

And I knew one other thing.

As it grew darker, I plodded on deeper into the Zoo. The layout of the interior was not simple. A series of avenues led out from the central elephant house to each major phylum of the Zoo's contents. I had to head inward a hundred and fifty yards towards the center, around a circular footpath by the aviaries, then out again along another one of the spokes of the wheel. It took longer than I wanted, though I forced myself to hobble along as fast as I possibly could. By the time I reached the reptile section the last of the sunset was a burnish of brass to the west. I slipped along from one enclosure to the next, looking down at the signs in the last of the cold desert light.

Popular names were given only in Arabic—completely unintelligible to me. I had to rely on my memory of the full Latin names of each family.

Anilidae, Uropeltidae, Typhlopidae, Colubridae—not what I needed at all (but I shivered to myself when I thought about what I did need). The snakes had all been assigned to one set of enclosures, within the general area of the reptiles. Here were the egg-eaters, *Dasypeltidae*, and farther on I found *Pythonidae*—the big constrictors. I could handle them, but they wouldn't do. Nor would the large tanked enclosure of *Hydrophidae*, the sea snakes.

At last, three large fenced areas next to each other. *Crotalidae, Viperidae, Elapidae*: all the worst of the poisonous snakes. I stood in deepening darkness and pondered what I would find in each habitat. *Crotalidae* meant diamondback rattlesnake, water moccasins, copperheads, ferde-lance, and pit vipers. Perhaps bushmasters, too, though it was hard to keep them alive in captivity. *Elapidae* would be most dangerous of all, hooded and spitting cobras, coral snakes, kraits, mambas, and death adders. Neurotoxic venom, nerve poisons that would kill but might not cause instant agony; also, I didn't think I could handle them—they were bad-tempered, agile, and unpredictable. A black mamba would be up to twelve feet long, and in my present condition it could travel a lot faster than me. *Steer clear of the Elapidae.*

Steer clear of all of them. The shadow

thought quivered in my brain, and I paused for a moment. This was one area where I would be a lot braver than Leo. And I had to be.

Each fenced area was protected by chain gates with double safety catches. They were designed to keep out small and inquisitive children, but not a determined adult. After a few moments of careful manipulation I eased open the gate of the middle enclosure and went inside. I left it open behind me. This was the home of the *Viperidae*, the vipers and adders. Hemolytic poisons, instant agony when you were struck by one of the worse species. I had seen the effects of the hemotoxins, and I knew how quickly the swelling and the pain would start. It took all of my will power to go down onto my hands and knees, ignore the pain from my bleeding calf, and begin to inch forward into the darkness. The enclosure was big, perhaps fifty yards across, and in that space the surface varied from dry desert to a lush irrigated area.

Just enough light left for me to see where I was going. I knew what I wanted: *Bitis gabonica*, the Gaboon Viper.

No matter which snake I went near, there was a high risk. The Gaboon Viper had two big advantages. It was nocturnal, so it would just now be waking; and although it looks hideous it is sluggish in habits and doesn't attack or run away when you get near. It flattens into the sand.

I knew where to look. Along the western side of the rocks, where the sun's heat still lingered. The big danger was that I would in my dizzy and exhausted condition stumble across a snake and annoy it enough to strike. A big Gaboon Viper has fangs two inches long, and injects enough venom to kill five men.

The one that I found was a huge specimen, six feet long and four inches across the body. The heart-shaped head turned lazily as I came close, and the thick body snuggled closer to the side of the ledge of rock. It made no attempt to escape, but sounded an angry blowing hiss and jabbed at my handkerchief when I held it forward.

The sand was cooling rapidly, giving up its stored heat to the cloudless sky. I took off my jacket, draped it around the body of the snake, and lifted it with both hands just behind the head. The lidless eyes shone a glassy silver-white in the darkness, and the elliptical pupils stared up at me. As the bloated body wriggled from side to side, the blowing hiss became a steady rhythm. As each breath was expelled the top of the ugly head flattened a little. I shivered, and held on tightly. Gradually, the noise grew less. The snake was infuriated, but it could do no more than open its jaws wide and reveal the monstrous fangs.

I slid my way, step by cautious step, up a rocky incline that led to the artificial peak at the center of the enclosure. This was a dangerous time. It was too dark to see what lay in front of my feet, and the nocturnal snakes were waking.

Behind me I heard muttered words from outside the main enclosure, and saw the reflected flame of a cigarette lighter. Scouse came first, with Zan just behind him. He was following my tracks across the sand. Pudd'n was a reluctant third, well behind the other two.

"Salkind! We know you're there. Better give up

now, an' we'll go easy on you." Scouse sounded furious, his voice cold and calm. I felt sorry for anyone who had to rely on his goodwill. "We'll have you soon. Don't think you can get away. Come out of hiding, or we'll make it that much worse for you."

They were inside the sandy arena, no more than twenty paces from me. I didn't dare to breathe. My arms were aching from holding the weight of the snake, and my head chose this moment to turn the whole world into dizzy pinwheeling patterns of colored stars. I gritted my teeth and hung on, willing the whirling scene to stabilize.

Scouse was ten paces away. Five, coming confidently forward with his gun in one hand. He knew I was unarmed, and Zan and Pudd'n were backing him up.

Three paces. Two. It had to be timed precisely.

As he moved up to the last ledge, I shook the snake to bring it to a higher point of fury, and swung it forward.

Scouse had been walking with his eyes still down to the bloodied track my feet had made. The Gaboon Viper opened its jaws wide and sank the fangs into his exposed neck, just to the right of his Adam's apple. For one moment Scouse was quite motionless, rigid against the sudden weight of the snake. Then he gave a high-pitched, horrified scream, dropped the gun to the sand, and grabbed at the bloated body. The viper hung on for a few seconds, then the jaws slackened. As it came free of his throat, the fangs sank deep into his right forearm.

The pain came at once. Unlike Dixie, Scouse

carried no prototype of the Belur introsomatic chips. He was screaming, thrashing at the snake and staggering from side to side on the rocky hillside.

Behind him, Zan flicked on her cigarette lighter. By its light she caught her first good view of Scouse and his murderer. He had stopped screaming now, and was reduced to a horrible gargle, deep in his swelling throat.

Most people are afraid of snakes, perhaps because they don't understand them. But for one person in twenty, phobia goes beyond normal fear to absolute panic and horror. Zan was the one in twenty. When she saw the twisting body of the Gaboon Viper her mouth stretched wide in a silent scream. The flickering flame of the lighter showed neck tendons strained to dark cords, and her whole body began to tremble. Her eyes bulged white against the flawless tan complexion. Without making any move to help Scouse, she dropped the cigarette lighter, turned, and ran blindly across the broad arena. At the edge of it lay a smooth wall, waist high. She scrambled over, a pale blur in the night.

I opened my mouth to shout a warning.

Don't help her. She deserves whatever she gets.

The warning words stuck in my throat. Zan was out of this area and into the enclosure that held the *Elapidae*. She was making a mindless run straight across the rock-strewn surface.

Sixty yards would take her to the outer wall. Before her lay a *terra incognita* that could hold anything: spectacled cobras, a lurking hamadryad, or tiny and deadly kraits. A few drops of venom from an Australian tiger snake would kill a man or woman in a few minutes.

Zan ran on.

It is over now, but we were close. Long before I understood Tippy's mind, I knew her body. I never fathomed what drove her to offer agony rather than ecstasy, but I remember the treasure-house of warm secrets beneath her fashionable clothing. All that is gone, forever past recall. Weep for Tippy, the way she might have been. The way I thought she was.

She was running on; twenty yards, then thirty. Nothing tangled her feet, nothing flashed fangs at her calves. I stooped to the sand, feeling about for the lighter that she had dropped. Scouse had staggered to lean against the rock, and slowly subsided to lie groaning facedown on the rough surface. I ignored him, reaching cautiously past the Gaboon Viper to pick up the lighter.

Ten yards more and Zan would be at the wall. As I straightened up, she was suddenly gone from view. Another moment, and she gave a scream of pure terror, a heartstopping ululation that rose higher and higher in pitch and seemed to go on forever.

All around me, the Zoo woke to the sound. I heard the answering bark and howl of desert dogs, cracking screams from the macaque monkeys, the angry roar and bellow of the big cats. My head seemed to split open with the sounds.

I was drowning, choking on the warm blood in my throat. The helicopter was down, I had fallen away from the controls, and part of the broken rotor had skewered me neatly through the right side. I had to hold on, pass on the word... **

More sounds and sights. Colored ribbons danced around me, red and green and violet, matching their sinuous movement to the animal cries that filled the zoo. In the other enclosure, something had jerked upright and was running blindly back towards me. It collided with the waist-high wall and scrabbled at the smooth surface, while an eerie *portamento* wail came muffled from its throat.

I took four hesitant paces towards the wall and flicked the lighter to the maximum setting of its gas jet.

Zan was leaning against the wall. Squirming dark tendrils hung from her face and shoulders, and another dark band circled her neck. As I watched, one clinging to her cheek dropped loose and wriggled away across the sand.

She had fallen face-first into a nest of the spectacled cobra, and a dozen of the young had attacked her. The foot-long snakes, venomous from the moment of birth, had buried their fangs in her cheeks and neck. One clung fast to her lower lip. Another, entangled in her blouse, wriggled with fangs buried in her right breast. An ooze of blood and gelatinous liquid ran from a deep wound on her left eye, past a flap of torn eyelid that hung loose against her cheek.

"Zan! Pull them off—they inject more venom, the longer they bite."

She was past hearing. After a few more seconds shuddering against the wall, she turned and ran headlong back across the open enclosure. In a few paces she was too far away to be seen with the cigarette lighter's flame. I heard an angry hissing, another scream of horror from the darkness, and a frenzied threshing.

Then I had to think of myself. Every movement I made brought nausea and confusion. I lurched back to where Scouse lay silent on the sand. His neck had swollen until it was as wide as his head, and his face was a purple-black mask. He had asphyxiated as his windpipe was flattened in the congested throat.

"Don't go near the snake. Get the jacket—got to get the jacket."

Slowly, weak and shaky as a ninety-year-old, I carefully bent and picked up my rumpled coat. Dark drops of venom spattered the sleeve, but the thin box of the Belur Package still sat in the left pocket. I put the jacket on, rummaged in the sand and gravel for another thirty seconds, then wearily straightened.

I had one last barrier to surmount, and I knew in my aching bones that it would be too much for me. No matter how I tried, I would never be able to climb out of the Zoo, over that wall. And Pudd'n was somewhere in the darkness ahead. From the moment that I thrust the viper at Scouse, there had been no sound from the entrance to the enclosure, but I knew Pudd'n was there, waiting for me.

My left leg had lost all feeling. I dragged myself slowly forward on my hands and knees. My left hand was flat on the sand, my right supported me on its clenched knuckles. Each time that I allowed my head to hang down, the ground tilted and reared like a squall-hit ship.

"All the effort, two years and three continents, to end like this. Crawling, bleeding, weaker and weaker. But Scouse and Mansouri won't get it now."

In front of me, the gate to the enclosure; standing there like a statue in my path, Pudd'n. I came up to sit back on my haunches, fished the cigarette lighter from my left pocket, and snapped it into flame. Pudd'n blinked as the light met his eyes, but he did not move. I tried to speak, failed, cleared my throat and tried again.

"All right, Pudd'n. It's your move now. Scouse is dead, and Xantippe won't live more than an hour or two. Come and get it. The Belur Package is right here, in my pocket."

He stared down at me. His big face was pale, like a wax mask, and he looked sick and haggard. He shook his head slowly, without speaking.

"Did you hear me?" I said. "I'm done for. I couldn't fight a baby. What now, Pudd'n?"

He sighed, and a shudder shook his whole body. "I saw it," he said at last. "Saw what happened to Scouse an' Zan. Christ, I could spew my ring. I've always been scared of snakes."

"Well? What now? You still after the package?"

He shook his head again. "I'm done with that bleeder, it's been all bad luck. You get out of here. I won't stop you."

He took a step back, outside the enclosure.

I moved my right hand forward and up, to show him Scouse's pistol that had been hidden in my sleeve and closed fist. "You just bought your own life, Pudd'n. I won't stop you, either. Get out of this place. Don't go near the enclosures. Keep to

the paths, and go out over the wall. Better get a
move on, before I change my mind."

He had jerked backwards at the sight of the gun.
Now he nodded and moved again, turning towards
the dark path behind him. As the flame of the
lighter dimmed, he was gone, crunching away along
the gravel.

It made little difference to me. I had fallen
forward, vaguely aware of the sand against my
cheek. The clear desert sky was filling with stars,
bright points of green and blue and orange that
swelled and burst around me. The whole heavens
lit up, filling with pulsating rosy flame.

Hold tight. Don't give up now.

Dark nebulae were invading the field of stars.
All around, the heavens dimmed and faded.

I fought to put my hand in my pocket, pull out
the bottle of blue pills.

Too late. My fingers were losing their sense of
touch, I could not open the glass phial. I raised it to
my mouth and gripped the plastic in my teeth, biting
at the stopper. Glass broke, ground between my
molars. My tongue bled as I spat the broken bottle
out onto the sand, swallowed, swallowed again. Two
pills, ten pills, what difference did it make?

The last tide was going out, sweeping away from
the sandy shore. I was helpless to fight it, drifting into the night. Axons linking, synapses closing,
the floodgates wide open.

Goodbye, Ameera. Goodbye, Rabiyah.
Goodbye, Tess.

The old tall story again. "So what happened to
you then, Bill?"

"What happened to me? Why, I died, of course."

– 18 –

I was awake, flat on my back and staring up at a grey ceiling. Creaks and clattering came from all sides, then a whir of machinery and the sound of running water. Finally, I heard the squeak of leather boots.

Impossible to sleep. I sighed, gave up the fight, and opened my eyes. Sir Westcott Shaw slowly came into focus, frowning down at me. He grunted as he saw my eyes flicker open.

"What's the point of patchin' you up, when you go off and get torn to bits again? Open your mouth."

"Where am I?" It came out as a throaty gurgle.

"Where do you think? Back where you started, in Intensive Care. Wider, an' keep it open."

He was shining a light down my throat, and moving my tongue around with a spatula. It hurt like hell.

"How did I get here?" I mumbled, as soon

as he stopped poking about. "I thought I was dying."

"We're all dying." He looked across at the bank of meters sitting by the bedside. "But you don't seem to be goin' any faster than the rest of us. Move your eyes, an' follow my finger." He passed his hand slowly across my face: up, down, left, right.

"I was in the Riyadh Zoo." The memory blurred back like a bad dream. "Who brought me here?"

"I did, soon as you were stable enough to be moved." He stopped waving his fingers in front of my eyes. "The doctors out there wanted to slice open your skull—didn't like the EEG readings, said you had meningitis an' a brain tumor. They only phoned me because our hospital discharge was in your wallet. I had a lot of trouble with 'em. An' I had one hell of a job gettin' the Riyadh Police to let you go, what with a dead man an' a sick woman in that zoo with you. I told 'em—"

"Sick woman?" It took my fuzzied concentration a few seconds to interpret his words. "You mean a dead woman."

"Uh-uh." He shook his head firmly. "I saw her. She'd been bitten a lot, but they were small wounds—not much venom in 'em. They got you both out quick, so there wasn't much danger she'd die. I'll bet she's discharged by now."

Zan. Alive. The old blend of terror and excitement tingled inside me. Where was she now? On her way here? I started to lever myself toward the side of the bed.

"But you were somethin' else," went on Sir Westcott. He pushed me back firmly onto the pillow. "I told 'em you'd die for sure unless we got you over here sharpish. Does this hurt?"

He twisted the lower part of my left calf in a way that brought me upright and cursing, and nodded happily at my reaction. "Good. You're a madman, Salkind, I hope you know that. You were brought in here missing a quart of blood, with a skin infection, abrasions, a hundred and three temperature, two bullet wounds, and a blood pressure of fifty over twenty. I suppose that's your idea of takin' it easy?"

Infections, abrasions, bullet wounds—and all for nothing? I struggled to sit up straighter and grabbed at his arm. "My jacket. What happened to it? In the left hand pocket, a little box—"

"The Belur Package?" He again pushed me back to the pillow. "We got that all right—your friend Chandra told us you might be carrying somethin' interesting. We found it, an' it's being looked at by the right people. But some of the chips have 'em baffled."

Chandra.

I wanted to ask ten questions at once. Ameera, Zan, the Package, Tess . . .

"You mean Chandra's here?"

"Got here yesterday, along with that popsie of yours. Attractive girl, eh?" He sniffed. "We had a good long talk about everything last night, me an' Chandra an' Ameera—an' Tess. Matter of fact, they'll be poppin' in later—you weren't conscious when they stopped by yesterday." He began to fiddle with the tubes of my I.V., but he wouldn't look me in the eye as he went on: "Ameera's eye operation is tomorrow. Should be an easy one, a week or two here and she can go back home—if she wants to."

Tess and Ameera! There was trouble on the horizon, but I had to get something else out of the way before I could worry about that. I gritted my teeth and sat up again. My left hand was a ball of white bandages, my head was spinning, and I had an ache all the way from my crotch to my ribs.

"Sir Westcott, I have to talk to the police. I know what the Belur Package does—I don't know who's looking at it in London, but get them over here."

He raised his eyebrows at me and rubbed a hand over his bald head. "We've already realized they're implants. They've been takin' data dumps off the chips, an' tryin' to work out what the program code means."

"I can tell you more than that." Maybe it was some odd combination of fear and medication, but my muddled brain suddenly hit high gear. "I know what they do. Three of the implants are improved versions of Belur's old prototypes. They allow the person they're grafted into to ignore pain. But he made new ones, quite different ones, a couple of months before he was killed."

"An' you know what the new ones do?"

"Not in detail, but I can tell you enough to get started. I got the main clue in the British Embassy in Riyadh. That, plus the fact that the people peddling Nymphs were so interested in the Belur Package. Each wafer in the box is a different introsomatic chip, designed to be planted inside the body."

"We know that much. What else?"

"They hold programs that can override fatigue or hunger signals, or induce sleep for exactly the length of time that you want, or jump adrenaline and hormone levels, or increase or decrease blood flow to injured or infected areas—all under programmed control. Belur may not have known it, but he was creating the perfect soldier."

"But you said Nymphs were a clue, too." The fleshy jowls puffed out. Sir Westcott had paused in his examination of the monitors. "None of the effects you mentioned has a thing to do with the drug business."

"Not the drug business—the sex business. *Increased blood supply to any part of the body, under conscious control.* Can't you see what that means? Impotence a thing of the past. Some men—especially some old men—would pay fortunes for that implant. 'Specially if they could buy ones that control the female body reactions, too."

"That's what Nymphs do."

"Nymphs can only do so much. Combine the drug with programmed control of a girl's muscular and glandular system, and you have a dirty old man's dream. Young girls who respond to him exactly as he wants, with his own implants helping him to take advantage of it."

I let my head fall back on the pillow. Too much excitement; my head was turning back to a bowl of mush.

"The military implications may be biggest in the long run," I went on. "But that wasn't the game for Scouse and his buddies. They didn't know that market. They wanted the packages to use in their own business. It would be the biggest thing ever. They went after it—hard. But we beat them to it."

His eyes watched me closely most of the time, but every few seconds they would flick across to the monitors. He moved to look at a silver needle that quivered on its dial.

"How long before I get out of here?" I said.

"Give it a chance, man—I said you were mendin', not recovered." He looked casually off to the side, at the window, and shot the question at me suddenly.

"Who are you?"

"What? Why, I'm—I'm—" *Damn it, man, get the words out.* "I'm Li—Le—Lio—Lionel." My cut tongue struggled with the word. Sir Westcott nodded.

"Exactly. You're Lio-Leo-Lionel, that's who you are. An' that's why you need a few weeks of quiet, puttin' that lot together. What's the main road from San Diego to Los Angeles?"

"I-5." The words came automatically.

"From Glasgow to Edinburgh?"

"The M8."

"Fair enough." He sniffed. "You'll do, but don't get the wrong idea. You have a lot of mending to take care of before we'll let you out of here this time." He frowned down at me, and took another glance at the monitors.

"Mendin', and explainin'. I'll be back in here later, to sit guard when the lads from the Foreign Office come in to talk about the Belur Package. I'm as interested in the details as they are—be a dirty old man myself in a few years, if I get the chance." He moved across to me and lifted my hand. "For the moment, I think you need a bit of this before you're ready to explain any more."

The needle went into my left arm so smoothly and quickly that I had no time to resist. Ten seconds of protest, then I felt the urge to close my eyes for a moment. When I opened them again he was gone. A familiar white-tunic-clad figure stood by the bedside with her back to me.

"Tess!" I reached out and just managed to touch the back of her thigh.

"Now then!" She turned gracefully, and I had my first look at her face. It was a complete stranger.

"Nurse Thomson told me what you're like—all fingers," she said. "Keep your hands to yourself, or I'll have to tie them up." Her smile took the bite out of her words. While I was still groping for my apology she went to the panel of monitors and did her own quick review of the battery of gauges, fluid sacs, and dial readings. I saw our reflection in the metal of the machine. I was as pale as the sheets. She saw me looking and shook her auburn head. Plump, placid face, dazzling smile, sexy body—and even in my drugged condition I could see she didn't look at all like Tess.

She moved to the bedside. "You know, you're supposed to be sleeping. Sir Westcott was right. You have quite a constitution. When they brought you in here I didn't expect you to last the night. What have you been doing to yourself?"

"To myself. Not a thing. It was done to me."

"I'll bet. Some day I want to hear all the gory details. Not now, though. You're supposed to be resting. But I'll tell Tess you've recovered enough to have roving hands."

She headed for the door, then turned back to me.

"Did anybody give you your phone message? He rang earlier, when you were still unconscious."

"No. Who did?"

"I don't know. He didn't give his full name. Just asked how you were, and to tell you that Thomas called."

"Thomas? I don't know anybody called Thomas." Scrabbling around for names hurt my head. Good constitution or not, something wasn't right inside there.

"Well, he knows you. He wanted me to tell you that you've not seen the last of him. He said, give him a few months, then look out for his Godowsky."

Thomas. Thomas? Godowsky? A faint memory. *"Thomas, the Good Lord God has given you a talent . . ."* It was true enough, in spite of the cynical way that Pudd'n had said it. "You've not seen the last of him"? With Zan alive, that could mean anything.

My face must have mirrored my feelings, because the nurse came back into the room and peered at me anxiously.

"Are you feeling all right? Everything shows fine on the monitors."

"I'm all right. But—did he make any threats?"

"Threats?" She giggled. "Of course he didn't—he sounded real nice. He said he was the one who sent the police into the Zoo to get you out of there. If he hadn't done that you'd probably be dead by now. He helped you, he didn't threaten you."

Good old Pudd'n. So he had repaid the favor. Cast bread on the waters, and sometimes you get back a whole loaf. "Did he say anything else?"

She frowned. "Only that thing looking out for his Godowsky. What's a Godowsky?"

"A dead pianist. It's all right, I know what he means; and you're quite right, he wasn't threatening me."

She nodded formally. "All right. I'll be back in a little while. Tess comes on at four. I'll tell her you're having a sleep now."

I was left for a while with my own drugged thoughts . . .

. . . of Tess, bringing me carefully back from death's doorstep, mending my mind as much as my body . . . if it hadn't been for her, I might never have left this place to go off to India, to Calcutta, to Ameera, to my child bride who wanted to bear Leo's baby . . . if Sir Westcott had done his surgery well, the chances of that ought to be exactly fifty-fifty. . . .

. . . of Ameera's courage when we had been captured in the house in Cuttack . . . of her look at me, totally calm and trusting, convinced that I would get us safely out and back home . . . back to the hideaway, the secret shelter from the whole world . . .

. . . of Zan, the red lips parted above the white rose . . . the flush of heat on olive cheeks, lust and cruelty alight in amber eyes . . . she was moving towards me, silk dress tight across broad, swaying hips . . .

I woke up sweating, full of a perverse excitement. A month ago I had worried about my future. That was a problem no longer—I knew what I had to do, where I must go.

I opened my eyes. Ameera and Tess were

standing by the monitors, talking to each other in whispers. Their words were lost in the soft click and mutter of the medical equipment. They were talking about me; I was convinced of it. Now for the thunder and lightning. I wanted to cringe, but instead forced myself to lift my head.

"Er—I'm—er—I didn't mean to—er—ah . . ." I said intelligently.

They moved together to my bedside. Ameera leaned forward and ran her fingers lightly over my face. Tess took my right hand—the other one was no more than a mass of bandages—in both of hers. I couldn't believe my eyes.

They were both grinning like thieves.

"How are you feeling?" said Tess softly.

"Well, I'm—er—I suppose that I'm . . . are you two—I mean . . ." I mumbled .

Ameera didn't speak, but she stooped over and kissed me gently on the lips. "We were both being so worried about you," she said. Tess nodded, then in turn bent to give me a kiss.

I closed my eyes. In a few seconds I would open them again and wake up, but meanwhile I wanted to enjoy the moment—and sort out my plans. Somehow I had to make my peace with Tess and Ameera and explain to them how fond I was of both of them. But before I did that . . .

Other urgencies intruded. As soon as I could be up and about, I must trace Pudd'n—I had a few ideas on that already. If anyone could help me and lead me to Zan, he could. The business wasn't finished. Zan was alive and active, Mansouri still at large. Even with Scouse gone the crooked ring was unbroken.

The old quivering excitement was building in me. The highest form of living, the hunt, the chase. I would face Zan again, move into and through the jaws of danger.

Damn you, Big Brother. What about the quiet life?

Not yet, Little Brother. Not yet.

I opened my eyes again and looked up at Tess and Ameera. They were smiling down at me, waiting to hear how I was feeling. Wonderful women, marvelous women. Someday, might I find peace and happiness with one of them? **Not yet. Not yet. After the hunt is over.**

I sighed, fought back a shiver of anticipation (or fear), and forced a smile.

"I'm feeling fine," I said. "How long before they let me out of here?"

Got questions? We've got answers at

BAEN'S BAR!

Here's what some of our members have to say:

"Ever wanted to get involved in a newsgroup but were frightened off by rude know-it-alls? Stop by Baen's Bar. Our know-it-alls are the friendly, helpful type—and some write the hottest SF around."
>   —**Melody L** *melodyl@ccnmail.com*

"Baen's Bar . . . where you just might find people who understand what you are talking about!"
>   —**Tom Perry** *perry@airswitch.net*

"Lots of gentle teasing and numerous puns, mixed with various recipes for food and fun."
>   —**Ginger Tansey** *makautz@prodigy.net*

"Join the fun at Baen's Bar, where you can discuss the latest in books, Treecat Sign Language, ramifications of cloning, how military uniforms have changed, help an author do research, fuss about differences between American and European measurements—and top it off with being able to talk to the people who write and publish what you love."
>   —**Sun Shadow** *sun2shadow@hotmail.com*

"Thanks for a lovely first year at the Bar, where the only thing that's been intoxicating is conversation."
>   —**Al Jorgensen** *awjorgen@wolf.co.net*

   Join BAEN'S BAR at
WWW.BAEN.COM
"Bring your brain!"